PEREGRINE

BOSON BOOKS by Michael Aye

THE FIGHTING ANTHONYS
BOOK FIVE

PEREGRINE

by

Michael Aye

BOSON BOOKS
Raleigh

Michael Aye is a retired Naval Medical Officer. He has long been a student of early American and British Naval history. Since reading his first Kent novel, Mike has spent many hours reading the great authors of sea fiction, often while being "haze gray and underway" himself.

http://michaelaye.com

ISBN (paper): 978-0-917990-74-8
ISBN (ebook): 978-0-917990-73-1

Published by **Boson Books**
An imprint of **C & M Online Media, Inc.**
3905 Meadow Field Lane,
Raleigh, NC 27606-4470
email: cm@cmonline.com
http://www.bosonbooks.com

Cover art by Jan Julian
Graphic art by Carrie Skalla

Author's Note
This book is a work of fiction with a historical backdrop. I have taken liberties with historical figures, ships, and time frames to blend in with my story. Therefore, this book is not a reflection of actual historical events.

Dedication

This one is for Don

To Pat—without your dedication and devotion this book would never have been possible.

Contents

Acknowledgments

I continue to be amazed at how helpful Age of Sail authors are when another asks for guidance.

Douglas Reeman and Kim have never failed to help me out.

One rainy Saturday I was at a place where I couldn't go further. Dewey Lambdin answered his phone and answered my questions immediately.

Jim Nelson has never failed me and I feel like he's my sea daddy at times.

Bill Hammond continues to be an inspiration and I appreciate him very much.

I want to thank Johannes Ewers for allowing me to use his wonderful paintings as cover art. I hope my books justify the use of his art.

Alaric Bond has become a good friend. His in depth knowledge and willingness to share information about the business has been heartfelt. I'd love to buy you a wet, Alaric.

Characters in the Fighting Anthony Series

British Officers and Seamen:

Rear Admiral Lord Gilbert "Gil" Anthony – Commands British fleet in the Caribbean. First son of Retired Admiral Lord James Anthony (deceased) and Lady Anthony.

Captain Gabriel "Gabe" Anthony – Second son of Retired Admiral Lord James Anthony (deceased) and his mistress Maria Dupree.

Captain Rupert Buck – Admiral Lord Gil Anthony's flag captain.

Bart – Long time cox'n and friend to Admiral Lord Anthony.

Dagan Dupree – Supernumerary on *Peregrine*. Gabe's uncle and self-appointed guardian.

Lieutenant David Davy – *Peregrine's* third lieutenant. Gabe's friend.

Lord Ragland – British Governor of Barbados.

Captain Francis Markham – Captain of frigate *HMS Dasher*.

Captain Stephen Earl – British naval officer in earlier novels.

Lieutenant George Jepson – Commander of the small ship, *HMS Pegasus*.

Lieutenant Mahan – Commands *HMS Rapid*.

Lieutenant Wesley – *HMS Rapid's* first lieutenant.

Nathan Lavery – *HMS Peregrine's* first lieutenant.

Everette Hazard – Admiral Lord Anthony's flag lieutenant. Lost an arm in previous action.

x

Ambrose Taylor – Captain of *HMS Lizard*.
Gunnells – *Peregrine's* master.
Jacob (Jake) Hex – Gabe's new cox'n.
Silas – Lord Anthony's steward.
Dawkins – Gabe's servant and secretary.
Josiah Nesbit – A chef and a gentleman's gentleman.
Sir Victor McNeil – British Foreign Office agent/spy.
Lord Skalla – British Foreign Office agent who replaces Sir Victor.
Mr. Hawks – One of Gabe's midshipmen.
Mr. Alejandro a/k/a Mr. Ally – Son of Spanish parents in Saint Augustine. He becomes one of Gabe's midshipmen.
Paco – Gabe's cox'n. Friend to Mr. Ally and his parents.
Mr. Chase – Midshipman from the captured *HMS Drake*.

The Ladies:

Lady Deborah – Lord Anthony's wife. They met after pirates had attacked the ship Lady Deborah and her husband were on. The husband was killed by the pirates before Lord Anthony's ship came to the rescue. The marriage between Lady Deborah and her first husband had been one of convenience. When she and Lord Anthony met it was love at first sight. They later married and had a daughter, Macayla.
Faith – Gabe's wife. They met in *HMS SeaWolf* where Gabe had survived an explosion but was wounded. Faith and Nanny were walking on the beach and came upon him. They hid Gabe and nursed him back to health. Gabe and Faith fell in love but with her being an American and with Gabe being a British sea officer it was difficult.
Betsy – Dagan's love. She is the sister of American General Manning's deceased wife. She is a young widow who lives with the general. Dagan met Betsy during the time

General Manning was being held in Saint Augustine as a paroled prisoner of war.

Rebecca/Becky – Lord Anthony's sister. She lives in England with her husband, Hugh, and daughter, Gretchen.

Maria Dupree– She is Gabe's mother and Dagan's sister. She was Admiral Lord James Anthony's mistress of many years.

The Americans:

General Manning – America's chief negotiator for POW exchange.

Andre Dupree – Dagan's uncle. He moved to Virginia years ago.

Caleb McKean – Physician and surgeon. Gabe's friend. Loves Kitty Dupree.

Kitty – Andre Dupree's daughter who loves Caleb McKean.

Jubal – Andre Dupree's son. Still a youngster, he appears to have "the gift" as his cousin, Dagan.

Kawliga – American Indian who lives with Andre Dupree's family and looks after Jubal. Kawliga understands Jubal's "gift".

Ariel – A captive sex slave to privateer Witzenfeld.

Lum – Slave on Faith's family plantation. He kills a man attempting to rape Faith. He spends time with Gabe on board ship as his servant, and then when Faith and Gabe reunite, he leaves the sea to be with her and Nanny.

Nanny – Like Lum, she was a slave on Faith's family plantation. She was a personal servant to Faith's mother and has been Faith's nanny since birth. She loves Lum.

The Bad Guy:

Witzenfeld – American privateer blames Gabe and Dagan for the death of his brother.

PART I

Final Victory

The mighty ship entered port
Her yards set cockbill
A loyal crew mourned the death
Their brave captain killed
The battle had been fought and won
They fired the last broadside
As enemy colours floated down
The good captain died

...Michael Aye

Prologue

"Bloody 'ell...Deck thar," the mainmast lookout shouted down. "It's the whole Frog fleet."

"Where away," Lieutenant Mahan shouted back at the excited lookout.

"Dead astern, sir."

Lieutenant Mahan felt a sinking feeling in the pit of his stomach as he grabbed a glass and rushed aft. The glare from the rising sun made it difficult to focus but as the breeze wisped away an area of haze the fleet came into view. The lookout had been right. It looked like the whole Frog fleet.

"Did the Johnny Crapuads leave any ships at home?" Wesley, the ship's only other officer asked his captain.

Mahan didn't answer. He had just been given command of the sloop in March of 1778 and it was just July, of all the rotten luck. Rated a sloop, **HMS Rapid**, was a snow, a prize taken by his previous command. He had been placed in command of the prize with his captain's strongest recommendation for command. Lord Howe had in honour of his previous captain made him Master and Commander after determining the vessel a worth prize. Looking down the eighty-foot deck of **Rapid**, Mahan wondered how much longer he would continue to have a command.

Looking to Wesley he asked, "Is **HMS Haerlem** in sight?"

"No sir," the first lieutenant replied. He had been the third lieutenant on *Mahan's* previous ship and had come over with him.

They had been friends for several years and had come aboard **Rapid** together. He hoped they wouldn't become prisoners of war together...or worse.

Looking at the French fleet bearing down on them, Mahen gave the only order he could, "Make all sail."

"Deck thar," the lookout called down again. "Ship off the port bow." Then before anyone could question him further added, "Looks like **Haerlem**, sir."

Nodding to himself Mahan turned to his first lieutenant, "Make signal to **Haerlem**, enemy in sight. If he doesn't acknowledge, fire a cannon."

"Won't that give away our position, sir?"

Mahan answered with a snap, "You don't think the damn Frogs know where we are, sir? I just hope **Haerlem** makes it to warn Lord Howe."

"Deck thar, signals from the Frog flagship and two big frigates 'as left formation. They're bearing down on us, sir."

"Very well," Mahan acknowledged. "Mr. Wesley, you have the deck. Have the men toss everything overboard that they can. I'm going down to my cabin to look at my charts."

"Everything, sir, even the cannons?"

"Dammit, Mr. Wesley, must you question every order today?"

Seeing the hurt look on his friend's face, Mahan took a breath and said, "There is little we can do with sixteen six pounders with two big Frog frigates bearing down on us. Our only hope is to gain time to find a likely spot to beach the ship...and burn her."

Feeling somewhat foolish Wesley replied, "Aye aye, sir," and went to do as ordered.

Mahan then turned to the ship's master. "Mr. Love, would you join me as I peer over what charts we have?"

"Aye, Captain," Love responded. He could see the despair in the young captain's face. What bad luck, he thought. Damn the Frogs to hell.

Returning on deck, Mahan saw the wind was from the southwest. With the ship's anchors, cannons, and all supplies thrown overboard to lighten the ship a small advantage was gained for an hour or so. But the French held a more favourable position with the wind at their backs and it was soon realized the advantage once held was diminishing fast.

*Mahan called the crew together. "Men we have done all we can to outrun the French. It's obvious now that they will soon be within cannon range. According to the charts we are close to Assateague Island. The wake is deep then shoals very fast. I intend to run the ship aground under full sail then set fire to her. That way she will be of no use to our enemies. Get what little is left aboard that we can use to get a good blaze going. You've been a good crew and **Rapid** has been a fine ship. I wish you all the best."*

After finishing his speech, Mahan turned to the bosun. "Dismiss the crew."

Turning toward the quarterdeck, he was surprised when a cheer went up. "Huzza, huzza, for the captain." Will they cheer at my court martial, he wondered. Well, I've kept her from the French, he thought as he heard the report of cannon fire.

"Make an entry, Mr. Wesley, fired on by the enemy. Make that by the French."

"Aye aye, sir."

Assateague Island was now just off the larboard bow.

"There appears to be several American vessels at anchor," Wesley volunteered.

"I see them," Mahan replied. "I'd rather be an American prisoner than a French one. Now fire the ship, and then have the men find something to hold on to as we run aground."

"Aye aye, sir. Captain?"

"Yes, Mr. Wesley."

"It's been a pleasure, sir."

Chapter One

Lieutenant George "Jep" Jepson stood in the shrouds amazed at the sight of the approaching fleet as it approached Sandy Hook, New York. It was something to behold...even if it was French and their arrival could mean death before the sun set this day of our Lord, July 11, 1778. As he continued to watch from his vantage point, he could see Lord Howe's tiny line of defence...seven vessels – five sixty-fours, one fifty, and an armed store ship. Black Dick knew his business though.

When the ships were anchored, springs were placed on the ship's cables so that they could swing to rake any ship coming up the channel. They would also be able to face the French broadside to broadside if the Frogs succeeded in forcing a passage. This gave Jepson a shiver.

The French fleet was made up of one ninety-gun ship that carried Admiral Comte d'Estaing's flag, six seventy-fours, three sixty-fours, and one fifty. The French held a superior firepower such as Jepson had never seen before, and only the Lord knew what yet lay over the horizon. It was as hopeless a situation as he had ever encountered.

Climbing down the shrouds, Jepson was careful not to get any tar on his new uniform. *Hell*, he thought, *all my uniforms are new*. So new in fact they still held the sheen of new fabric. He'd only worn the uniform of a British navy officer for a few weeks. He'd been promoted to lieutenant from master by his Lordship Vice Admiral Anthony after they'd beaten a French squadron in the Caribbean. His Lordship had then surprised Jepson even more by offering him command of the brig, *HMS Pegasus*.

Pegasus was the winged horse of Greek mythology. She was not a big ship, only one hundred feet long with a beam of twenty-four feet. She mounted fourteen six pounders, seven down each side and two four pounders for bow chasers. The Americans who had built and armed her had definitely planned to use the ship as a commerce raider...a privateer, as she was also fitted out with twelve swivels. She might be small but she was his.

Chomping down on a cigar he retrieved from his senior midshipman, Joseph Bucklin, he looked about his ship. Never in all his days in the navy had he expected to command a ship. Yet here he was with the Frogs bearing down in such a belligerent and hellish manner. Well they'd have a hard time taking his first command and that was no error.

"Mr. Parks," Jepson called to his first lieutenant.

"Aye, sir."

"I'm going below to break my fast. Call me if anything further develops."

Parks watched as "the captain" made his way down the small companionway to his cabin. He had to be the oldest junior officer he'd ever laid eyes on. *I'll bet my date of rank is at least six months senior to his...maybe a year*. However, one didn't compare dates of rank with one's captain. Not that the captain didn't know his business. Parks had never sailed with anyone who knew the elements or how to get the most out of a ship better than the captain. No sir, the only thing lacking that he could see was polish. He knew the sea, but knew very little about the finer things in life. Taking a deep breath Parks gave a sigh. Right now he was glad the captain was an old salt. With the French fleet bearing down he'd put his money on the captain any day rather than some popinjay from Cambridge.

* * *

A knock on the door and the sentry announced, "First lieutenant, zur." Jepson had been looking over the ship's books and was glad for the interruption. He was trying to make sense of the purser's, Burford's, ledgers. *How could it be that two plus two made four one time but five the next? Learned his trade well, he did, but I'll let him know I know the ways of his kind and I'll be watching...watching closely.* Looking up at Parks he offered a glass of something cool.

"Thank you sir," Parks replied as he took the offered chair. "We just got word from a lieutenant in the guard boat, sir; the French has had to anchor." Seeing the captain raise his eyebrow over this news, he continued. "It seems the tide is low and the water over the sandbar at the channel entrance is only twenty-three feet whereas the French ships draw twenty-five feet. They can't cross the bar to attack," Parks said, excitement in his voice.

Jepson leaned back with his arm behind his head as he listened to Parks' news. He now rocked forward and slapped his legs with a twinkle in his blue eyes. "I knew there was a God in heaven, Mr. Parks."

Parks then produced a sealed document. "The guard lieutenant also brought this by, sir."

Taking the paper Jepson could see Lord Howe's seal. *It can't be sailing orders,* he thought and seemed to be a single page folded then sealed. "Have another glass, Mr. Parks, while I read this. Would you care for a cigar?"

"Thank you, Captain, I don't mind if I do."

Jepson pushed the box of cigars across the table and watched as Parks bit off the tip then opened the door to the lantern and expertly lit the cigar. *Humph...boy has got promise*, Jepson thought as he broke the seal and read the single page.

When he finished reading he spoke, "It seems we are ordered to provide passage and render all required assistance to Sir Victor MacNeil from his Majesty's Foreign Office."

"I've never met anyone from the foreign office, sir."

"I have," Jepson replied. "In fact this very same gentleman. It seems Gabe...ere, Captain Anthony, he's Admiral Anthony's younger brother, was given an assignment much as ours and the two hit it off fairly well. Sir Victor even took part in battling some privateers as I recall. I've no concern with this foreign office gentleman."

Parks couldn't help but ask, "I hear you have been ah...close to his Lordship for some time...off and on over the years."

Jepson replied, "If you live long enough and stay in the Navy, paths will usually cross here and there."

"Yes sir. Would it be imposing, sir, to ask if you would tell me a little about his Lordship; I've always heard he was a great man."

"Aye that he is, sir, in every way." Jepson then began his narrative of the times and ships the two of them had served on together, leaving out his saving the admiral's life.

Standing on deck, Lieutenant Barry could feel the first drops of an early afternoon shower. Walking aft he could hear portions of the conversation coming through an open stern window. *Lucky sod Parks is,* he thought, *down there rubbing elbows with the captain while I'm stuck on deck in this rain.*

"Mr. Bucklin," he called to the midshipman on watch. "Run down to my cabin and get my tarpaulin."

"Aye sir," Bucklin replied as he rushed off. *If I take my time,* he thought, *he'll already be soaked when I get back.* The temptation to tarry was strong but the midshipman made it back on deck just seconds before the rain came in earnest.

"I've got my eye on you, young sir," Barry said, snapping his watch closed.

A sheepish Bucklin could only reply, "Aye aye, sir."

* * *

For the next eleven days the British and French stared at each other over the sandbar. Lord Howe had formed a second line of defense with four galleys while an old sixty-four and a few small frigates were held in reserve. British General Clifton mounted a five-gun shore battery at the end of the hook to help defend the harbour. Meanwhile Admiral Comte d'Estaing was said to be so frustrated with the inability to get his ships across the sandbar so that he could engage the British that he offered a reward of fifty thousand crowns to any pilot who could lead his ships across the sandbar.

On the twenty-second day of July a fresh breeze blew from the northeast and a strong spring tide raised the water over the bar to thirty feet. Word was spread throughout Lord Howe's command and the British prepared to make battle.

Lieutenant Jepson stood with his glass and watched as the French weighed anchor and hoisted their sails. "Mr. Parks."

"Aye, Captain."

"Have the weapons broken out and have the men stand by."

"Do we beat to quarters sir?"

"No. The Frogs have to break through Lord Howe's two lines of defense before we could bring our guns into action, though little good we could do with our pop guns. No, I want the men prepared in case we are needed to augment one of the lines of defense."

"I see, sir."

"Mr. Parks."

"Aye sir," the first lieutenant replied, turning back to his captain.

"Have the man with the best pair of eyes sent aloft. I want to be kept abreast of things as they occur. Not told afterwards."

"Aye sir, Mr. Bucklin has a good set of peepers. I'll send him, sir."

"Very well," Jepson replied.

The sound of boat ahoy stopped Jepson as he started down to his cabin to get his pistols and sword. He was close enough to the entry port to hear the reply from the sentry, Midshipman Robinson's challenge, "Sir Victor MacNeil from his Majesty's Foreign Office," the boatman called up.

Humph, Jepson grunted. He'd wondered when Sir Victor would make his appearance. Normally a guest of Sir Victor's magnitude would require honours to be rendered but in the current state Jepson figured Sir Victor would understand the foregoing of pomp and ceremony.

Lieutenant Parks made his way toward his captain and when Sir Victor made his way on board the two removed their hats and gave a slight bow. Jepson then replaced his hat on his head and stretched out his hand to shake with his guest.

"Sir Victor, it's so nice to see you again."

Taking Jepson's hand, Sir Victor replied, "When I saw your name I wondered if it was the same 'Jep' Jepson who had served Lord Anthony so well. I'm glad to see you've been promoted and given a nice command to boot. Tell me, Captain," Sir Victor said, using Jepson's courtesy title, "how's our friend Bart doing?"

Jepson couldn't help but smile, recalling how Bart once had dressed down Sir Victor and let him know in no uncertain terms what to expect if he caused harm to befall either Gabe or Lord Anthony. "He was doing well when we last spoke, sir. Called me a traitor to the men forward by taking this promotion yet he was the one who bought me a new glass."

"That sounds like Bart but he's not one who should point a finger since he's been aft with his Lordship for so long. He'd probably fall out of his hammock and break his neck if he had to move forward again."

In the Navy "forward" was where the common sailors lived and slept while "aft" was for the officers.

"Mr. Robinson," Jep called.

"Sir," the midshipman answered.

"Please assist Sir Victor's man and have his chest placed in my cabin."

"Aye aye, sir."

"Nonsense," Sir Victor objected but hushed when Jepson quieted his objections by holding up his hand, cocking his head to the side.

"Deck there," Bucklin called down in an excited voice. "The French, sir...the French are hauling their wind."

Jepson couldn't believe his ears. He'd fully expected to shortly be engaged in a bloody battle to the end. "Mr. Robinson, my glass, sir."

The young midshipman dropped his end of Sir Victor's trunk as he rushed to do his captain's bidding. The chest hit the deck with a thud causing Sir Victor's servant to fall backward. He landed off balance against the bulwark then tumbled over the side, splashing into the harbour's water below, just missing the longboat. Wincing, the midshipman was torn between fetching the captain's glass and helping the poor servant below who was crying for help.

"I can't swim!" the servant yelled in a frantic voice while spitting out water.

Finally Robinson grabbed a coil of rope and tossed it overboard, hitting the servant squarely in the face and causing a shout of pain.

"Hold to the rope," Robinson called down, "I'll be right back."

In his haste, the midshipman neglected to secure the other end of the rope before he rushed off. The servant kept pulling on the rope but all he did was unwind the coil. As he bobbed up and down still shouting for help he swallowed more water, causing him to choke.

"Well damme," Jepson shouted as he quickly grabbed the bitter end of the rope before it went over the side. Looking at Lieutenant Parks he barked, "Grab a hold. Are we to let Sir Victor's man drown while lying to?"

Parks took the rope and by the time Robinson returned they had the dripping servant on deck, a huge whelp on his face where the rope had struck him.

"Here's your glass sir," the midshipman said with a quivering voice.

Embarrassed, Jepson just glared at the trembling youth. "Mr. Parks," Jepson growled taking the glass.

"I'll take care of it, sir," the first lieutenant responded as he turned to Robinson. "Have one of the crew take Sir Victor's servant to be examined by the surgeon, then have a couple of the crew carry Sir Victor's chest to the captain's cabin. After you've completed these tasks report back to me so that we may discuss setting one's priorities."

Climbing into the shrouds for a better viewing advantage Jepson was able to see the remaining ships of the French fleet as it bore away. Not understanding why the French had not pressed its advantage at high water he was nevertheless grateful to have survived the day. As he made his way back to the deck Sir Victor waited for him.

"So they've set sail?"

"Aye, sir."

"Humph. Well, they didn't press the advantage today but I doubt we've been spared a taste of their metal. Just postponed, I'd say."

"My thoughts as well, Sir Victor, my thoughts as well," Jepson replied, wondering not when but where they would meet. "A glass, Sir Victor?"

"By all means, Captain, and if my chest survived that crash on deck I have a couple of good bottles of some French wine. We'll use it to toast the French admiral."

"The French admiral, sir?" Jepson asked.

"Aye, Captain, to his hurried departure."

Then as an afterthought Sir Victor added, "And we'll raise a glass to a smooth passage to Barbados."

Chapter Two

The Caribbean sun beat down on the island of Barbados. A stiff land breeze did little to relieve the heat but made rowing the admiral's barge more difficult than usual. Bart, the admiral's cox'n, snarled at the crew.

"Ye row like a bunch of laggards off a bumboat."

One of the crewmen, braver than his comrades, whispered under his breath, "We's pulling into the wind."

Hearing this Bart retorted, "Ye should be thankful for the breeze what cools ye so on such a warmish day."

Admiral Lord Anthony sat in the stern sheets and listened as Bart growled at the barge crew. *He must be feeling some malady today,* Anthony thought. Bart had not eaten much that morning and he hadn't been out having a wet or gambling the previous evening. Anthony decided he'd have to keep a weather eye out for his friend.

"Lord Ragland's men are already waiting, sir."

Deep in thought, Anthony had not seen the carriage arrive.

"Bart."

"Aye sir."

"You come with me and send the barge back to the ship."

"Aye sir. Up oars," Bart commanded, then pushed the tiller over as the barge sided up to the pier and a mooring line was expertly tossed over by one of the barge men both forward and aft.

The slack was taken up and the line was quickly made secure after two or three turns. Lord Anthony stepped from the barge but turned just in time to see Bart hand the senior bargeman enough coins for a wet before rowing back to the flagship. *Bart's way of making up for being grumpy*, Anthony thought. *A lot of officers could learn from his cox'n*, he thought, and then, just as quickly, realized several had.

Waiting at the carriage, the coachman and footman stood patiently waiting in their fine livery. As Lord Anthony approached, the footman quickly opened the carriage door and placed a white wooden step in front of it to make the entrance easier. The ride to Government House was fairly short but by the time a person walked the distance their clothes would be wet and clingy from perspiration.

"So, Sir Victor is back stirring up things is he?" Bart said.

Anthony couldn't help but smile. While Bart didn't exactly dislike the foreign office fellow he didn't go out of his way for him.

"Now Bart, Sir Victor is a fine sort. Why, he even made sure you were invited to our meeting today."

"Wants to keep 'is eye on me 'e does. Scared I might bounce a belaying pin off 'is 'ead for all the trouble 'e brings us when 'e's around."

"Well, I expect you to treat him as befitting a man of his office," Anthony replied firmly.

"Oh, I intends too."

"Bart!"

Taking a deep breath Bart replied, "I know, the bugger's a King's officer."

"He's not a bugger, Bart."

"How yews know?"

"I know, Bart, we were at this party..."

"Whoa! Whoa!" The driver stopping the horses interrupted Lord Anthony's explanation.

The footman was down and had the door open. Seeing Bart was all ears made Anthony chuckle.

"I'll tell you later."

"Damme," Bart snorted. "Have me beat to quarters then tells me to stand down before I even catches a glimpse of the enemy."

The doorman was waiting and as Anthony and Bart entered Government House he made a noise. "Ahem! Perhaps your man could follow me, your Lordship."

Not liking the little man's snooty attitude, Anthony replied, "And perhaps he'd rather not."

Realizing he'd committed an error in judgment, the doorman cocked his head and gazed at Bart. "As you say, my Lord; Lord Ragland and Sir Victor are waiting."

As the man attempted to lead them down the hall Anthony spoke, "We know our way. I'm sure you have other duties that need your attention."

The man did an about face that would have made any sergeant happy. Once he was past earshot Bart looked at Anthony and said, "Now tell me that one ain't no bugger."

* * *

Lord Ragland and Sir Victor were sitting casually in the library. As Lord Anthony and Bart entered, the men rose to greet them. After a round of handshakes, Lord Ragland spoke.

"Sir Victor has presented me with a case of fine hock. We've just opened a bottle. Shall I pour each of you a glass?" Without waiting for an answer, the glasses were filled.

Taking a sip, Bart thought, *I'd rather have rum*, as he walked over by the window and looked down toward the harbour. He was amazed at the amount of activity on such a sweltering day.

Lord Ragland started the meeting. "Sir Victor has returned to us requesting assistance from you, Lord Anthony."

This caused Bart's ears to perk up and he turned his full attention to the conversation. Waiting, Anthony did not speak.

"My reason for requesting your assistance, Lord Anthony, is I understand you have firsthand knowledge of Saint Augustine and at one point knew several of the prisoners held there."

"That's correct."

"Good," Sir Victor replied. "We are at a point where negotiations have been agreed upon to have a large prisoner exchange. However, the agreement was reached before the French entered the war. Now we have several...shall we say...key officers and officials that we would like to have back in our fold before the French have time to influence the exchange."

Spies he means, Anthony thought.

"However, we can't make our desires for these certain people known. We will, therefore, be exchanging a number of prisoners in all aspects. Officers, government officials, enlisted men, sailors, and so on. We want a man of sufficient rank to represent his Majesty. That is to be you, Lord Anthony. However, we want someone with, say, a more common knowledge of the average soldier or sailor so they won't be able to slip in an agent or two. Bart, that's where you come in. From our previous conversations I feel you can spot or flush out a government agent as well as anyone."

Bart couldn't help but recall his not too friendly conversation with Sir Victor in a tavern one afternoon. Without replying, Bart just nodded.

Lord Anthony had heard of the Colonial General George Washington's cadre of spies. Many of them were able to fit into various walks of life and had a variety of social skills. Bart would be as good a choice as anyone to flush them out, with the possible exception of Dagan.

"When we do depart?" Anthony asked.

"Soon, my Lord. The exchange is scheduled to take place in Norfolk, Virginia, in September. This place was chosen as sort of a halfway point for us to meet. A Colonel Manning will be the Colonial officer in charge of the exchange."

Anthony nodded again. *It has to be the same Manning I met some time ago in Saint Augustine*, he thought, *a man of substance and honour.*

"You will, of course, stop in Saint Augustine and pick up the Colonial prisoners to be exchanged," Sir Victor was saying.

"When I was there before, a lot of families were being held along with their servants."

"Yes, that's my understanding as well," Sir Victor replied.

"How many prisoners are we talking about?" Anthony asked.

"Approximately three hundred all together, but of course we don't as of yet have the exact total as family members and servants haven't been counted yet."

"Damme, sir, but that is a large exchange."

A knock on the door interrupted the conversation. It was one of Lord Ragland's clerks who entered, leaned forward, and whispered to the governor. Once the clerk had departed, Lord Ragland rose.

"I'm sorry, gentlemen. Other matters require my attention." Seeing he still had a swallow of hock he lifted his glass. "A toast, gentlemen, to a swift and successful exchange."

After the toast was drunk, Ragland spoke again, "We will, of course, prepare a formal reception for Sir Victor. I will see your invitations are sent forthwith, Admiral. Now, gentlemen, I must take my leave."

Once Lord Ragland had departed, Sir Victor turned back to Anthony and Bart. "You realize this mission is probably our last chance to get some very key people back before their identity is discovered and they are hanged as spies."

Seeing the look on Anthony and Bart's faces, Sir Victor nodded. "Yes, we have men who could ruin us to save their own necks if they were to choose to do so."

"Does the war depend that much on these individuals?" Anthony asked.

"Yes...well no. Damme sir, but the war is lost."

Lord Anthony looked stunned.

Then, agitated at his loss of control, Sir Victor poured himself another glass. "The damnable politicians have looked at this war as a lark. Not really willing to supply the forces or provide the resources to bring a quick end to the conflict. Meanwhile, the French have been rebuilding their navy and biding their time. Now it's here. With their alliance with the Colonials they have been given the perfect opportunity to settle some scores from the Seven Year War. We cannot protect our borders at home and fight a long distance war. If something is not done soon we could be forced to dine on frog stew."

Chapter Three

The door opened and Bart padded into the captain's cabin aboard *HMS Peregrine*. After spending the last few years aboard a flagship he'd forgotten how small the space was aboard a frigate.

HMS Peregrine was one of the larger frigates of the time. It was larger than Lord Anthony's first frigate but smaller than *HMS Drakkar*, which had been a razed sixty-four, turning the ship into a heavy frigate of forty-four guns. Thinking back, it was hard to believe all the water that had gone beneath the keel since that time. His Lordship's brother, Gabe, had been a midshipman on *Drakkar* and now here he was a captain in command of *HMS Peregrine*. Lord Anthony had just put his boots on and looked Bart's way. Eyeing the two jugs in Bart's hand, he said, "I hope one is coffee."

"Aye," Bart replied. "The other is hot water for yew's shave."

"How are things on deck?" Anthony inquired.

Setting the jugs down, Bart was about to shout for Silas to fetch his Lordship a cup but recalled, just as he opened his mouth, that Silas was back aboard the flagship.

"Mr. Gunnells says it'll be another roaster," he informed Anthony.

Bart had been facing Lord Anthony as he was speaking and therefore didn't see Nesbit, Gabe's servant, as he entered the pantry. The two collided, with Nesbit hitting the deck with a thud.

"Clumsy oaf," Nesbit hissed. Bart couldn't believe his ears. Clumsy oaf!

"You little bugger," Bart snarled. "For a man sitting on his arse you got a lot of wind and I'm the salt what will take some of that wind out of yews sails."

"Bart."

"Aye."

"Leave Gabe's man alone."

"Don't worry, my Lord. It's too early to keelhaul this poor Christian soul." With that Bart strode out of the captain's cabin.

Something's definitely amiss with Bart, Anthony decided as he walked over to help Nesbit to his feet.

"I apologize for Bart's behaviour," Anthony offered. "He's usually not like this."

Nesbit didn't know how to respond. He had never had a cross word with Bart so he knew his Lordship was right. However, what amazed him the most was his Lordship actually cared enough to apologize.

Making his way on deck, it was light enough for Anthony to make out a group of officers on the quarterdeck. Bart and Dagan were sitting on the taffrail. *Hopefully Dagan will help Bart work out whatever ails him*, Anthony thought as he made his way to the quarterdeck.

Gabe had his back to his brother but the gentle nudge and eye movement by Lieutenant Davy did not go unnoticed. Even if the admiral was the captain's brother he was still the admiral. *A good officer Lieutenant Davy*, Anthony thought. *His actions show loyalty.* An officer who was trying to seek favour with the admiral and having an axe to grind with the captain would have waited until the admiral was present and then make a show of greeting him.

"Good morning, my Lord," Gabe greeted his brother in the official manner. "Wind is almost directly astern and blowing to the north-northeast. Mr. Gunnells promises a blistering day. Except for *Dasher* and *Pegasus*, the horizon is free of sails."

"Very well," Anthony replied to the report. "Any word as to whether our passenger has roused out as yet?"

"No, my Lord. Lieutenant Lavery said he could hear snoring when he passed his cabin. I would say Sir Victor is sleeping a peaceful, much needed and deserved sleep."

"Aye," Anthony agreed.

From the conversation last evening, Sir Victor had confided he'd not had many peaceful sleeps of late. There had been several attempts on his life. He wondered if somebody didn't want this prisoner exchange to take place. Who and for what reason was yet to be discussed. Unless...they had a spy in the midst of the prisoners that was having success gaining and passing information. Or was he just being jumpy?

Lord Anthony had offered to share Gabe's cabin with the Foreign Office gentleman but Sir Victor had declined and borrowed the first lieutenant's cabin.

Gabe had slept in the chart room but the three men had taken their dinner together. Nesbit's cooking was not to be passed up. Thinking of the evening meal, Anthony looked at the officers, Gabe's officers, standing but not speaking. Protocol demanded they remain until dismissed by the admiral. *I'm in the way.* He thought, *these men have their duties to attend. I know how Gabe must feel. I wish the admiral would go below so we could go about our routine.* Gabe would never say a word but Anthony knew what he was thinking. *It hadn't been that long ago he'd been standing in the captain's shoes and thinking I'd give anything if the admiral would just go below. Well, he wouldn't keep Gabe and his officers in agony any longer; he'd go below. Besides, Nesbit was sure to have something to tempt the palate.*

"Captain, I think I shall go break my fast. If you have the time, please join me."

"Thank you, sir."

"Bart."

"Aye sir."

"Shall we break our fast?"

"Aye," the burly cox'n replied and started toward his admiral.

Anthony was almost to the companionway then as an afterthought turned. "Captain, if Sir Victor wakes before the noon meal, extend the invitation for morning coffee to him as well."

This brought a smile to all within hearing. A little jape at the Foreign Officer's expense would do no harm.

* * *

Mr. Gunnells, the master, gripped the quarterdeck rail and peered blindly into the foggy abyss. "Damn this mist," he snarled.

Gabe said nothing as he watched the mist drip from his hat. They should have raised the Florida coast off Saint Augustine at dawn. He listened as the leadsman standing in the chains heaved the lead and, marking the depth, called out his findings from the weather side of the ship. The crashing surf could now be heard.

Looking aft and to the starboard, *Dasher* would appear and disappear like a ghost in the fog. *Pegasus* had not been spotted. An early morning fog was not unusual in these waters at this time of year but this was lasting longer than expected. The sound of the crashing surf had the crew on edge.

Turning to Midshipman Hawks, Gabe ordered, "My compliments to the admiral and I think I'll anchor and wait till this soup clears before closing with the land."

"I'm here, Gabe." Anthony had made his way on deck without being spotted; every eye was concentrating on the fog. Catching his brother's questioning look, Anthony replied, "She's your ship, Captain."

Nodding, Gabe turned to the first lieutenant. "Mr. Lavery, prepare to anchor. Mr. Ally."

"Aye sir."

"You profess to have a good set of lungs. Take yonder speaking trumpet and see if you can raise Captain Markham aboard *Dasher*. We need to advise them of our anchor...else he's likely to run his jib boom right up our arse."

"Aye, Captain, alert them I will."

Once *Dasher* was alerted to anchor, the ship took on an eerie silence. Looking skyward, not a thread of sunlight seemed to penetrate the fog. The slapping sounds of waves lapping against the hull and the groan of timbers as the ship tugged on its anchor cable added to the mystique. It was like a phantom. Not a man whispered as each listened and waited.

It was Ally who broke the silence and was hushed by his fellow midshipmen. Ignoring Hawks, Ally made his way to the nearest officer. "Lieutenant Davy, sir...Lieutenant Davy," Ally whispered.

"Yes, what is it, Alejandro?"

The use of his full name was not lost on the midshipman. "Permission to speak to the captain, sir."

"Speak to the captain?" Lieutenant Davy asked, not believing what he'd heard. The immediate reaction was to deny permission but the look on the youth's face made Davy reconsider. "Very well, young sir, follow me quietly."

Gabe could see the two approaching the quarterdeck. "Yes," he asked without giving the two a chance to speak.

"I'm...I'm sure I heard the sound of small arms to larboard, sir."

Gabe had never known the boy to speak lightly so he believed him. Almost like magic, Dagan appeared.

"I think the boy is right," he said.

"Mr. Lavery."

"Sir."

"I want you to take a boarding party in two longboats toward the sound of gunfire. Alejandro will be your guide. Mr. Wiley, send a boat over to *Dasher* and let them know what's about."

"Aye Captain."

The longboats were put over the side quickly and quietly. Seeing Dagan about to go over the rail, Gabe spoke, "You don't have to go."

"Might help the boy if I did."

Gabe nodded. His lieutenants may question Alejandro but they'd never question Dagan. Turning back Gabe saw his brother standing. *Damme,* he thought, *I didn't even ask his permission.* He then recalled his brother's words: *She's your ship, Captain.* Well, this went a bit farther than anchoring so he'd better inform his...ah...the admiral as to his actions.

Chapter Four

Dagan watched as the armed men quickly lowered themselves into the longboats. Tough, seasoned men, every jack tar, marine, and officer. Lieutenant Lavery had instructed Mr. Ally to take the lead as he had a better sense of the direction the sounds had come from. Taking his job seriously the midshipman sat down next to the tiller, "Cast off. Out oars, give way all."

Sitting in the stern sheets Dagan wiped the mist from his eyes and strained to hear anything that would direct them in this hellish fog. Toward the bow of the boat somebody's hands slipped off his oar, causing another to chuckle.

"Silence there," Ally hissed, iron in his voice.

"A boat, fine to larboard," the bowman called, his voice barely a whisper.

"Up oars," Ally ordered.

The movement of the boat slowed significantly and soon the other longboat with Lieutenant Lavery was up to them.

"The buggers are going to ram us!" the man sitting next to Dagan cried out. But the look on Dagan's face silenced him before he could say more.

The men rested on their thwarts, letting their muscles relax from rowing. When alongside,

Lieutenant Lavery's men hooked on to the other longboat. Ally told of sighting the boat just ahead. Nodding, the lieutenant started to speak when another gunshot broke the silence, then a second.

"Move out with caution," Lavery ordered. "We'll stick close."

The men were all alert now. There was no doubt as to what Mr. Ally had heard. They were headed in the right direction, but the exact bearing and distance could not be judged. The men had only been at their oars for a few minutes when the bowman again called out.

"Something's in the water." Before the bowman could get his boat hook, it thudded into the bow, causing ripples of waves to slosh inboard. Taking the boat hook and pulling on the object the bowman gave a sudden gasp.

"What is it?" Ally hissed as he stood up to see better, taking Dagan's offered hand to help maintain his balance.

"It's a man...a dead man, sir."

Gazing at the naked corpse it dawned on Ally that the man had a third eye. He still had powder burns on his forehead where he'd been shot at point blank range. The men stared at the man's dead fixed eyes.

"Why did they strip him?" Ally asked.

"Wanted his uniform," Dagan replied. "They shot him in the head so as to not ruin it."

Turning aft to seat himself, Ally watched as Lieutenant Lavery and his crew looked on spellbound as the body floated past.

"Can't be far," Dagan advised. "Body was not stiff yet."

This news sent a shiver through Ally as he firmly gripped the tiller. As the boatmen took up the oars Dagan touched Ally's hand and nodded. The boy had gripped the tiller so hard his knuckles had turned white.

In the distance voices could be heard: curses, shouts, and then a scream followed by a splash.

"Another one done for," someone volunteered.

"Silence in the boat," Ally responded.

"A ship...a small ship," the bowman called.

"Ease your helm," Dagan whispered to Ally.

"Toss your oars," Ally ordered.

Lieutenant Lavery drifted up as voices could clearly be heard coming from the dense fog.

"A small ship directly ahead," Ally reported.

Lieutenant Lavery spoke, looking to Dagan. "Come up on both sides and board her from two directions?"

"Aye. I think that would be best," Dagan replied.

"Give me a five minutes head start," Lavery said. "However, if we're spotted you row like hell."

"Aye sir," Ally replied then asked, "In which direction?"

Lavery looked thunderstruck for a moment then a smile creased his face. "To the sound of gunfire, you sod."

This caused a chuckle from the boatmen. Ally peered at his watch as Lavery's boat disappeared into the fog. In five minutes he ordered the men to start rowing. The fog, which had been their enemy, was now on their side as they closed with the unsuspecting vessel.

"She's a pinnace, sir," the bowman called again.

"Probably used as a pilot's boat or a guard boat," Dagan explained.

Suddenly they were alongside.

"Ship your oars."

The bowman hooked onto the main chains without being told as Ally swung the tiller hard over. A loud clink came from the bow as a discarded wine bottle bounced off the longboat's bow.

"Damnation," a voice cried out and a shot was fired.

"They've spotted Lavery," Ally said.

Dagan held his fingers to his lips. "Quietly board her. Let them rush to the other side then we'll attack once their backs are to us. Once we are aboard scream like bloody hell and watch for your mates with Lieutenant Lavery."

"I wished we'd tied on armbands," Ally whispered.

A lesson he'll not likely forget, Dagan thought then wondered why he hadn't suggested it before they left the ship. Silently the men boarded the ship while the rogues' attention was drawn to the other side.

Seeing the last man crawl over the rail, Ally shouted, "Attack...attack, at 'em lads."

Men rushed toward the enemy, screaming curses at the top of their lungs. Cutlasses waved in the air and another gunshot was heard. A mixed bag of rogues turned to face this new onslaught. A few clangs and grunts were heard and one yelled out in pain before slumping to the deck.

Dagan parried a boarding pike then struck down his assailant. Another rogue hacked awkwardly and Dagan clubbed him with his pistol.

"Stand fast!" Ally shouted. "Stand fast or die!"

The fire in the midshipman's commands brought the fight to a halt. In his Spanish accent Ally called out, "In the king's name I order you to surrender."

That was the end of it. Hemmed in from both sides the rogues had two choices: jump ship or surrender. They put down their weapons and begged mercy. Lieutenant Lavery walked over to Dagan, a grin on his face.

"Regular fire-eater, Mr. Ally is."

"Aye," Dagan replied. "More-n-likely mad at the delay in seeing his folks; had to take it out on somebody."

"Huzza! Huzza! Cheers for Mr. Ally."

"That's something he won't forget," Dagan said.

"Nor I," Lavery added. Then he added, "Tell me, Dagan. When our midshipman yelled 'In the king's name', do you reckon they knew which one he was talking about?"

Thinking on Ally's Spanish accent, Dagan replied, "I wouldn't bet on it. My question is why the devils wanted the pinnace."

"Maybe we can find out," Lavery answered. "Faced with a hanging, I'm sure some of them will find their tongue."

"Aye," Dagan replied. "Might be after they've seen a mate dance on air but one of them will talk to save his skin."

Recalling the eyes of the floating corpse, Lavery shivered. "I'd hang a few of the whoresons regardless."

Nodding, Dagan cocked his head as he heard a rustle overhead. *The wind has picked up. Won't be long before the fog clears.*

Chapter Five

Gabe smiled as the pinnace was brought into position alongside *Peregrine* towing the longboats astern. The wind had freshened and only small patches of fog remained. The prisoners were brought on board *Peregrine* and placed under guard of the marines while Lieutenant Lavery, Midshipman Ally, and Dagan went below to make their report.

"The pilot and the pinnace's master were both murdered outright and the mate was about to get his turn had we not shown up."

"Did you discover what they were after?" Lord Anthony asked.

"Aye," Lavery replied. "Ere...actually it was Dagan who came to the bottom of it."

"How so?" Lord Anthony asked.

This brought smiles to Lavery and Ally. "It was actually a ruse," Lavery volunteered. "We had the men lined up facing forward, and when nobody would speak up, Dagan called to Dunmore, a bosun's mate, and said sling a noose over the yard arm. A few heads turned as a rope was slung over. Dagan ordered eyes front. *I'll shoot the next one that turns his head.* Dagan then goes to the rear of the men and whispers to Dunmore again. Dunmore

motions to a couple of his mates and they go take up
station beside him as Dagan passes back and forth
only pausing to give Mr. Ally and me a wink. He
then says, 'Lieutenant Lavery, I recall once when we
captured a band of pirates his Lordship had to hang
near half of the whoresons before he got one to talk.
Started at the rear he did and had nearly a dozen
doing the Newgate shuffle before some bloke broke
down. It was a fine day for the sharks once we cut
them down, course they didn't know any difference.
Mr. Ally, I said. Yes, Lieutenant Lavery. If that's the
way his Lordship handled it should we do any
different. No, sir, Ally replied. Seems to me the way
has been set. I nodded my agreement then spoke to
Dagan. How would you proceed; Dagan, I asked.
Dagan paused crossed his arms and rubbed his chin
as if in deep thought. Finally he said you're the
officer, sir, but was it me I'd hang one of the sods just
to let the rest know we mean business. Make it
happen, I replied. Dagan then called to Dunmore
again and said to hang that man and pointed toward
the rear. Men went to turn but stilled themselves as
Dagan cocked the hammer on his pistols. The men
kept looking forward even though a hellish
commotion went on behind them. Finally the man
started to scream but soon the screams were choked
off. I then told the men to face aft. Seeing a man
swinging from a noose will loosen tongues quicker
than anything I know. I ordered Dunmore to cut the
man down and toss him over the side."

"You actually hanged one?" Lord Anthony
asked, not sure he was believing his ears.

"Aye sir," Lavery replied. "We strung up one of the men who'd been cut down when we boarded. It was Dunmore's mate what took on so."

"Well damme," Sir Victor replied. "What did you learn?"

"They were hoping to board an unsuspecting supply ship from a convoy that's due in, sir. That was the main objective. The second was to steal the signal and recognition codes."

"Good work. I will mention each of you in my report," Lord Anthony said. "I know your worth but it won't hurt to get your name in the Gazette."

"Thank you, sir," Lieutenant Lavery and Ally replied.

"Once the fog is clear," Anthony said, speaking to Gabe, "we'll take the pinnace in and report to the governor. I'm sure he'll be surprised." Then, as an afterthought, Anthony spoke again, "I would not think it amiss if you were to give Mr. Alejandro leave, Captain Anthony. From what I know of our orders, we are to return here once the exchange is over. Several of the families will reside here and the soldiers exchanged will augment those at the fort."

"Thank you, sir. I had considered that very thing but without knowing the very extent of our orders I didn't want to make the offer until I was sure."

That was for Sir Victor's benefit, Anthony thought. *I've told Gabe everything but Sir Victor doesn't know that and this last statement will keep him guessing.*

* * *

Governor Tonyn must have been more than a little surprised when his secretary reported the pilot boat was returning from the anchorage with an admiral's flag flying from the mast. However surprised, by the time the pinnace dropped anchor, the governor had a carriage waiting at the waterfront.

"A very capable man," Sir Victor offered and asked what Lord Anthony knew of Saint Augustine's governor.

"He's well informed as you can tell by the carriage awaiting us," Lord Anthony replied, then went on to speak of his time at Saint Augustine and his relationship with the governor.

Andrew Chiswick sat in the seat across from Sir Victor and Lord Anthony. He relaxed and enjoyed the heat of the Florida sun. *Dry land*, he thought. *How good it feels to be on dry land*. He'd not felt the land beneath his feet for more than a few hours since the clumsy midshipman knocked him arse over teakettle into New York harbour. When he took the job as Sir Victor's man at the Foreign Office he never thought he'd spend so much time aboard a ship at sea. Well, they'd be here a week or so. He'd enjoy it. *Who knows?* he thought. *A job for a man of his talents might be open here. He'd have to keep an ear open.*

Governor Tonyn had cool refreshments waiting by the time the carriage arrived at Government House. Lord Anthony was quick to note how fast Sir Victor downed his first glass.

"Careful sir," Anthony warned. "Our host is partial to the fruity wine, sangria. But don't let the sweetness or the sliced fruit floating atop the pitcher fool you. A quick glass or two on a hot day like today will put you in your cups before you know it."

Chiswick was already feeling the effects of the heady liquid.

"Ah yes," Tonyn said to Lord Anthony's comments. "One of the pleasant surprises I picked up from the Spanish. A cool glass is meant to be savoured on such days."

"What's in it?" Sir Victor asked.

"A sweet red wine topped with a mixture of spice and lemon juice, or a mixture of fruits and juices. I prefer the orange sliced on top. The mixture is then poured over a pitcher of ice to chill and let stand until even the ice is rich in flavor."

"Humm," Sir Victor uttered as he put the glass to his lips. After a swallow he commented, "I'd soon be out of ice."

"Yes, of all the ingredients ice is the most difficult to keep. I have a merchantman who supplies me twice a year from Nova Scotia but it never lasts. So enjoy, gentlemen, a toast to ice."

"Hear, hear," they all toasted.

After the toast Lord Anthony explained how the pilot boat had been taken by a band of rebels out of Georgia but thanks to the keen ear of one of his midshipmen the boat had been retaken...unfortunately not before murder and mayhem had taken place.

Nodding, Tonyn said, "We still have the odd raid but no more attacks from the sea or upon shipping. Thank God you put a stop to that, Lord Anthony. This is the first attempt at such since you left. Hopefully the rogues will be surprised enough

to figure the chance of warships being at anchorage
is too great to chance such attacks. I can't tell you
how surprised I was to see the pilot boat dropping
anchor with a vice admiral's flag flying." Having said
that, Tonyn rose and raised his glass, "A toast
gentlemen...to Lord Anthony's promotion."

After a servant had refilled the glasses, Lord
Anthony explained why they were here and inquired
as to whether Tonyn had been notified.

"I have been," Tonyn admitted but was too
skeptical to believe it would really happen; the
magnitude of such an undertaking was unbelievable.

There's that word again, Anthony thought.
Magnitude. Lord Anthony stood and looked out
toward Anastasia Island. In his mind he could still
see the broken schooner, *HMS Swan* that had been
thrown upon the beach like something insignificant
during a sudden squall. Looking back toward the
talking men, he thought just how insignificant all this
was. Feeling a touch melancholy, he thought of his
wife and daughter and how he missed them...how
much he loved them. Now that is significant!

* * *

The next week was spent meeting with prisoners to
be exchanged, explaining what was to take place and
where, as well as finding out how many family
members was involved. Those prisoners who had
given their parole to the British had led a relatively
normal existence, which included allowing entire
families to join them if they could afford it. This
group was treated much the same as other wealthy
Floridians and were invited to the social events and

balls. Those who had refused had been kept under lock and key, most of them on the sloop *Otter*, which had been turned into a prison ship while others were held on Anastasia Island. A few were even kept at the fort. By the time the final number had been established, Lord Anthony realized he didn't have the ships to transport all the people.

Sir Victor reluctantly admitted that no thought had been given to the transport of slaves, servants, or extended family. It was finally decided a pass would be a given and household goods, slaves, and servants would travel overland in wagons. The prisoners would be allowed to take two servants per family of four or more but only one in smaller families.

The night before the families were to be taken aboard ship, Gabe and Dagan stopped at the Mermaid for a wet. Alejandro had been given permission to sleep ashore and had spent most of his evenings at the tavern since they had arrived in Saint Augustine. Tonight Ally's mother, who the men had started calling Mama Chavez, had cooked a special meal for them. During the meal, small talk about the tavern took place. The fight between Midshipman Lancaster and the soldier was discussed and how at the subsequent trail the courtroom had erupted in near hysteria and laughter at Lum's testimony.

Talk then turned to the prisoner exchange. At this point Mama Chavez asked the question Gabe had been considering. "Norfolk, Virginia, is that not where Colonel Manning's family is from?"

"Aye," Dagan replied.

"Good," Mama Chavez continued. "I hope it's possible you will be able to visit if the war allows. I know Senora Betsy would be most glad to see you."

"And I her," Dagan answered.

Seeing Dagan was uncomfortable with the line of discussion, Gabe spoke out. "Well, Domingo, have you enjoyed Alejandro's presence this past week?"

"Si, it has been good. We will be sad to see him leave tomorrow, his madre and I."

"Well," Gabe started with a smile, "do you think you could find something to keep him busy until we return? I'd not like to think he'd just lie around and get fat and lazy."

"Oh, si, we will of course have plenty for him to do."

"Good! It's settled then. Mr. Ally!"

"Si...ah yes sir," the midshipman replied, still in a state of shock over what he had been hearing.

"You are hereby granted leave until we return. I expect that will be between two to four weeks. I will trust Domingo will limit your sea tales of daring to all the young ladies until my return."

"I will, Captain," Domingo replied. "And gracias."

"Well Dagan, we'd best head back to the ship."

"Aye," Dagan replied. Rising, he cuffed Ally behind the head good-naturedly.

As the two headed out the tavern, Ally and his parents watched, not believing they'd have several weeks together.

"Vaya con dios," Domingo whispered. "Vaya con dios."

Chapter Six

The first day out of Saint Augustine brought with it a stiff breeze and a choppy sea. To the northwest, clouds were building up causing the sea to roll. The ship would rise up with one large roller then crash down, sending a constant spray over the bow that ran down each side of the deck creating a continuous flow of water draining from the scuppers. More than one of the passengers found out firsthand the meaning of being seasick. As bad as it was on *Peregrine,* Gabe couldn't help but wonder about the passengers aboard *Pegasus.* Colonel Meacham, the senior prisoner of war, had walked up without Gabe hearing him due to the sound of the wind blowing through the riggings. Sensing someone close at hand, Gabe turned to find himself face to face with the colonel.

"My apologies, Captain. I didn't mean to intrude upon your space," Meacham volunteered.

"No apology needed," Gabe replied. He had dined with the colonel and his family on a few occasions since their pulling into Saint Augustine and had quickly come to like the gentleman.

Gabe noticed the colonel had his feet spread apart and, with the aid of a cane, managed to steady himself as the sea tossed the ship about. Grasping a shroud to keep his balance, the colonel used his cane to point at *Pegasus*.

"Not unlike a thoroughbred colt after the first frost," the colonel said.

Gabe smiled. He would never have made the analogy, but it was easy to see once mentioned.

The colonel had been a breeder from Williamsburg before the war and had made the acquaintance of Dagan's Uncle Andre. It had been good for Dagan to spend time and talk with someone who knew his family. Watching the two share a bowl of tobacco after dinner last night, Gabe recalled the words that had been spoken to him a year or so back.

"Your problem, Gabe, is you don't hate those you're fighting against and you don't necessarily love the ones we're fighting for." Troubled, he recently had discussed this with Sir Victor over drinks one night while in Saint Augustine. Gabe had tried to explain that one did his duty as ordered, with the faith that while he might not agree it was what was best for King and country.

Hearing this, Sir Victor gave such a vicious snort it echoed throughout the Mermaid. The tavern had been closed for hours. Even Domingo had retired, leaving the two to fend for themselves.

"I might believe as you do, Gabe, if I felt it was for King and country, but it's not. It's the bloody politicians leading our country with very little regard for the monarch."

"Well, hopefully they are mostly true and just in their governing our country," Gabe replied. "One would hope they put the country first in their hearts and mind."

Shaking his head, Sir Victor drained the last of the liquid in his cup then scraped the legs of the chair backwards as he stood. Walking behind the bar, Sir Victor reached for another bottle of wine, paying no attention to the label or selection. Removing the cork with his teeth and banging the open bottle on the table before seating himself. Sir Victor reminded Gabe more of some rogue of a seadog than of an English nobleman.

"Humph," Sir Victor snorted again. "You are an excellent captain and seaman, Gabe, but you are out of your element when it comes to politicians. I hardly know of any who's not more concerned with filling his purse than the needs of England."

Taking a deep swallow, Sir Victor gave a sigh then continued, "Gabe, my friend, you are more likely to find a virgin in a whorehouse than an honest politician in Parliament."

Unable to resist the thought that came to his head, Gabe asked, "And what about you, sir?"

The Foreign Office agent paused, his glass in midair and peered at Gabe over the rim, "Aye, I bear considerable watching myself."

Then after a moment of silence Gabe burst out in laughter, "An honest Englishman," he quipped.

This caused Sir Victor to smile and reply, "But don't tell a soul."

* * *

Gunnells, the sailing master, was looking at the distant clouds, which seemed to be moving fast.

"Think we're in for a blow?" Gabe asked.

"Nay, I'd say calm before a storm," the master replied.

Gabe opened his mouth to question the man's comments but closed it without a word. In all the time the two had sailed together, he'd never been wrong.

"Deck there," the masthead lookout called down, "signal from *Dasher*."

Instantly Hawks, the senior midshipman, had a glass in his hand and bounded to the shrouds and up the ratlines until he could get a good view of *Dasher's* signals. "Strange sail to windward," he read out.

"Who could that be?" Gabe asked as he turned and saw his brother mounting the quarterdeck.

One usually requested permission to come on the quarterdeck but when it was not only the captain's brother but a vice admiral as well, people just moved to make way.

"Any recognition signal?" Lord Anthony asked.

"No sir, none reported. Should I signal *Dasher* to investigate?"

Lord Anthony gazed up at the white flag of truce flying over the British flag. "Ours is a mission of peace," Lord Anthony replied. "We will keep a watchful eye but no more at the moment."

Realizing Bart wasn't accompanying his brother as usual, Gabe asked, "Where's Bart? I haven't seen much of him in the last day or so."

A frown creased Lord Anthony's brow. "Bart has been under the weather with miseries of the gut. Your man, Livesey, states he's more of a surgeon than a physician but he thinks Bart has picked up some ill humour or contagion. Hopefully the fresh sea air and a bland diet should see his symptoms resolve. Thus far, Bart has not run any fever."

Gabe could see the look of worry that enveloped his brother's face. He and Bart had been together for a very long time. They had enjoyed a relationship that few could only dream about. They had survived fierce sea battles with cannon balls flying about, the joys of Gil's marriage to Lady Deborah and the birth of Macayla. Bart had been there when Lord Anthony had been a junior lieutenant and he'd been present when Anthony became vice admiral. Gabe could not recall a single moment when Bart had not been at his brother's side.

As Lord Anthony took his leave, Dagan walked up. "I like Mr. Livesey but I wish Caleb was here."

"Aye," Gabe responded. "Hopefully in two or three days we will be in Norfolk and you can find Caleb and have him take a look at Bart."

"We'll go see Caleb when we reach Norfolk," Dagan replied. "But it won't be in a couple of days. A week, maybe."

Seeing Gabe's questioning look, Dagan continued. "Did you forget the master said we'll likely find ourselves in a calm...then I expect squalls." Dagan added as he turned, speaking over his shoulder, "Think I'll go see Bart, may make him feel better."

"Aye," Gabe answered. "Tell him I'll be down directly." Looking up at the full press of sails, he found himself somewhat of a Doubting Thomas regarding the master's prediction.

"Captain."

Gabe took his gaze from aloft and found his First Lieutenant, Nathan Lavery, standing there. *Damn,* Gabe thought, *where is my mind, my attention? People have been sneaking up on me all day.*

"Yes, Mr. Lavery."

"We may have a problem, sir."

"A problem, Mr. Lavery?"

"Yes sir. It seems Cradock has gotten himself into an altercation."

Cradock...an altercation? He was an experienced bosun's mate who had great potential to become a bosun one day. Lavery would normally handle such matters in a way that it would not go on a man's record. Therefore Gabe knew this was not the usual petty infraction.

"Who was the altercation with?" Gabe asked.

Taking a breath, Lavery exhaled, and then answered, "Colonel Meacham's man. Ashley is his name, sir."

Gabe knew the man. Somewhat of a giant, he'd worked with the colonel's horses since he was a lad, it was said.

"How did this incident happen?" Gabe found himself asking.

"It happened as the men were scrubbing decks, sir. Ashley accidentally kicked a seaman's bucket which caused him to curse and call Ashley a clumsy oaf."

Picturing a bucket of water being kicked over a deck that had just been flogged dry made Gabe smile in spite of himself. No wonder the seaman spoke out. Now he had a task that had to be done all over again.

"When the seaman spoke out," Lavery continued, "Ashley grabbed his shirt and jerked him to his feet. Seeing this, Cradock said let the man down, we'll be having none of that. Ashley then looked at Cradock and hissed, 'You make me little man'. So Cradock did," Lavery finished.

Realizing there had to be more, Gabe looked Lavery in the eye and questioned, "How did he make him let go of the seaman?"

Lavery gave a sigh not relishing this part but answered, "Cradock kicked Ashley in the testicles and when the big man bent double he rapped him a good one with a belaying pin."

"Damme, sir, but that's a hellish way to bring one down to size," Gabe said, and then realized this was a sensitive issue indeed. He'd have to walk a tightrope to not anger Colonel Meacham, who, as a prisoner being exchanged, was somewhat of a guest aboard and needed to be treated appropriately; still, Gabe had to maintain the respect of his crew by not overly punishing a shipmate for taking up for one of their own. He'd have to ponder this one, possibly discuss it with his brother and, maybe, Sir Victor. Realizing Lavery was waiting on an answer Gabe started to speak but was interrupted by the bells for the first dog watch. It was time to feed the crew.

Once the ringing of the bell fell silent, Gabe answered Lavery. "I'll think on it tonight and we'll address the problem tomorrow."

"Aye aye, sir," Lavery responded, wondering exactly what his captain meant with the "we'll" address the problem.

Chapter Seven

Gabe woke with a start. Something was not as it should be. The pounding headache from too much wine and brandy consumed last evening, combined with the foul aftertaste of Colonel Meacham's cigars, did little to improve Gabe's mood. Never a good riser, Gabe tried to clear his head as he sat up. Nesbit could be heard in the pantry as he went about preparing coffee and, possibly, a pastry that would serve as his captain's breakfast. He had learned early of Gabe's difficulty rising and his lack of desire with regard to a full morning meal.

However, Lord Anthony, who was sharing the captain's quarters, had risen almost an hour earlier and had drunk two cups of coffee and then carried a cup to the ailing Bart. It was strange the burly admiral's cox'n had not already made an appearance before the admiral was fully dressed.

While Nesbit had only been a captain's man for a short period of time, he'd learned how unusual it was for a captain to share his quarters with a flag officer. The first lieutenant had told him the admiral usually took over the captain's quarters and the captain took over the first lieutenant's quarters and on down the chain of command. He'd also been told by Dagan that if the time aboard for a flag officer was to be of short duration, the ship's captain would usually sling a hammock and sleep in the chart room. He guessed that, with the captain and the admiral being brothers, it did not seem amiss that the admiral insisted the captain sleep in his quarters even if it was the cushions underneath the stern windows.

Meanwhile, trying to focus, Gabe could see Nesbit's shadow as he moved around the pantry. The overhead lantern...it was not swaying. That was what Gabe had sensed. Years of waking with the roll of a ship as it cut through the seas had been enough to alert Gabe to a change. *Damme, but the master was right...we've been becalmed.* Gabe's mind then trailed off and his thoughts were on Faith. *Would she be taking Sampson out for a walk when the sun came up?* She would he knew, rain or shine. He had on occasion offered but when he'd tried to get the big ugly brute to come along, he just sat down and ignored him. Then Faith would laughingly rise and the dog would jump about as if he were a puppy. Faith called the dog her baby. When hearing these comments Lum would roll his eyes and say, "He sho don't eat like no baby, Missy and that's the truth." After what had happened to Faith by Montague and his rogues, Gabe didn't care how ornery the dog could be, he was Faith's protector and God help the soul who tried to harm her with Sampson around.

Hearing the cabin door open, Gabe saw Dagan entering. The marine sentry had learned who to announce and who to let pass. Dagan was let pass.

"Glad to see you've decided to join the rest of us who serve aboard his Majesty's ships."

Gabe cut his eyes but didn't speak. He was the ship's captain but Dagan was still his uncle and, when not in public, he liked to give Gabe the devil about his difficulty rising.

"We're at a calm," Gabe said, more a statement than a question.

"Aye," Dagan replied. "The sea is as smooth as a baby's arse."

Taking a deep breath, Gabe clutched the empty pouch around his neck and thought once more of Faith. In a romantic moment, Gabe had given a huge red ruby to Faith, declaring, "You have my stone and my heart." When she went to take the pouch he said, "No, this is how empty my heart is when you're not around."

Seeing Gabe clutch the pouch, Dagan thought of Betsy, sweet Betsy in Norfolk. He would find a way to see her. He could understand Gabe's love for Faith as he had discovered what love was when he'd met Betsy. "Damn this war to hell," he said without realizing it.

"I agree," Gabe said, causing Dagan to flush. He'd not meant to speak out loud.

* * *

On deck, Gabe gave his usual greeting. "Good morning, Mr. Lavery, Mr. Gunnells." The two responded in unison as usual. "I see you were right as always, Mr. Gunnells. Any idea how long we'll be becalmed?"

"I'd say a day, two at the most." Looking up, the flags hung limp and the sails didn't even flap.

"I've doused the sails," Lavery volunteered. "Still nothing."

"Ahem!" was Gabe's only reply.

"After we secure from quarters, we could put out the longboats and tow the ship," Lavery offered.

"No ..." Gabe said shaking his head. "In this heat, it would be too hard on the men."

"Well, maybe it will give the passengers time to recover from their miseries," Lavery remarked.

Those within hearing distance on the quarterdeck couldn't help but chuckle. Then, seeing his brother, the chuckle was quickly forgotten. Bart's miseries must not be improving for Gil to look so worried.

"Morning sir," Gabe greeted his brother as per protocol.

"Captain, I trust you had a comfortable evening."

"It went well." *Damn*, thought Gabe, *this is not the Gil I know*. "Nesbit is heating up another pot of coffee if you'd care for a cup."

"Maybe later."

"Aye sir."

The sun was just breaking day when the lookout called down. "*Dasher* and *Pegasus* on station."

"Very well," Lavery called up.

Turning back to his brother, Gabe asked, "Any instructions sir?"

"No, Captain, she's your ship." And with those comments, he made his way below.

Lavery walked up and spoke, "Begging your pardon, sir, but I've never seen the admiral like this."

"You've never seen Bart down either, have you, Nathan?"

Swallowing, the first lieutenant mumbled, "No sir. Even back when we were just snottys, Bart has been...well...Bart."

"Aye," Gabe smiled, "and didn't he give us the devil?"

"Yes sir, he did. In a good sort of way, but he did."

The laughter caused more than one seaman to look toward the quarterdeck. *Lucky sods*, one seaman thought, *got nothing to do but find things to break a poor tar's back when they ain't laughing.*

After enjoying his second cup of coffee, Gabe was using his index finger to pick up crumbs from the pastry he'd just devoured. Watching the captain, Nesbit shook his head and raised his eyebrows.

"There are more pastries Captain. You don't have to pick at the crumbs."

His comments were totally ignored, as the captain's mind seemed to be far off. Gabe absently stabbed at another crust as he sat in his chair with his boots propped on another chair.

Nesbit stared at the captain's boots; hopefully he wouldn't ruin the green leather seat cushions. He had spent hours cleaning the tar from a cushion in preparation for the evening guests just yesterday.

"Nesbit!"

Hearing his name called so unexpectedly startled the man. "Yes sir."

"Would you please give the first lieutenant my compliments, and would he please come down as soon as convenient."

"Yes sir," Nesbit replied. As he passed the sentry on the way topside, he thought, *That's a nice way of saying get your arse down here.* Something the bosun had whispered to him when he'd remarked how cordial the captain was when addressing his officers. *Ah,* he thought, *so much to learn about the Royal Navy.*

Within a few minutes, the sentry knocked. "First lieutenant, suh!"

* * *

A ring was rigged in the forward part of the ship. Most of the Colonials stood aft and to the starboard side while the ship's company lined the larboard and forward aspect of the ring. Some stood in the shrouds, trying for a better viewing advantage as the way was otherwise blocked so that they could not see.

Gabe had mentioned the incident to the colonel two nights previous. The colonel was apologetic his man had caused a rift until he'd been told Ashley had been soundly trounced by a very tough but smaller man.

"It was due to surprise," Colonel Meacham said in bluster. "I've never seen his equal in a fair fight."

Not sure what the colonel called "fair", Gabe responded, "Well, my men don't abide by any set of rules, but they are a scrappy bunch. They've had to be to survive. Unfortunately, I now have to punish a good petty officer for fighting."

Turning his neck from side to side the colonel's chin seemed to rise as he quickly replied, "But Captain, I see no need for punishment of, as you say, a good petty officer. My man was out of line then your seaman was out of line. In the Army of Virginia, we would let the men settle the issue...in the proper manner, of course."

The colonel quickly turned toward Lord Anthony, "With your permission of course, Admiral."

Anthony thought a minute then replied, "It's up to the captain, of course, but I see no reason an exhibition of the manly art of self-defense cannot be carried out within the right setting. There can be no betting, however, for then it would be more than an exhibition."

"Well, then Captain it's up to you," the colonel said with a glint in his eye.

Gabe was more than a little concerned about Cradock taking on Ashley but refused to show it. With a poker face he stated, "If the conditions remain favourable, we will put on the...ah...exhibition."

Gabe had talked with Lavery, who in turn had a private conversation with Cradock, who was more than willing to face Ashley. Lavery then talked with the carpenter who, with his mates, constructed a ring of sorts. The next morning the sea was like a sheet of glass. After quarters, Gabe gave Lavery the go-ahead to schedule the bout during the forenoon watch if the wind didn't pick up.

"Who do we choose for a referee?" Lavery asked.

"My choice would be Dagan, but ask the colonel if he has a preference."

The colonel, who had come to know and like Dagan, had no objections.

Cradock and Ashley now stood at opposite sides of the rope ring. Lord Anthony had been seated in one of Gabe's dinner table chairs with Bart, still sick, sitting next to him on one side, while Sir Victor occupied the other. Gabe stood behind his brother with his officers.

Dagan stood in the ring laying down the rules. "No biting, no eye gouging, no squeezing or kicking the opponent's testicles."

A voice rang out, "Do the big sod have any?"

This caused Gabe to flush in anger. "A taste of the cat to the next man who speaks out," he snorted.

"Ahem..." the colonel cleared his voice and replied, "and I'll trouble the captain to have his bosun lay on a dozen if one of my men speaks out."

Lord Anthony had officially prohibited betting on the match but Gabe had seen more than one wager take place. Dagan called the two men forward and advised them to abide by the rules. The winner had to take two out of three rounds. A round would be called when a man was downed and could not rise by the count of ten or did not answer the call to return to the centre of the ring after the previous round. With that, Dagan nodded to the bosun who gave a shrill whistle and the match began.

Watching the two men circle, it was obvious to all that the advantages went to Ashley. He had height, weight, arm length, plus he was strong as an ox. Cradock had the experience that only open battle could bring, and he had heart. The two circled each other warily, each seeking an opening. Several times

Ashley pushed in to grab hold of Cradock in an attempt to squeeze the breath out of the smaller man. However, Cradock was much quicker and all Ashley got for his efforts were hard fists to the face, which did little to slow the big man.

After several minutes, both men were drenched in sweat and starting to breathe a little harder. Ashley swung a hard right that was slow and missed. Cradock dove in for a kidney punch that landed and caused a gasp from Ashley. That would have ended the round, if not fight, with most men. Ashley was not most men. He swung his body backwards, his elbow catching Cradock on the side of the head and the man was down. The colonel's men cheered. Dagan had to forcefully push Ashley back to his side.

Cradock was dazed but was up on his knees by the count of ten. He stood and went to his side of the ring. "I didn't see that one coming," he said, trying to act cheerful.

As the men were given a cup of water and a wet cloth to wipe down with, Dagan went to the center of the ring, "First round goes to Ashley."

Dagan then walked to the side of the ring, looking at his watch. Three minutes had been agreed upon as the time between rounds. The first round had lasted over fifteen minutes. Dagan was soon in the center of the ring again.

"Time!" he called.

Both men came forward amid a cheer from their supporters. When the bosun's pipe sounded, Ashley rushed in but Cradock darted beneath his foe and again gave a tremendous blow to Ashley's kidney area. However, this time Craddock dropped down to avoid the back swing that had ended the first round. He then immediately faked left, then darted right and this time a hard fist caught Ashley just above the eye, lacerating the eyebrow and causing blood to spurt.

Ashley then swung around and was just able to grab Cradock's arm. He then spun, slinging Cradock across the ring onto the hard deck. Cradock was up in a flash and avoided the bigger man's rush to finish the job. He had gained his feet and, just when it seemed Ashley was upon him, he dropped to the deck, using one hand on the deck for support. Cradock gave a leg sweep. Ashley fell backwards, his head hitting the oak planking with a thud. Dagan counted to ten and it looked like Ashley was out for good. He first let go a deep moan, and then, very wobbly, he finally got to his feet, not sure what had happened.

"Second round to Cradock," Dagan called.

Several things took place almost at once. Standing in the middle of the ring, Dagan gazed upward. Gabe and Lord Anthony followed his gaze and saw the admiral's flag wave, lift, drop, then gather life and lift up again.

The masthead lookout that obviously had been paying attention to duty called down, "*Pegasus* has the wind. She's making sail."

Gabe cupped his hands and shouted, "A draw! The match is a tie. Mr. Lavery."

"Aye, Captain."

"Man the braces, all hands prepare to make sail."

Lord Anthony saw the look of dismay on Meacham's face. "Sorry, Colonel," he explained, "the needs of the ship come first. It was good entertainment while it lasted but as the captain had said, weather permitting."

Looking at Ashley's still dazed features, Meacham acknowledged Lord Anthony's comment with a shake of his head and headed below where his wife awaited. She had decided to not take part of such vulgar activities.

Seeing the colonel disappear down the companionway, Gabe spoke to his brother, "I hope the colonel is not too upset I called the fight a draw."

"He shouldn't be," Anthony replied. "In all likelihood, you just saved him a hundred pounds."

Gabe stood there, his mouth ajar. "Surely you didn't bet," he asked incredibly.

"No, not me, Sir Victor. He's the one that might need an apology."

"I'd a bet too," Bart spoke, the pain obvious on his face. "I didn't 'ave any bloody doubts. If Cradock 'ad of been paying attention, 'e wouldn't 'ave gotten his block rattled in the first place and we'd all been a bit richer."

"Now Bart."

"Yew know," Bart replied to Anthony.

"Let's go below," Anthony said, changing the subject. "You've been up enough today."

Gabe watched as they disappeared, and then realized something. *Damn, Bart must be sick; he didn't put in the last word.*

Chapter Eight

Barely an hour had passed when the sentry announced, "Mr. Gunnells, sir."

Gabe had been going over the charts. His dividers, compass, and ruler lay before him on the unrolled chart. Looking up at the master, Gabe was surprised to see the worried look that creased his face.

"What is it, Mr. Gunnells?"

"I think we're in for a blow, sir. The barometer has dropped to twenty-nine and thunderheads are building up to the southeast."

Nodding, Gabe threw down the ruler he'd picked up and had been tapping the palm of his hands with. Going on deck, the sun, which had been very bright, was now hardly visible through a leaden sky. The heat was still intense but the wind was picking up. Well, the master had said a calm then a squall.

A woman's shout made Gabe turn. The colonel's wife had just lost her hat to a sudden gust of wind that was also tugging at her daughter's dress. One of the seamen was able to retrieve Mrs. Meacham's hat and return it, his eyes on the colonel's daughter. The wind pushed the material of her dress against her body, revealing a well-proportioned young woman.

"Poor Christian souls," Gunnells volunteered. "The weather has got them so frustrated they don't know whether to shite or go blind."

"Aren't you the wise one," Gabe quipped, thinking the sight of the young lady was enough to frustrate his sailors.

"Comes from years of experience," Gunnells replied. "I've been there a time or two myself."

Feeling a bit frustrated himself, Gabe turned and called to the officer of the watch. "Mr. Davy!"

"Aye sir."

"The master says we're in for a blow. Have the anchor and deck secured...then reduce to storm sail."

"Aye, aye Captain," Lieutenant Davy replied as he called for the bosun. He knew the captain wanted to carry all the sail he could but with the Colonials aboard he would also have their welfare at mind. Otherwise, they'd be tossed about like bait in a bucket.

"Mr. Davy!"

"Aye, Captain."

"Put two men on the wheel before it gets too lively."

"Yes sir."

Lord Anthony came on deck and watched as the ship was prepared for the oncoming storm. Thunder rumbled and lightning pierced the sky.

The surgeon made his way toward the admiral, speaking as he approached. "I have always loved a storm. It's amazing to me to see God's earth change so drastically from one moment to the next."

"Have you been at sea during a storm?" Anthony asked.

"Oh yes, my Lord. Many a time and I've always enjoyed the excitement."

Well, you wouldn't enjoy it so much if you were the ship's captain, Anthony thought. "Well, I'll leave you to enjoy the storm, sir. I'm going below."

Lord Anthony had just cleared the deck when the rain came: a hard rain coming down in wind driven sheets. Drops so big they hurt when they hit you.

Suddenly the masthead lookout slid down a backstay and ran to the quarterdeck in a panic. "A ship, sir...a ship is bearing down on us. I reported but you couldn't hear me hail."

Gabe, Lieutenant Davy, and Lieutenant Wiley were in a group when the lookout shouted his report. Gabe grabbed a glass and hurried aft. He'd just focused the glass in time to see a ship appear through the squall and swing to larboard, bringing her starboard guns to bear.

Seeing the gunports open, Gabe screamed to be heard, "Get down, get down."

The crash was deafening as cannon ball, canister, and chain shot tore into *Peregrine*. Parts of transom and flag locker exploded from the impact of the enemy's broadside. When he didn't hear another gun go off, Gabe stood up and focused his glass just in time to see the stern of the attacking ship disappear into the squall. Lieutenant Davy was up and ordering to the bosun to call all hands. Gabe walked forward and stopped. Lieutenant Wiley lay in a mangled heap. Lieutenant Lavery, Dagan, and

Lord Anthony had all come on deck and rushed up to Gabe.

"You're bleeding all down your back," a concerned Dagan informed Gabe.

"There's no pain. I'll have the surgeon see to it directly."

"He can't. He's a goner, sir. Looks like he caught a chest full of canister," Lavery advised.

"The surgeon was killed?" Gabe asked, not believing his ears.

"Yes sir," Lavery replied stoically.

"Anybody else?" Gabe asked.

"Aye, the two helmsmen. Lieutenant Davy and the master have the helm now. Looks like the master may have a broke hand."

"Were the other ships involved?" Gabe asked.

"Doesn't look like it," Lavery answered.

"Send up a distress flare, Mr. Lavery," Lord Anthony ordered. "If we can find the flags to make a signal send close on flag."

"Aye," Lavery answered, his gaze following the admiral's to the demolished flag locker.

"Dagan!"

"Yes, my Lord."

"Get Gabe below and have one of the surgeon's mates check his injuries."

"But sir," Gabe started but closed his mouth when his brother said, "That's an order, Captain."

* * *

It was a solemn group that gathered for the burial service. Death was a common enough part of life at sea and the men usually took it in stride as with the other hardships one faced. But damnation, they were under a flag of truce. It was not supposed to happen. If it had been during a sea battle or even caused by the storm it would have been accepted. But nobody expected or accepted this, not the lowest deckhand to the captain. Neither could the admiral, the foreign agent, or even the Colonials. Not a living soul could understand or accept the brutal way their shipmates and friends were needlessly slaughtered.

A knock at the cabin door sounded as the sentry announced, "Midshipman Chase, sir."

Gabe was putting on his dress coat in spite of a very sore back where half a dozen splinters had penetrated his uniform just as he dove for the deck. A split second later and he'd likely have ended up like any of those stretched out on the deck, awaiting his final words before having their bodies committed to the deep.

Trying to clear his thoughts Gabe looked at the midshipman. He was taking the deaths hard. His eyes were red and swollen from crying. Lieutenant Wiley had taken him under his wing while the surgeon had been teaching the boy to play chess.

"Yes, Mr. Chase."

The midshipman's voice was broken as he tried to control his emotions. "Mr. Lavery's respects, sir, and the men are gathered."

"Thank you, Mr. Chase. I will be up directly."

As the boy turned to leave, Gabe called after him, "I will miss them too, Mr. Chase. They were fine officers. But don't you worry. Whoever did this will be brought to justice; you can rest assured of that."

"Thank you, sir," the boy muttered. "I hope we do find them and send their hateful souls straight to hell." The boy then burst into tears and rushed out.

"I know how he feels," Dagan commented, catching himself just as he was going to clap Gabe on the back.

Looking at Dagan, Gabe half whispered, "You knew there was something about to happen. You said there'd be squalls."

"Aye. Something," Dagan admitted. "Not what or when it would happen." What he didn't say was his mind had been on Betsy too much of late for him to see things clearly. That would have to change...at least till after the war.

Lavery saluted Gabe as he came on deck. "Sir, the crew is formed up for burial services."

Gabe straightened his back and saw not only the crew but Bart, his brother, Sir Victor, and the Colonials all standing. As Dagan walked up, Gabe barely brushed his shoulder with his arm. Dagan paused, looked at Gabe, then followed his gaze to Bart, who was sweating and extremely pale. The briefest of nods was passed then Dagan walked up to the bosun and whispered in his ear. Within a minute chairs were provided for Lord Anthony, Bart, and Sir Victor as well as Colonel Meacham and his family.

Once everyone was seated, Lavery took a step forward, "Attention on deck, hats off."

Bart made to rise but Dagan, with his hands on his shoulders, gave a gentle push and Bart remained seated. A look of thanks passed from Lord Anthony to Dagan. Gabe tucked his hat beneath his arm and opened his "Book of Common Prayer" to the pages he'd marked "service for the burial of the dead at sea."

Gabe could feel the wind in his hair and couldn't decide whether to put his hat back on to keep his hair out of his eyes or just proceed. With the pages rustling in the breeze he decided to just go forth. While he was reading, Gabe could hear Mrs. Meacham sob and more than one sniffle from the crew. When the final plank had been tipped up and the last shrouded body dropped into the sea, the splash echoing through Gabe's mind he paused a few seconds and turned to the Twenty-Third Psalm.

"Let us pray," and read as the men followed along. "The Lord is my shepherd..." Once the prayer was finished, Gabe turned to his first lieutenant. "Dismiss the crew then prepare to make all sail."

"Aye aye, sir."

Gabe had considered making the rest of the day make and mend but decided the men didn't need time on their hands. He didn't need time on his hands. Seeing Bart being helped, he thought, *He might not have much time.*

Chapter Nine

The remainder of the voyage was uneventful. The transom as well as the flag locker was repaired as best as the carpenter could with the material available. The sharp contrast of the freshly made repairs compared with the rest of the weather worn transom was enough to alert even a landsman that some tragedy had struck the ship. The strange ship that had attacked *Peregrine* had not been sighted again.

Captain Francis Markham, commanding the frigate *HMS Dasher,* had requested permission to seek out the rogue who had dishonoured the flag of truce so violently. Lord Anthony denied the request, citing their mission and, with the civilians on board *Dasher,* it would be putting them at unnecessary risk.

Gabe came on deck just as the sun was setting over the horizon. This was the most peaceful time of day for him. Hearing the bell, he realized it was time for the second dogwatch. Thinking back he remembered his father, Admiral James Anthony, explaining the significance of the dogwatch: "If we didn't have the dogwatch men would find themselves standing watch at the same time each day. There are seven watches a day. The first watch is from 8 p.m. till midnight, the second watch called the middle watch goes from midnight to 4 a.m. when the morning watch starts. This goes till 8 a.m. at which time you have the forenoon watch, which goes to noon of course. From noon to 4 p.m. is the afternoon watch. Then comes the dogwatches, this is the time between 4 p.m. and 8 p.m. It has been divided into two separate watches. The first dogwatch which is 4 p.m. till 6 p.m. and the second dogwatch which runs from 6 p.m. to 8 p.m. This allows a change in schedules so a man is not always stuck with the same watch."

Gabe couldn't help but smile recalling how his father had so patiently explained it to him. *I wonder if he explained it to Gil in the same way*, Gabe thought to himself.

"It's a pretty sunset, Captain." The master had approached.

"Aye, that it is, Mr. Gunnells."

"We'll be off Chesapeake Bay at sunup."

Gabe nodded. "And none too soon, Mr. Gunnells. Damme if this hasn't turned out to be more than I expected."

"I believe we all feel that way, Captain. We lost some good people to those mean-souled, poxed sons of sodomites," the master replied vehemently.

Gabe had never heard Gunnells speak so strongly. Dagan had approached the two men. Seeing Dagan, Gunnells made his departure, leaving room for the two men to talk. Nesbit had just taken some soup down to Bart, who felt too sick to eat solid food.

"He is now running a fever. His Lordship asked Nesbit to have you come speak with him. I expect he wants to make his apologies for not being able to dine tonight as planned."

Bart's worse, Gabe thought, *so Gil will not leave his side*. This was to be the last night the group would dine together before arriving at Norfolk.

"I'm sure Colonel Meacham and Sir Victor will understand," Gabe said.

"My thoughts as well," Dagan responded.

"The master says we'll be there tomorrow. I hope it's not too late for Bart."

"No, I don't think so. We'll get Caleb to look at Bart right off."

"You expect him to be there?" Gabe asked.

"I'd be surprised if he wasn't."

"How come?" Gabe asked.

"Gabe, you haven't been hearing what has been said have you?"

"When?" Gabe asked.

Dagan lifted his brow and replied, "After the evening meals, when Sir Victor and the Colonel break out the cigars. One of the men in charge of the British prisoners to be exchanged is a Colonel Manning, who was a former British prisoner himself. Now they might be more than one but I doubt it. When negotiations for the exchange to take place began Sir Victor mentioned Gil as his choice to carry out the logistics on behalf of the British. Knowing him from Saint Augustine the colonel was in agreement. Now, with Colonel Manning knowing who's coming, and his knowing my uncle, it only stands to reason he would have told them. So it's more than likely they'll be waiting when we get there."

"Humph!" Gabe grunted. "Well I can see you are well informed. Did you win any money?"

"Money?"

"Yes. Every time that I know of, when the cigars and brandy were broken out, so were the cards."

Dagan looked sheepish but did not reply so Gabe continued. "I didn't feel as ship's captain it was appropriate for me to play so I made my excuses citing duty."

"Well, I did win a few rounds...here and there," Dagan admitted.

"I see," Gabe responded, not surprised but acting so. "Tell me then," Gabe added, "did you learn anymore important information?" Gabe almost smiled seeing the quizzical look on Dagan's face.

"Like what?" Dagan finally asked.

"Like if a lady named Betsy would be there?"

"I didn't ask specific like," Dagan said, grinning. "But I feel like she will."

Lord Anthony's small squadron was met at the mouth of the Chesapeake Bay by a pilot boat at three bells in the forenoon watch. An hour before they had met up with a British frigate patrolling an area to intercept ships attempting to enter or leave the entrance of the bay. The frigate's captain, who had several years' seniority, was surprised when he was summoned to repair on board by a vice admiral. Lord Anthony informed the captain of the incident with the mystery ship and the need to keep vigilant.

As the pilot boat got closer to *Peregrine*, Gabe was approached by Gunnells. "It wouldn't take much to bottle up the Chesapeake and what do we have patrolling the area?" Without giving Gabe a chance to reply, he went on, "A single frigate commanded by an overage captain."

Pointing to larboard with his glass, the master continued, "There lies Cape Henry and to starboard is Cape Charles. Just off Cape Charles, to say the middle of the mouth of the bay, lies a dangerous shallow area known as middle ground. To actually enter the bay you have to pass through a funnel between Cape Henry and the middle ground. A squadron of ships could keep the place bottled up."

"You seem to know a great deal about the area," Gabe commented as he watched the approaching pilot boat.

"Aye, Captain. I was at the shipyard during the Seven Years War, what the Americans called the French and Indian War. The shipyard is called the Gosport Shipyard. It has a deep channel and the harbour offers natural protection from storms plus it's close to the bay. I don't know why some say it's in Norfolk as it is actually in Portsmouth. Until the war it was the best facility we had in North America. Until the war," Gunnells repeated.

"Aye," Gabe replied. "Until the war." Then eyeing Midshipman Chase, Gabe called the youth.

"Yes sir, Captain."

"My compliments to the admiral and Sir Victor and inform them the pilot boat is approaching."

"Aye aye, sir."

Gabe watched the boat as it approached. As the boat grew closer, he picked up a glass for a quick look. Closing the glass with a snap he called to his first lieutenant, "I believe yonder boat has a general officer on board."

Embarrassed that his captain, not one of his lookouts, had to inform him of the situation, Lavery swallowed and said, "I'll have the sides manned." Then, as an afterthought, asked, "Do we fire a salute?"

"We do not salute a country whose ownership is in dispute."

Lavery and Gabe both turned to see Sir Victor. "My apologies, Captain, I shouldn't have spoken out."

"No need to apologize, Sir Victor. In truth, I was not sure," Gabe said.

Lavery called to the bosun to prepare the side party.

"Aye sir."

The air was suddenly filled with the twitter of the bosun pipes and the trample of feet on the deck as men rushed to their station. Lord Anthony came on deck just as General Manning was piped aboard. His aide followed closely behind. Hands were shook and Manning introduced his aide, Captain Cade. Gabe's officers were then introduced as was Colonel Meacham and his family.

General Manning shook Sir Victor's hand and said, "It's a pleasure to see you again, sir. It seems months of negotiations are about to become complete."

"As it should be, sir," the foreign office agent replied.

"May I offer you a glass of refreshment, General?" Gabe asked.

"Yes and a toast to your promotion," Anthony added. He had been a guest at then Colonel

Manning's quarters when he'd been held a prisoner at Saint Augustine.

As the group moved from the entry port aft to the companionway, Manning spied another visitor...a frequent visitor, during the time at Saint Augustine.

"Dagan, how do you do?"

"Fine sir."

"You look healthy. A young lady has asked me to give her regards, should I see you."

Flushing, Dagan nodded. "I have hope of calling later with your permission, General."

"Of course, I'd be run out of my own home if you were not welcomed," the general joked.

Standing to the side, Nesbit took a deep breath. *This is a hellish fine way to treat the enemy*, he thought. Once in the captain's dining area drinks were poured.

"A toast to your promotion," Anthony said, congratulating Manning.

"Well, it was promote me or put me to pasture. I'm getting too old to command a combat brigade so they promoted me and made me a diplomat. Experience I gained from Tonyn's parties helped," the general joked.

This brought the expected chuckles. The Florida governor was known for his lavish parties and those prisoners of suitable class, who'd given their parole, were usually invited. Once the toast was completed Lord Anthony took the general aside and explained Bart's condition and his concern that he needed immediate attention.

"We'll take him to my home immediately upon anchoring," Manning offered. "A friend of yours who I'm told is a very capable surgeon is waiting to greet you there."

Hearing this Gabe turned to Dagan and gave a slight nod.

"I told you so," Dagan mouthed.

Thank God, Gabe thought.

Chapter Ten

The locals had gathered at the waterfront, not sure of what was taking place. As the pilot boat led the three ships from the bay and into the James River, word had quickly spread that British warships were approaching under a flag of truce. Rumour was rampant throughout the crowd.

"Maybe they changed sides," said one old man with tobacco stained gray whiskers.

"Naw," his companion answered. "More likely we done whipped 'em and they's surrendering."

British warships had not been seen in the James River since Lord Dunmore had bombarded the city in his retreat. It was said that most of the waterfront and hundreds of homes were burned. It was later found that the British had destroyed only nineteen houses while Rebels destroyed over eight hundred homes that belonged to the loyalists.

When the ships finally came to their anchorage, the captain's gig was readied for Bart to be transferred to General Manning's house. A bosun's chair was rigged to lower the ailing man into the waiting boat. At first Bart objected, but waves of pain cut off his refusal.

Turning to Lord Anthony, General Manning spoke. "My aide will escort you to my home."

Glancing at the crowded waterfront the general continued, "When I boarded the pilot boat, my carriage was waiting on the dock. Hopefully, it's still there."

"Thank you," Lord Anthony replied, as he again shook hands with the general, and then made his way to the entry port.

As he started down the battens, Anthony heard Manning talking to Captain Cade. "Make sure everything that the surgeon or the admiral needs is provided."

The aide's response was not heard but Cade gave a smart salute and hurried after the admiral.

"Are you going?" Gabe asked Dagan. Gabe could see the man was torn between duty and giving a helping hand.

"Go ahead," Sir Victor said, overhearing the conversation. "I'll not need you for what I have in mind until tomorrow at the earliest." Dagan rushed to the entry port to catch the gig before it pulled away.

Speaking to Gabe, Sir Victor commented, "Do you think he even thought that he'd just breached naval protocol by getting into the gig after the admiral?"

Smiling, Gabe answered, "The general's aide already blew protocol to hell. Dagan's last minute departure won't make any difference."

"Aye, and I would imagine his Lordship is more concerned with Bart than who gets in or out of a boat in a certain order."

Before Gabe could answer, the general approached Sir Victor, "We've set up temporary accommodations in a couple of warehouses and at St. Paul's church. I'm sure some will be anxious to be returning to their homes but, with your permission, we will gather them together and explain the processing procedures."

This had already been done while at Saint Augustine but Sir Victor didn't feel going over it again would hurt.

* * *

The trip to General Manning's house took longer than normal as people rushed to gawk at the British admiral. Once they arrived, greetings were cut short once Bart's condition was realized.

"So, you have a bellyache?" Caleb asked Bart, trying to not sound concerned.

"Aye," Bart replied. "One that has gone on for days; having a wet helped for a while but now it doesn't help at all. The surgeon gave me a purgative which only made it worse."

"Where did it start?" Caleb asked.

"Here," Bart said pointing to his belly button, "but now it's over here." This time Bart pointed to the right lower aspect of his abdomen. "At first I thought it was just sore from where I got stuck with a blade." Caleb could see the still pinkish scar, and Bart continued, "But now it's way over here."

Caleb tried to help Bart relax as he examined him. When he placed his hand on Bart's abdomen it felt very hot and was extremely tender. Bart cried out in pain when he gently pushed down then suddenly released the abdomen.

"I'm sorry, Bart," Caleb said, and then had one of Manning's servants apply a cool cloth on Bart's forehead. Once out of hearing, Caleb spoke in a voice barely more than a whisper, "Bart has a colic caused by inflammation and infection of the vermiform appendix."

"What's that?" Anthony asked.

"It's a small, finger-size attachment at the right lower quadrant of the large intestine. If it ruptures, and I'm surprised it hasn't already, Bart will die from putrefaction of the viscera."

Anthony turned pale and suddenly felt faint at hearing this. "What...what can be done?" he stammered.

"At this stage, the only thing to do is cut into the gut and amputate the affected organ."

"Then do it," Anthony said.

"It's not that easy. I've closed the gut on men with wounds to the bowel or the stomach. Most of them died later either from shock or infection. The problem, as I see it, is shock or exsanguinations. You hold a man down to cut off a leg or arm then give him an anodyne for pain. You can't do that for a malady of the gut."

"What do we do? We can't let Bart die," Anthony said, desperation in his voice. He then looked at Caleb. "Have you done such an operation?"

"I have."

"Then think of something. You're a doctor."

"I have read the Chinese have performed such surgeries by having the patient smoke opium before they operate. I don't know how well it worked;

however, it's a moot point as we don't have any in Norfolk that I know about."

Kawliga, an Indian who had been with Dagan's Uncle Andre for many years, was standing to one side listening. Hearing the word opium caused him to respond, "Mr. Andre say smoking hemp leaves much like smoking opium. Make man crazy sometime but always make man sleep."

Caleb was suddenly excited. "You may have something there, Kawliga." Turning back to Anthony, Caleb continued, "A lot of people in the Tidewater grow hemp. Some will take the superior seeds and grow plants where they harvest the leaves and use it in place of tobacco or alcohol."

"How do we get it?" Anthony asked.

Captain Cade, who had been standing by, said, "I know a man who grows it for such purposes. How much do we need?"

"A leather pouch full," Caleb replied, noticing one lying on a table.

Cade took the pouch and left. "I will be back as soon as I can."

"While he's gone," Caleb said to those gathered around, "let's boil some water, tear up some cloth for bandages, and get a bottle of brandy to soak my instruments in."

"Do you have enough?" Anthony asked.

"I think so but we don't have time to go get more. Now let's clean off the kitchen table and place a clean sheet on it. Let's bring in a couple more lanterns. I'm going to need help." Looking at Kitty, Caleb asked, "You feel up to it?"

The girl had helped Caleb often in the past year; she had proven to be a good nurse. Caleb wished for the day she would not only be his nurse but also his wife.

"I can help," Dagan volunteered.

"No," Caleb said. "You take care of his Lordship."

"Aye," Dagan replied. He knew things would turn out now that Caleb was involved but was also glad he wasn't needed for the surgery.

Cade was back within the hour. The leather pouch was stuffed full of dried hemp leaves. "Mr. Keith says these are his best leaves," he said, handing the pouch to Caleb. "He said if you use a long stem pipe it cuts down on the bite somewhat."

Caleb didn't care about the bite; he only hoped the leaf would work. "Bart."

"Aye."

"I'm going to give you a pipe of hemp leaves to smoke. This should help you sleep so that I can operate on your belly and take out your appendix."

"Does yew have to?" Bart asked.

"If I don't, Bart, you're likely to die."

"Yew has to then. Don't let 'is Lordship fret."

"Don't worry. Now, when you smoke the pipe take deep breaths, inhale deeply. When you start to feel lightheaded, I will give you a dose of laudanum to help with any pain. I can't give you much as I don't want to make you nauseated."

Trying to be brave, Bart said, "Well, light up the pipe and let's be done with it."

Kawliga had taken a white long stem clay pipe off the fireplace mantle. He crushed up the leaves in the palm of his hand, and then filled the pipe. He lit the pipe and held the stem over to Bart who inhaled deeply.

After a few minutes, the grimace of pain left Bart's face and he smiled. Looking at Lord Anthony, he said, "You need to try this. It's better 'n a wet."

"Maybe I will," Anthony replied.

After five minutes Caleb began to worry the concoction wasn't going to work. Bart had finished the bowl and while droopy-eyed, he didn't appear to be sedate.

"Pipe has small bowl," Kawliga said and repacked the bowl after knocking out the ashes. While Kawliga was relighting the fresh bowl of leaves, Caleb decided to go ahead and give Bart the laudanum. Bart had to be held up to drink the liquid. He was again given the pipe.

"Breathe deeply, Bart," Caleb said.

He did, and then had to be told to do so again. After the third round of instruction Bart didn't respond.

"Let's move quickly," Caleb ordered. "Let's tie his chest, hands, and legs down just to be on the safe side."

This was done quickly. Caleb's instruments had been soaking in a pan filled with General Manning's brandy. Bart's clothes had been removed so that, when the sheet was pulled down, his white abdomen was exposed. Caleb took one of the cloth bandages and dipped it in the brandy and wiped the skin down.

"Does that help?" Cade asked.

"I don't know," Caleb said. "My professor put a worm in a glass of brandy once and it died. He felt many such things not seen by the eye existed on the skin and therefore a good cleaning hurt nothing. He used brandy in such a way as I have and he washed his hands with it before every surgery. Records were kept and he had far fewer patients to die from infections than those who didn't. Well, it is now or never," Caleb said, taking a deep breath and exhaling slowly.

He then took a scalpel and made an incision about four inches along the right lower quadrant of Bart's abdomen. Kitty expertly wiped at the blood. After another minute or so, Caleb gained the abdominal cavity. He took a two-prong retractor and applied it to the abdominal wall, then gave the handle to Kitty. "Keep traction on this if you please."

By retracting the incision Caleb was able to see and place his hand in the wound and visualize the swollen and angry appearing organ. "It's not ruptured," Caleb volunteered with a sigh of relief. "Captain Cade, if you will be so kind as to heat the tip of this scalpel in the candle flame, taking care to keep the soot off of it, I will be obliged."

While Cade was heating the blade, Caleb took a ligature made from waxed shoemaker's thread and tied it around the base of the appendix using a surgeon's knot. After cutting the excess off, he then tied another ligature closer to the intestine. Caleb then took the heated scalpel and excised the appendix, cutting between the ligatures. The smell of burning flesh temporarily filled the room. Using the hot tip of the scalpel, Caleb cauterized some of the bleeders in the incision site but a few had to be tied off with ligatures. Caleb was almost finished closing his incision when Bart began to moan and pull on the ropes.

"You may release his hands," Caleb instructed, "but keep the rope on his chest and legs for now."

When Caleb turned, Lord Anthony was standing in the doorway. "It's finished?"

"It is."

"Will he live?"

"The organ had not yet ruptured so the cavity had not been filled with infection. Therefore, I believe he will, but I've never done this before on a live person so we can only pray."

"What do you mean, on a live person?" York asked.

"The procedures I'd done in the past were practiced on cadavers."

"Damme!" Lord Anthony exclaimed and took the offered glass of wine, downing it in one gulp.

Chapter Eleven

When General Manning and Sir Victor arrived at the general's house, Bart was resting. Lord Anthony and Dagan's Uncle Andre were smoking their pipes and discussing how to appraise a good horse by certain features. Anthony listened intently and did not notice the general and Sir Victor's entrance. Caleb and Kitty were playing cards with Dagan and Betsy while Jubal and Kawliga were walking the streets of Norfolk, taking in the bustling port city.

Betsy had returned home after visiting a friend and found her house had been turned into a hospital. She was watching the man being moved to a bedroom when she felt a hand on her shoulder. She knew without turning the hand belonged to only one person...Dagan. Now as she sat across the table from him, little thought was given to the fact that not two hours ago the table was being used to operate on a man. Her mind was on how could the two of them get away for a while when she saw the door open.

"How is our sick friend doing?" Manning asked as he entered.

"He's asleep," Caleb volunteered. "It's the best thing for him at this point."

"Good," Manning replied. He then looked at Anthony. "You've been made comfortable I hope."

"Of course, General, your aide has been most helpful and accommodating."

"Well," Manning said drawing out the word. "I see you've met the best horse thief...I mean the best horse trader in all of Virginia."

It was obvious Manning and Andre were friends.

"Ah..." Andre replied, lifting his hands in surrender. "If you only knew, Admiral. Some expect to pay no more for the finest horses in America than what you'd pay for a mule. To even be near one of my magnificent animals is an experience in itself. Still, some would haggle when you'd think their station in life would preclude such behaviour."

Shaking his head Manning defended himself. "It's only by haggling that I'm able to maintain my station."

"That's enough you two." This from Betsy.

"I know when to send up a white flag," Manning replied, giving a bow of surrender. "Speaking of white flags, Lord Anthony, your brother and Sir Victor have informed me of the rogue who so cowardly fired on your ship. I assure you I have no knowledge of who would engage in such an act."

"I'd never believe you did," Anthony replied as graciously as he could. "I believe I'm a good enough judge of character to know when a man is not what he makes himself out to be; and, General, I believe you to be an honourable man."

"Thank you for that, Admiral, and while our countries are at war, I hope we will be best of friends when this calamity is over."

Standing to the side Sir Victor thought to himself, *Damned if I don't believe him.*

* * *

The following day the process of exchanging prisoners began. The exchange began with those well known to be who they stated themselves to be. These were the ones whose identities were not in doubt by either side...the elite group of civilians and high-ranking officers. There was much pomp and fuss made over these individuals, which included fond farewells from their captors.

Next in line were the officers of lesser rank, a major for a major and so on. It was on the third day of exchange that a navy officer was presented.

"Lieutenant Mahan, sir, late master and commander of *HMS Rapid.*"

Gabe had been assigned the duty of interviewing naval officers. He shook Mahan's hand and asked how he came to be taken. After a thorough report, Gabe asked about his first officer, warrant officers, and members of the crew.

"I know Lieutenant Wesley is waiting to be processed, sir, but as far as the others, I'm not sure. I do have a list," Mahan added, taking a paper from his pocket.

The paper was old and stained. He'd probably made the list soon after he was captured.

Calling to Sir Victor's man, Chiswick, Gabe handed him the list. "See how many of these names match those on our list."

Once Chiswick had departed, Gabe turned back to Mahan. "You know when you lose one of his Majesty's ships you have to face a court martial."

"Aye."

"Were you allowed to keep any records?"

"No sir. Only those I wrote after we surrendered."

"Well, official records would have been better but I don't think you will have any problems," Gabe said, trying to reassure the man. "Lord Anthony will likely be the convening authority and he is a fair man."

"Thank you," Mahan replied.

Gabe then called a petty officer over. "Please have Captain Mahan taken out to *Peregrine*."

"For the record, sir," Gabe again addressed Mahan, "you realize you are, in effect, under arrest."

"I understand, sir, and thank you for presenting me as captain."

"No thanks necessary." Then turning his attention to the petty officer, Gabe added, "My compliments and ask Lieutenant Lavery if he would be kind enough to offer the hospitality of the wardroom to our guest."

"Aye aye, sir," the petty officer replied and with Mahan in tow, he rowed out to the ship.

Several more prisoners were brought forward before Lieutenant Wesley was brought forth. After a short conversation, Gabe had him taken out to *Pegasus. Jep will find out if all is as it's made out to be,* Gabe thought. He didn't doubt either man's story but by putting them on separate ships he could not be accused of letting the two conspire. Not that they'd not already had time to do so while being held captive.

Later, when the processing came to a halt for the day, Sir Victor met with Chiswick, Gabe, and Dagan.

"Well, Dagan, have you come upon any of the prisoners in which you question their legitimacy?"

"Aye, one...a corporal who claims to have been taken when Lord Dunmore evacuated. He claims to have been part of the supply column that got cut off. He states he was knocked unconscious when his wagon overturned and when he came to, he was surrounded. His name is Pate and though he claims to never have known a fellow named Keith, I've watched them speak in passing far more frequently than any two strangers would normally do."

"Do you think they are...of a certain perversion?" Chiswick asked. "They usually recog-nize one another."

This made Dagan smile; some of the crew wondered if Chiswick was a sodomite. "No, I don't think so. I believe they may have been planted to spy on us as Sir Victor thought."

"What do we do?" Chiswick asked.

"I would hate to ruin a relationship with General Manning by rejecting them," Sir Victor said, rubbing his brow.

"Why not take them?" Dagan volunteered. "Once we get back to Barbados put the corporal on the first ship back to England to rejoin his regiment."

Now Sir Victor was smiling, "Damme, but that's a bloody good idea. What about the other bloke? What does he claim to be?"

"A minister."

"A minister?" both Sir Victor and Chiswick asked in unison, neither believing their ears.

"Aye, that's his claim. We could leave him in Saint Augustine if you don't have any other ideas."

Sir Victor seemed to be in deep thought then asked, "He's not 'Church of England' is he?"

"I didn't ask," Dagan answered.

"Let's ask around before we decide on a course for...the Reverend Keith," Sir Victor said.

* * *

Bart was sitting up when Sir Victor and Dagan arrived at General Manning's. His colour was much better and he was talking. "What happened to Mr. Jewells?" he was asking Caleb.

"He's at home. He's getting up in age and not as active as he used to be. I think the Virginia winters may be too cold for him."

"Yew could give 'im to 'is Lordship for little Macayla to play with. It's warm year round on Antigua."

"Bart! I'm sure Caleb is too attached to the monkey," Lord Anthony responded quickly.

"Ape!" Bart interrupted. "Did yew forget it's an ape? Just think of little Macayla with an ape for a pet."

Sir Victor leaned over and whispered to Dagan, "Bart's on the mend."

Seeing the two men come in, Anthony greeted them. "Where's Gabe?" he asked.

"He and Chiswick went back to the ship," Dagan replied.

"Are we about finished?" Anthony asked.

"I think one more day, perhaps two, will finish the process," Sir Victor said.

"Damn little help I've been," Anthony said.

"Nonsense, my Lord. You were present for those of nobility or of flag rank. No one would expect a vice admiral to involve himself in the mundane. Besides sir, it was in part your relationship with General Manning that brought this exchange together."

Jubal walked in and seeing Dagan called out, as a young man will do. "Dagan. I thought you was gonna take me and Kawliga to see a ship."

Before Dagan could answer, Anthony spoke. "I will be glad to take you on a tour of one of the Navy's finest ships. Your whole family is invited."

The youth's eyes lit up. "Everybody, even Kitty?"

"Even Kitty."

"Hear that, Kawliga, we are going to go see the ship before they have another fight."

The others in the room laughed, except Dagan, who caught Andre's eye. Dagan remembered his uncle's words from years ago just like they were spoken yesterday: *He has the gift; he can see things though he doesn't know it yet.*

Chapter Twelve

The prisoner exchange was completed the next morning. The people would soon be ferried out to the waiting ships for the first leg of their journey home. Jubal woke up excited. He'd never been on a ship the size of *Peregrine*. He did recall with excitement the trip from Beaufort, South Carolina to Norfolk when Gabe had been captured but that had been on small ships.

Now he was going on a much bigger ship and he was going with a navy admiral. He had talked to Kitty, who had tried to explain that they were all in the same family: Father, Dagan, Gabe, and even the admiral.

"Then why are we on different sides of the war?" he asked.

Before this could be answered, Dagan came in with a smile. "You ready for lunch on a king's ship?"

Jubal was out the door in a flash. As the family filed out, Dagan lingered then embraced Betsy. "You sure you don't want to come?"

"I would love to," Betsy said as she drew Dagan to her. "However, it would not look good."

"I hope we have not caused problems for you and the general," Dagan replied, concern in his voice.

"No, everyone understands what has transpired has been diplomatic protocol. We'd be poor hosts not to extend the hospitality of our home, even more so with a sick man involved. I will be glad when this terrible war is over, Dagan. I worry so much. It tears my heart apart to think something may happen to you."

"I will survive and I'll be back," Dagan whispered.

"You better," she replied and they kissed...a deep loving kiss.

"Dagan!"

"That's Jubal. He's impatient."

Betsy smiled as the two broke away. "He's excited," she said.

"I was getting that way myself," Dagan replied, only to receive a slap to his arm.

"You sailors, you're all alike," Betsy said, feigning anger.

* * *

The sides were manned and honours were rendered when the admiral's hat broke the entry port. However, the person under the hat was a smiling youngster with the admiral in tow. Gabe greeted each as they came aboard. Captains Markham and Jepson had been invited and introductions were made, in addition to *Peregrine's* officers.

Francis Markham smiled at Caleb and whispered, "So this is the lady that tamed the terror of the taverns."

A frown creased Caleb's brow and he replied in a whisper, "Open your mouth and I'll amputate your wedding tackle."

Markham tried to keep a smile on his face as he gulped.

"So, you are one of Caleb's randy bunch are you?" Kitty asked.

This time it was Caleb who gulped.

"Oh yes! I've heard...overheard that is, stories of how the two of you, along with Gabe, were the biggest womanizers in the West Indies."

Markham bowed and tried to sound contrite. "I assure you, madam, those stories are over-exaggerated and unfounded for the most part."

"Humph," Kitty snorted. "I wonder where the exaggeration started." She then smiled and held her hand to Markham, who kissed it. "It's Francis, is it not, or do you prefer Captain Markham?"

"Francis is fine, madam, when at social functions."

"Do you consider this a social function, Captain?"

"Yes, madam."

"Then you may call me Kitty."

Nesbit had prepared a feast. The main courses had been cleared away and dessert was being served amid stories of Mr. Jewells running amuck through the riggings, screeching loud enough to raise the dead.

"This was within a hundred yards of Admiral Graves' flagship and it being the wee morning hours, mind you," Anthony interjected.

A knock at the door quieted the laughter as the sentry announced, "Midshipman of the watch, sir."

Gabe stood. He, as well as the other naval officers, knew something had to be wrong: dreadfully wrong to interrupt the admiral's party.

"What is it, Mr. Chase?"

"Lieutenant Davy's compliments, sir, and he feels that your presence is required on deck."

When his captain didn't immediately respond, Chase quickly added, "It's one of our frigates, sir. It has been taken."

Gabe didn't reply but bounded up the ladder and to the quarterdeck.

"There sir," Lieutenant Davy said, pointing toward two ships coming up the river.

Gabe took the offered glass. The lead ship was a brigantine, a damn big brigantine to be sure. Much larger than *SeaWolf* had been and behind it the British frigate that had been patrolling just off the mouth of the bay.

"What is it, Gabe?" Lord Anthony had come on deck.

"It appears our frigate has been taken, sir. I don't recognize the flag but there is one over our colors. I can't be sure, sir, but I believe that's the ship that fired on us."

Lord Anthony nodded. "How did it take the frigate? It's...it's unthinkable."

"Permission to take a boat to inquire about prisoners when they anchor?" Gabe asked.

"No! We'll let Manning do that," Anthony replied.

The ships were now almost directly off the stern when Lieutenant Davy exclaimed, "Damn! Sir, they've thrown a man over the side."

"Where's the sentry boat, Mr. Davy?"

"Off to larboard, sir."

Gabe snatched up a speaking trumpet and shouted his orders. "Go get that man." He didn't hear the reply but the boat was being rowed to intercept the swimmer.

As the ship passed by, Gabe peered at the stern, *Tidewater Witch*. He'd not forget that name.

* * *

The shivering boy stood dripping on the deck as Midshipman Lacy handed him a blanket to wrap around him.

"Who are you, young sir?" Anthony asked.

The youth had never even seen an admiral up close and had never been spoken to by one. He was already scared, wet, and cold. He tried to speak but only stammered. It was Bart, who had come aboard earlier that morning, who came to the boy's aid.

"Here lad, have a wet. It will warm your innards. Yew look like a drowned rat, you do. Now let's get you settled down so yew can tell 'is Lordship what happened."

The boy calmed down quickly and after downing the glass of brandy, he cleared his throat and spoke. "I'm Cooper White, sir, midshipman on *HMS Drake*, Captain Cunningham, sir."

"Yes, I've met your captain. Now what happened so that the ship was taken?" Anthony asked impatiently.

"I'm not completely sure, sir. I was asleep and when I woke up we'd been taken."

Jepson, who was standing close, couldn't believe his ears. "Gawd boy."

"Didn't you talk to anyone?" Anthony asked.

"Yes sir," the boy whimpered. "A bosun's mate said the ship approached at dawn and had a flag of truce like you did when we met up. Then, suddenly when they were alongside, they sent boarders over. The captain and first lieutenant were shot right off. That's all I know except to tell you Captain Witzenfeld wanted you to know that it was he that sent you his respects during the squall."

"Captain Witzenfeld," Anthony and Gabe said in disbelief.

"Aye sir, that's what he said."

* * *

Lord Anthony called a meeting with his captains and requested Sir Victor's presence at the meeting. Prior to the meeting, Gabe and Dagan had a chance to speak.

"It's not the same man," Dagan assured Gabe. "I can promise you that."

A Lieutenant Witzenfeld had been the third lieutenant on *Drakkar*. He had been a very sadistic person and had been constantly thinking of ways to make the ship's midshipman's lives hell. He was particularly cruel to now Lieutenant Davy and Gabe. Part of his cruelty to Gabe had been due to an embarrassing moment when a smuggler held a knife to Witzenfeld's neck, threatening to slit his gullet and causing the scared man to lose control of his bladder and piss in his pants. Gabe had come to Witzenfeld's rescue and allowed the smuggler a choice: die or let Witzenfeld go. If he did the latter, he could go free. The man released his victim who immediately wanted to kill him for embarrassing him so. Gabe refused to allow Witzenfeld to retaliate, stating he'd given the smuggler his word. Witzenfeld was soon transferred and the two did not meet again until they were both assigned to *Drakkar*. Gabe had suffered much under the man until he went crazy and jumped overboard. Some thought it was because of Dagan. It was known he was the last to speak to the man but several had heard his words: "Careful where thy step, sir. Accidents happen, a misstep could haunt you a lifetime." Witnesses said the lieutenant turned ghost white pale, screamed at the top of his lungs, and then jumped over the side.

That had been years ago and no one had thought of the devilish man since. Now here was someone with the same last name raising havoc. How eerie it seemed.

The officers were all gathered in the captain's cabin and Nesbit had poured each a glass of brandy. Bart, who was recovering well, was sitting on the leather cushions beneath the stern window while Dagan stood behind Gabe's chair.

After hearing Lord Anthony's narrative of *Drakkar's* third lieutenant, Sir Victor cleared his throat and spoke. "Well, obviously there's a personal vendetta in all of this but let's look at the other aspects. The man is obviously a traitor to his country and must undoubtedly be a Colonial privateer. I can talk to General Manning about the frigate's prisoners and even complain about this man Witzenfeld's tactics. Both when he attacked us when we were under a flag of truce and using the flag of truce as a *ruse de guerre*. That clearly violates any honourable condition of war. But I know of no instances where a person who was not in the Army, Navy, or Marines was to be punished for such acts. We'll have to leave it up to General Manning. He's an honourable man and I'm confident he will do as much as a man in his position is able."

Dagan listened to the conversation. He'd let the admiral and Sir Victor talk to General Manning. Protocol demanded it from where they stood. However, Dagan knew it would do little good, if any. When they had finished playing diplomats he'd take action. Not a public action, not one that would bring recrimination on the peaceful exchange of prisoners or to Betsy and the general. But a very private action. For a dishonourable rogue like Witzenfeld, who hurt a woman, it would be no more than shooting a snake. Should he discover his and Betsy's relationship, Dagan was sure her life would be in danger. No, he'd act...maybe before the general got involved.

Chapter Thirteen

The Rathskeller had, at one time, tried to cater to the wealthy merchants and sea officers who did their business in and around the Portsmouth Shipyard. It was a respectful rooming house upstairs and a tavern in the cellar. However, when the business day concluded, men of wealth seemed to distance themselves from the waterfront.

Now the rooming house was a brothel filled with whores from all over the world. Many had been bought and brought to the Skeller, as sailors called the place, by Captain Witzenfeld. Here they would ply their wares until they were so old or so poxed that they couldn't perform. A few were killed in quarrels with other whores, sickness, or they just happened to be in the wrong spot when men were fighting. More than one had been shot down when they couldn't move fast enough. This would usually cost the men anywhere from a month to a year's wages, depending on how young, how pretty, or how well versed the woman was in plying her trade. Nobody was ever arrested or tried for killing a whore. If you ruined the merchandise, you paid for it.

The sun had barely set when Dagan walked down the crumbling steps to the Skeller. The only fresh air to the place came from the open doorway at street level. At one time there had been several small windows at street level as well, but these had long since been boarded up. The place was dimly lit in spite of a wagon wheel tied to a beam that was circled with candles. Oil lamps were fixed at each of the four corners and behind a well used bar. A narrow staircase in one corner led upstairs but it was roped off and a man with an old-fashioned broad sword sat next to it. The size of the man alone was enough to discourage most who would attempt to climb the stairs.

Dagan, dressed as a sailor off any of the merchant ships, made his way to the bar, ordered a wet and made small talk with the man behind the bar until others required the man's attention. Several wenches sashayed, showing more of their wares than covering them up. The man behind the bar proved talkative after Dagan bought him a mug of ale. When Dagan hinted interest in a particular wench, the man shook his head and whispered, "Poxed wench."

Nodding his appreciation, Dagan slid a couple of shillings across the bar, which the man deftly scooped up and into his pocket. After a while, a beautiful black-haired vixen walked down the staircase and spoke to the big man, who motioned Dagan's newfound friend over. The man returned behind the bar, washed a glass and poured it half full from a private bottle. He carried the drink back to the man, who handed it to the girl. When the man came back to the bar he was sweating.

"Who is she?" Dagan asked.

"She is death," the man whispered.

Dagan had seen death many times and this girl was not death. She was a beauty, dressed in an outfit that did little to hide her nakedness beneath. She had ample breasts that stretched the material, black hair, dark eyes, and full lips. She was enough to excite any man. She looked, Dagan realized, much as his sister, Maria, had in her younger years. However, Maria had never dressed so...so provocatively.

Dagan asked again. "Who is she?"

"She is the captain's very own. In five years she has never left this building without her bodyguard," the man said, his eyes pointing to the giant in the corner.

"Five years," Dagan whispered. "She must have been a child."

"She was not a child for long. The captain had her trained by his best girls in the ways to please a man. When he tires of her, he will sell her to some Chinaman or trade her for opium."

"Opium...here?" Dagan asked, surprised.

The man nodded but didn't speak.

Damn, I wish that I had known, Dagan thought. Caleb could have used it on Bart. Maybe he'd get some for Caleb after...after his business was done. He ordered another mug then stared at the girl. It wasn't long before she gazed back and held his gaze, almost as if longing, wishing for him to take her away.

Noticing Dagan's stare, it didn't take long for the bodyguard to speak out. Dagan ignored him. The man scrubbed the legs of his chair on the rough plank flooring as he pushed the chair back and stood up. Dagan still kept his gaze on the girl as the giant man picked up the broad sword and flicked his wrist on one hand and slapped the palm of his other hand with the blade. Dagan still held the girl's gaze. The big man was used to scaring people and was surprised when Dagan didn't flee as he approached.

Finally, he towered over Dagan and leaned forward to get in his face as he spoke. It was a mistake...the giant's last mistake. Dagan's hand had been resting on his hip. When the man leaned forward to speak, Dagan's hand shot out like a snake striking its prey. His aim was true. The hidden dagger entered just below the Adam's apple and, when it hit bone, Dagan sliced both ways, severing the spine. The man dropped to the tobacco and dirt stained floor, staring at the smoky ceiling for a few seconds before the light dimmed forever, and he could see no more.

Dagan quickly rushed to the stairs and took hold of the girl's hand and started toward the door, pausing only long enough to cut away a section of the dead man's coat. He then cut a slice midway through the coat to make a poncho of sorts to cover the girl.

He turned to the man at the bar. "Whatever is in his pockets is yours. I'd search quickly. Tell the captain I will be in touch."

Holding the girl's hand Dagan guided her up the steps and onto the streets. Once away from the place, he paused to think. He'd acted on impulse. An idea had come to mind and he'd taken advantage of it. Now he had to hide the girl, but where? Jepson! He'd take her to *Pegasus*. Ducking into an alley, Dagan whispered to the girl he'd take care of her and she wouldn't have to go back.

"I trust you," the girl replied.

"What's your name?" Dagan asked realizing he hadn't inquired.

"Ariel."

"That's a pretty name. Now I'm gonna find a place to hide you till I can get you something to wear. I don't want you to be scared."

"I won't be."

No, I don't think you will, Dagan thought, *not after what you've been through.* Walking down the alley, Dagan found a woodshed still standing where a house had burned down.

"Stay here till I get back. I should be back soon, but even if I'm not, you stay here at least for a day. Then go across the river to General Manning's house. But don't go until its dark and wait a full day."

Walking down the street, Dagan removed his hat and tossed it over a fence. It didn't change his appearance much but very few people knew what he looked like anyway. Besides they'd never expect him back down near the waterfront. Lighting his pipe Dagan made his way back to a shop that sold clothes for sailors. He was haggling with the shop's owner for a set of used sailors slops when the captain and a group of men passed by with the bar man in tow. Dagan and the bar man's eyes met but the man never blinked and the group kept going.

The shop owner did comment, "A dangerous group. Out for blood I'd say."

"Aye," Dagan replied. "Glad it is not mine."

* * *

Dagan turned as Ariel removed her poncho and scanty clothing. She had thought nothing of removing her clothes in front of him. *Something they'll have to teach her not to do*, Dagan thought. He used a small length of twine to tie the waist of the slops. He'd stopped and retrieved his hat. He now pulled the girl's hair back and pulled the hat down low. At first glance she looked like a ship's boy...at first glance, but it was hard to hide the way her breasts stuck out. Dagan reached down and picked up her old clothing. He cut a piece out of the linen shift. He held up her shirt and had the girl wrap it around her chest then tied it in the back. He then looked again. That was better...somewhat. Some things you just couldn't hide. Well, say what you want, that damnable captain knew women. This girl if given the time would make some man happy. She was also the reason duels were fought.

Taking a deep breath and exhaling slowly, Dagan asked, "Are you ready?"

"If you are," Ariel said.

"Well let us be at it then," he said.

Dagan found a boat easy enough and used it to row across the river and back towards the ships. He was challenged by the guard boat and then by the midshipman on *Pegasus*.

"Captain, Captain."

"Yes."

"It's Bucklin, sir."

"I know damn well who it is," Jepson snarled. "What do you want?"

"It's...it's Mr. Dagan, sir. He requests a private conversation."

"Dagan?"

"Aye, sir, Dagan."

"Well show him in," Jepson said through a yawn.

"You might want to put on some clothes, sir. He has someone with him."

"Yes well..." another yawn. "Give me five minutes then show Dagan and his visitor in."

"Aye sir."

"Bucklin."

"Yes sir, Captain."

"Find a damn candle and light it before you go."

"Yes sir."

Humph, Jep thought, stifling another yawn. *What the devil does Dagan want at this hour?*

Chapter Fourteen

Dagan awoke at first light. Years of getting up in the predawn hours made it a hard habit to break, regardless of how late he was up. Knowing he had no duties that needed his attention, Dagan made himself lie in his hammock and think. To take stock of his actions...and actions still left to be taken.

He'd involved Jepson by taking the girl...young woman, to his ship last evening. After his explanation of events, Jepson didn't seem put out at all. For the admiral and Gabe's sake he hadn't brought her to *Peregrine*. That way, even if asked, they could truthfully say they had no knowledge of the girl or the events surrounding her abduction. Jepson would not lie if asked, but the probability was he wouldn't be.

Now, how to get Witzenfeld? He would arrange a meeting in which he'd use the girl as bait. As he lay in his hammock, he thought of all the burned out buildings and homes and a plan was decided on. However, he'd need help. Every way he looked at it he'd have to have someone who could move as silently, and if need be as deadly, as a cobra. He could only think of one person: Kawliga. They had travelled and fought together in the past so Dagan knew his abilities. All he had to do was scout out the locations he'd use and, of course, speak to Kawliga. He could hear feet moving on deck and decided to go topside. *Today,* Dagan kept thinking as he dressed, *it has to be today.* In all likelihood they'd sail on the morrow.

Thinking of this made Dagan curse to himself. Today was the last time for some time he'd get to spend with Betsy. Then another thought crossed his mind. *It might be his last day on earth. Damn Witzenfeld! Damn this war!*

* * *

After coffee and a hurried breakfast of cheese and one of Nesbit's pastries, Dagan told Gabe he was going ashore and would be late returning. A pastry was halfway to Gabe's mouth when he stopped it in mid-air. He was about to speak but the words were left unspoken as Dagan looked eye to eye with him. *The boy I swore to protect is a man now,* Dagan realized.

"There is a letter in my chest if ..." Dagan paused, "if needed."

Gabe suddenly felt his eyes moisten as the extent of Dagan's words struck home. He knew he was going to deal with Witzenfeld. "Have a care uncle," Gabe muttered, his voice trembling.

"Aye, that I will." As he passed Gabe on the way out Dagan quickly grabbed his nephew and bit his ear.

"Ohhh! You ..." Gabe didn't finish as Dagan was gone.

Once ashore Dagan scouted out the places he felt would serve his purpose. Though he'd tell

Witzenfeld to come alone, Dagan knew he'd bring reinforcements. The trick was to separate the rendezvous in a way in which those reinforcements could be neutralized. After carefully selecting his choices, Dagan got a boatman to take him across the river.

After landing on the other side of the river, Dagan searched and soon found the woodshed he'd hid Ariel the previous evening. Once there, he found what he was looking for...part of the flimsy material she'd been wearing the previous evening. This would show his note was bona fide. Looking at the sun, Dagan decided that by the time he got back across the river, it would be a respectable time to call on Betsy...and talk with Kawliga.

* * *

The day seemed to pass all too quickly. It was almost 9 p.m. General Manning had invited Lord Anthony, Sir Victor, and Gabe to dine their last evening in port. Markham had already accepted another invitation and Jepson feigned illness. Dagan was thankful. Lord Anthony didn't take notice, feeling Jepson would feel out of place. Dagan knew differently.

Over brandy and cigars, Manning brought up the subject of Witzenfeld. "A damnable, arrogant individual he is. He refused to see me. Oh, his lieutenant said he was not available, but I was sure he was. I did find out the *Tidewater Witch* was once the *Norfolk Bell*. The owner, a Marlowe Prescott, had her built for the China trade till the war came along. She was then fitted out as a privateer after he talked with the man Witzenfeld. It seems that Witzenfeld was a gambler and a rogue who couldn't pay his debts, and killed the man who came to demand payment. He was in the East India Company and had to flee from a court martial. His brother was a Royal Navy lieutenant and was somehow lost at sea. He still has a few family members alive in England but, overall, he has no love for the British."

"You learned all of this today?" Anthony asked, incredulous.

"Yes."

"If I'm not out of line, may I ask how?"

"It appears one of Prescott's clerks is a man of many talents. He frequently does...shall we say, checks on a man before Marlowe Prescott turns him loose on one of his ships. The problem is, Marlowe doesn't pay the man enough to keep his mouth shut."

"What about the *Drake's* crew?" Anthony inquired.

"The ship's mate wouldn't say, but I talked with Prescott. He is willing to release the crew...those that haven't agreed to sign on with him, for one pound per man."

Sir Victor couldn't believe his ears. "That's twenty shillings per man."

"Yes," Manning agreed. "He wanted a guinea a man and that would have been twenty-one shillings per man. The way I see it is, I've saved you ten pounds at least."

"Aye," Sir Victor agreed reluctantly.

"General," Anthony said, using Manning's official title. "I think you should know it was my ship on which Witzenfeld's brother was lost."

A short narrative followed. At the end, Manning took a sip of his brandy then replied, "It's a good thing I dealt with Prescott then, isn't it? Otherwise, you'd never have gotten your seamen back."

* * *

Dagan and Betsy sat on the porch drinking tea and picking over their dessert.

"Do you know when you'll be back?" Betsy asked.

"No," Dagan admitted.

"Do you love me, Dagan?"

"You know I do."

"Then walk with me."

Taking Dagan's hand, Betsy led him down the street then took a path between two houses. In the backyard of the house on the left, a gazebo was dimly lit and the smell of citronella lingered in the air. A string held up a mosquito net. As the two ducked under the net, Betsy tugged gently on the string and the net fell. Turning to Dagan, Betsy pulled him close and their lips met.

After a long passionate kiss, Dagan asked, "Are you not concerned we'll be discovered?"

To answer, Betsy sat down on a padded bench. She tugged on another string. This time it was not the net that fell. Dagan stood speechless.

"Come here," Betsy barely whispered as she leaned over and blew out the nearest lamp.

After a time, Dagan lay on his side with Betsy pulled close to him. Both, spent from their passion, watched the flicker that the flame made as it jumped back and forth...casting tiny shadows on the illuminated whitewash.

"I will always be fond of citronella," Dagan said.

"You better be fond of me for thinking of it," Betsy replied. As she spoke, she went to turn and almost fell off the narrow bench.

Dagan grabbed her quickly and pulled her on top of him. "I love you," he said as he looked into her eyes. Tears were building up and he felt one drop on his chest. "You could come with me."

"Oh, I want to Dagan, but it would ruin the general. Besides, everyone is gone now. I'm the only one left to care for him. You will come back won't you, Dagan?"

"Aye, every chance I get."

"Then, I'll be here and after the war I'll make you the best wife you could ever hope for."

"You are already more than I ever hoped for," Dagan whispered as they kissed and came together again.

Chapter Fifteen

Dagan found a sailor loitering outside the Rathskeller. He pressed a guinea into the man's hand then said, "Deliver this note to Captain Witzenfeld. To Captain Witzenfeld...you understand?"

"Course I does," the sailor slurred. "And I recognize this cloth, I does. I'll deliver this note but iffen you don't want yew gullet slit, I'd be gone by the time I goes into the Skeller."

"Just deliver the note," Dagan hissed.

"Oh I wills, Gov'ner, I just hate to think you'd throw your life away so careless like."

Dagan crossed the street and stood in the shadows watching the entrance to the Skeller. It wasn't long before a man in a captain's coat, long shaggy hair, and a red beard rushed into the street. *So this is Captain Witzenfeld*, Dagan thought to himself. The hapless sailor was being dragged along roughly by two of Witzenfeld's henchmen.

"He took off, Cap'n. I told yew that. He said to give you the cloth and the note and you'd give me a guinea."

Dagan smiled in spite of the danger. *Bloody lout*, he thought, *trying to get paid for what I already paid him to do, but it worked.*

"Smith, you worthless sod, I ought to skin you alive," the captain bellowed but he cast down a handful of coins that Smith, who dropped to his knees, started to pick up.

The note had directed Witzenfeld to the burned out building that Dagan and Ariel had hid behind the previous night. There, another note directed him to a location a mile beyond. Once he reached that location, another note directed him back to the original location. The reason for the multiple locations was to find out who would follow the captain.

Dagan's note had stated to come alone and to bring one hundred pounds or the girl would die. He was sure Witzenfeld would not bring the ransom and he was just as sure he would not come alone. To have his woman stolen would infuriate Witzenfeld. To be led back and forth in such a manner would just increase his anger. Mad men make mistakes.

It was almost midnight when Kawliga let Dagan know someone was coming. It didn't take long for Dagan to make out the shadow of a horse and its rider. Pausing, the rider looked around listening. The horse pawed at the damp grass and stretched its neck when the rider didn't slacken the reins. From his vantage place, Dagan could see a saddle pistol as well as the sword and the pistol tucked into the rider's belt. Dagan didn't see a sack that would hold the ransom. *Damn.*

"Ariel," the man called, and then inched the horse forward.

A gentle breeze caused the note to flutter which caught the man's eye. Dismounting, Witzenfeld walked over and snatched the note from where it was tucked. Reading the note, he cursed. He then looked around and found a small charred stick that he used to write the words "meet me," and drew an arrow pointing to the other side where the directions were scribbled.

It was then Dagan considered a flaw in his plan. What if the followers couldn't read? What if Witzenfeld waited on them? Well, no matter, he'd still pick them off if he could...a big if.

Witzenfeld was mounting his horse when Kawliga let him know others were coming. After a moment, Kawliga made the sign for two. *So, he's only bringing two is he? Must be sure of himself.* As Dagan moved to position himself so that he and Kawliga would have the men in their crossfire, the Indian made a sound like an owl. When Dagan looked Kawliga held up three fingers. Is it three men or three more men? Dagan wondered. He didn't have long to find out.

"Bloody 'ell, what's this? Nobody is around."

"Hush you sod. Look about, but be quiet like."

As the first man looked about, a third man moved out of the trees. Swish...ahh. Dagan didn't take time to look at the man who had an arrow protruding from his neck. He took his knife and gave it a throw, hitting his man square in the chest. Another swish and the last man cried out. Dagan had been right in his choice of partners; Kawliga had silently dispatched two men without there ever being any hint of danger. His throw was accurate but compared to Kawliga's bow and arrow it was nothing. It was said many of the Colonials used such tactics on the British infantry. This had the British generals crying foul. Cry what they may, Dagan decided, the results were obvious. Look who was winning the war. Not the men marching in formation. *It may work in Europe*, Dagan thought, *but never in this wild land where the only rule to fighting was to win.*

Dagan and Kawliga removed the arrows and knife from the dead men then dragged their bodies out of sight. The men would be found, but by then, they would be long gone. Looking up at the sky, Dagan could see the clouds moving in the moonlight. The clouds were heavy and dark and were blotting out the stars. *Possibly a blow later*, he thought.

It wasn't long before the hooves of a horse could be heard. This time the horse was running, its rider being very impatient. Dagan had told Kawliga he would face Witzenfeld; it was a matter of honour. Something the Indian understood.

The rider pulled back roughly on the reins and the horse's hooves skidded on the damp road.

"Ariel...Ariel ..." Witzenfeld called as he slid from the horse, grabbing the saddle pistol as he dismounted. The metallic click rang out in the stillness as the pistol was cocked. In the distance, the faint rumble of thunder was heard. The wind had picked up so that the trees seemed to bend and sway.

"Ariel...Foster...Thomas ..."

"They're not here," Dagan spoke from the corner of the still standing chimney.

Witzenfeld swung around and fired, the ball glancing off the bricks and harmlessly into the night.

Dagan wasn't sure if it was the wind or Witzenfeld's whirling movement but his hat came off his head and now lay on the ground.

"Damn jumpy for a dangerous man," Dagan spoke again, only this time he was standing by a charred wall that had collapsed. Another shot rang out and the thud let Dagan know the ball had embedded in timber close by...but not close enough for the man to have been aiming.

Dropping the pistol, Witzenfeld pulled his sword out of its scabbard, making a rasping sound. Seeing this Dagan stepped from behind the wall as lightning lit up the sky. The wind had picked up more, blowing not only Witzenfeld's long hair but also his coat. Dagan pulled a cutlass from his belt and walked out to meet his enemy.

"Did you bring Ariel?"

"No, I did not. She was tired of you and decided to find a real man."

"You bastard."

He's mad, Dagan thought as he said, "No, unlike you, I knew both of my parents."

The moon reflected off the polished steel of Witzenfeld's blade as it slashed down and he rushed forward. Dagan parried the blow and stepped to the side, jumping as Witzenfeld slashed at his feet and legs then made a backhand slash that would have decapitated him if he hadn't ducked.

Another flash of lightning revealed a maniacal appearance to Witzenfeld as he cursed and slashed, the blades clanging together then parting. Rain started to come down pelting the combatants with large drops. Seeing Dagan shake the drops from his eyes, his foe rushed in to take advantage of the rainy distraction, but Dagan was ready. He dropped his shoulder and thrust forward and upward. The ground was now wet and slick. Though his opponent planted his foot, it slid on the wet grass and he was impaled by Dagan's cutlass. The look of surprise crossed the man's face. Dagan jerked his blade from his foe's chest which made a sucking sound. Free of the blade, he fell to the ground.

"Witzenfeld," Dagan spoke to the man, "Ariel is safe. I would never harm her. I just used her to get to you for your actions against my family."

The man tried to speak and blood came from his mouth. He spat it out. "You think I'm Witzenfeld."

Dagan was not sure if it was a laugh or the death rattle. The man spit more blood then spoke again.

"I'm Captain Morgan. I run the Rathskeller for Witzenfeld."

"Why did you come after me?" Dagan asked, shocked by this revelation.

"My life wouldn't be worth a fiddler's fart if Ariel was gone when the captain came back."

"Where is he?" Dagan asked.

The man coughed again, tried to speak as he slumped back and was gone. Dagan wiped his blade clean and walked over to the man's horse. He didn't see a sack hanging from the saddle but, when he checked the saddlebags, they were full. He took a handful of sovereigns and tried to give them to Kawliga, who refused them.

Dagan then hefted the saddlebags over his shoulder and the two of them headed toward General Manning's house. Kawliga had been sleeping in a small barn behind the main house. The two men went inside and Dagan lit a lantern. The rain had stopped but the two men were soaking. Looking toward the main house, it was dark as was expected. Dagan felt a loneliness fall over him. He had failed to bring Witzenfeld to justice. He was leaving the woman he loved and was also leaving a part of his family.

Dagan was surprised when Uncle Andre called his name. "It's done?" Andre asked.

"No sir," Dagan answered and told his uncle about what had taken place. "He's a cruel man, Uncle. He will stop at nothing to bring pain to Gabe or his family even if it means hurting someone else."

"I will watch over Betsy," Andre volunteered. It was as if he was reading Dagan's mind. "She will be safe in Petersburg. We will keep her there till it's safe to return."

Dagan knew that words could not describe how he felt. Feeling the weight of the saddlebags, he looked around the barn until he saw a bucket. He poured one side of the bag's contents into the bucket.

"An investment," Dagan said as he handed the gold to his uncle. Andre nodded...an investment.

PART II

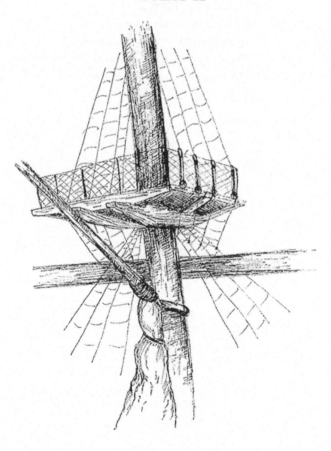

Spell of the Deep

What magic spell does the sea
Cast upon a man
To sail away from all he loves
It's hard to understand
Fearing not the wind and wave
The deep that has no sound.
The captain walks his quarterdeck
A ship that's fit-n-found

...Michael Aye

Chapter Sixteen

It was six bells in the day watch, three in the afternoon, when *Peregrine* and her sister ships made it to the anchorage at Saint Augustine.

"Ready forward," Lavery shouted, the speaking trumpet unused and dangling in his hand at his side.

As *Peregrine* rounded up, everything seemed in disarray. Sails were flogging as hands tried to go about their duties without bowling over some colonel's wife or stepping on some young boy who was so totally engrossed in the evolution that he was constantly in the way.

"Let go forward," Lavery yelled.

As the best bower anchor splashed into the warm water, Gunnells spoke to the helmsman. "Larboard your helm."

Orders were barked and the ship began to spin. "Let go main course halyards."

"Round up, Mr. Gunnells," Lavery called to the master. "Meet her. Let go second bower. Hand the courses handsomely now." Lavery seemed to be all over the quarterdeck as Gabe stood to windward watching his first lieutenant bring the ship to anchor. Down came the remaining sails.

"She's snubbed, sir," the bosun reported to Lavery.

"Very well," Lavery answered. "Summon the boat crews. You never know when it'll rain in Florida so let's get as many of our guests ashore as we possibly can before they get soaked in a cloud burst." What Lavery didn't say was Gabe, the captain, had let him know that if the guests were not on shore by sunset he'd think the first lieutenant would be amiss.

"'Peers Mr. Lavery is in a hurry to off-load our live lumber," Bart spoke as he made his way to where Gabe was standing.

"He's not the only one," Gabe replied barely above a whisper.

"Aye," Bart agreed. "'Is Lordship 'as bout 'ad 'is fill of the colonel's little un."

Gabe had a vivid picture of the little wench squealing or screaming at every turn. A closed door meant nothing to the colonel's children.

Smiling, Gabe leaned forward and again spoke softly. "See what's in the future for daddy and Uncle Bart."

"Humph," Bart snorted. "I believes in the Bible."

"I didn't realize you were so religious," Gabe chivvied his friend.

"Oh I is, special like when it comes to discipline."

"Discipline."

"Aye, I believes in spare the rod, spoil the child."

"Where is that verse?" Gabe asked. It had been awhile since he'd had any fun with Bart and was now on a subject he wouldn't let go.

"I don't rightly know but it's in the scriptures same as honour yews mother and father."

"Well, tell me what you are going to do when you take up the rod to Lady Deborah's little girl and she takes up a belaying pin to you?" Gabe asked.

"I guess that's when I finds a billet at sea. But that ain't gonna happen."

"You seem mighty sure, Bart."

"Oh I am. The colonel's girl done fixed that. I done seen 'is Lordship jump too many times. The little...little she devil always seems to be at 'is ear when she screams. Iffen she 'ad been a tar or bullock she'd been flogged round the fleet by now."

Gabe couldn't keep a straight face, "She devil?"

"Aye, makes you kind of believe in hants and such."

"How so?" Gabe asked, not understanding Bart's analogy.

Rolling his eyes Bart snorted, "And yew's a King's officer. Why she's pretty and a little angel one minute. Next she's a screaming she devil. They's got to be something unnatural bout that, bound to be a hant."

"I thought you believed in the Bible, Bart."

"I told you I does."

"The Bible doesn't talk about hants."

Bart was speechless for a moment as he stared at Gabe. Finally he spoke. "Yew need to talk with Lum and get educated 'bout the scriptures. Lum can tell you all kinds o' places where Jesus and his disciples cast out devils and if there ever were a person what had a devil in them, it's the colonel's daughter."

Seeing Lieutenant Davy standing close by, but not sure whether to interrupt, Gabe threw up his hands in surrender. "Yes, Mr. Davy."

"A barge is approaching, sir. Looks like the governor's barge."

"Is Governor Tonyn aboard?" Gabe questioned. If so a side party would have to be assembled.

"Not that I can see," Davy replied. "But it appears Mr. Ally is in charge of it."

* * *

A bowl of conch chowder was placed in front of each of the men seated at a table in the Mermaid Tavern. Bart attacked his with gusto as would be expected of a man who had been on a prolonged diet due to stomach ailments.

"I see your appetite is back," Lieutenant George "Jep" Jepson volunteered.

Bart's only reply was a burp and a smile. It was hard to believe that less than six months ago Jep had been a ship's master and now he commanded *Pegasus*. He had spent many an off duty hour playing cards with Bart and Dagan. They had become close friends. Jep was thankful that friendship had not come to an end with his step up. It was his friendship with Dagan that caused him to agree to give temporary hiding to the girl, Ariel. She was now the topic of conversation.

Dagan had gone to Gabe and Lord Anthony and explained his actions with regard to the girl and his failed attempt to draw out the traitor and privateer, Witzenfeld. Neither Lord Anthony nor Gabe had condemned Dagan; each was sure he had taken the appropriate action. Ariel had been brought aboard *Peregrine* as more women were aboard to act as chaperones. Now Ariel was being asked to live with one of the colonels and his family; however, Ariel wanted to go with Dagan.

Gabe had said Faith would welcome the girl as would Lady Deborah. Dagan was concerned that her presence might bring harm to those he loved.

"Face it," Jep was saying. "Witzenfeld is a scoundrel and will do what he can whether Ariel is around or not. Look what he's already done. What kind of man will dishonour a flag of truce?"

"Aye," Bart agreed, putting down his spoon and taking a pull from his tankard. He belched again, causing his friends to stare. "It's me innards," he said by way of apology. "Caleb said it may take awhile for 'em to work their way back toward normal."

"This Witzenfeld," Bart continued, "don't know it yet but 'e 'as got 'isself in a bad way with 'is Lordship. I wouldn't be surprised iffen once we get rid of the rest of our live lumber 'is Lordship don't send a ship or two on a witch hunting trip."

Bart had just informed his friends of the admiral's intentions regarding the rogue. He knew his words would go no further but it did set their minds in motion.

"Don't forget we got a court martial what 'as to be tended to first," Bart reminded his friends.

The men turned as a man at the bar banged his tankard and called for service. *It's not like Domingo not to keep man's glass full*, Dagan thought, then realized their lobster had not been served nor their tankards replenished.

Mama Chavez heard the noise and came out from the kitchen. She had almost made it to the bar when suddenly she stopped. Her hands went to her

face and she cried out. Seeing the woman turn
ghostly white, the friends bounded from the table to
behind the bar. Domingo lay face down in the floor.
Dagan knelt and checked the man; he was dead.
Shaking his head, Bart understood Dagan's
unspoken word. He and Jep helped Mama Chavez to
a chair where she broke down.

"I was just talking to him ten minutes ago!" she
cried.

"Aye," Jep responded.

It hadn't been much longer when Domingo had
been at their table serving the chowder and drinks,
laughing and joking as he did so. Walking from
behind the bar Dagan thought of Alejandro.

"I will go to Mr. Ally," he volunteered. "He's
probably still ferrying baggage and such."

Mama Chavez thanked him as Bart went behind
the bar and got a bottle of brandy. "Try this," he said
softly. "It will 'elp calm you for what lies ahead."

Damme, thought Jep, *I've just seen another side of
Bart most wouldn't believe.*

Chapter Seventeen

Gabe stood at the fife rail looking down at the men in the waist. The ship was now underway and making a good five knots with the winds out of the nor-northwest. Looking at the men, Gabe quickly thought of two he'd left behind in Saint Augustine. He would surely miss Alejandro and Paco.

The ever cheerful Mr. Ally, who as a young midshipman, had gained the respect of most of the men now gathered in the waist. By gaining their respect he had, in turn, benefited from their vast knowledge of ships and the sea. Given time, he would have commanded a ship like *Peregrine* or even a ship of the line. But time and fate have a way of changing the best laid plans. When Alejandro's father, Domingo, died suddenly from heart failure, Alejandro's dreams of being a sea officer had died also. Gabe had been present for many sea burials but the one and only shore funeral had been that of his father, Admiral Lord James Anthony. When a man died at sea he was buried usually by the next day. It had taken three days for Domingo to be laid to rest. Each day, Mama Chavez seemed to become weaker and weaker with grief.

Father Pedro Camps did a wonderful job, Gabe thought, *sending Domingo to live with the angels until such time as he was joined by his loved ones*. Alejandro approached Gabe soon after the funeral and tearfully asked if he could resign. Governor Tonyn had decided to offer the youth the pilot's job and Paco could help. Other times Paco would be of use at the tavern if Gabe agreed to discharge him. Paco had been a good man...all a captain could want in a cox'n but Gabe knew that the two men had developed a relationship not unlike his and Dagan.

Walking to windward, Gabe could see *Dasher* and just aft was *Pegasus*. The sight of the ships with the wind in their sails was breathtaking. *How could anyone want anything more?* Gabe wondered, then quickly realized there was a lot more. His wife, his brother, Dagan, even Francis Markham across the way commanding *Dasher*. The two had been midshipmen together and had fought together as well as imbibed together. Life was short. Domingo's death had brought this to the forefront of his thoughts. There were some things that needed to be said to certain people and some things should not be put off until tomorrow. Well, he intended on making some changes and that was no error, as Bart was fond of saying.

* * *

The small squadron made good time from Saint Augustine to Barbados. Winds were fair and no squalls were encountered. Departing Saint Augustine, they sailed to the eastward of the Bahama Islands then, after passing Saint Kitts, they sailed to the westward of Antigua to Barbados. During their time sailing, only one other ship had been sighted until they were off Saint Kitts.

The sun was bright and shining down on the houses at Bridgetown. Several of the passengers were on deck and commented on the brightly colered houses. Gabe had been in the West Indies, off and on, since 1774 and had gotten used to the floral pink, blue, and green houses. They were far different than those that dotted the English coast and countryside. It seemed gray, white, and natural wood or stone were the predominant colours there.

Hearing female laughter, Gabe focused on a group standing amidships. Lord Anthony was at the center of the group and holding onto his arm like a true lady was Ariel. Nesbit had spent countless hours tutoring the girl on the ways of a lady. Gabe was not sure if Dagan had instigated the tutoring or if Ariel had spoken to Nesbit herself.

Once away from Witzenfeld, the girl had blossomed into a very open and articulate young lady. Dagan had watched over her like a hawk in the early days but, while he still watched, he was not constantly at her side. *Give her room,* Gil had said in one of the rare moments when it was just the admiral, Bart, Gabe, and Dagan together.

Lord Mifflin and his wife had approached Dagan and stated, "We just love your ward."

"Damme," Dagan had whispered to Gabe. "It's not enough I spend most of my day looking after you. Look what I've done got myself into."

Gabe had noticed Mr. Davy spent as much time as he could with the girl when his duties allowed. After fighting a duel over the honour of Sir William Bolton's daughter, Annabelle, the two seemed to have drifted away from each other. Gabe was sure

Sir William didn't feel a mere Navy lieutenant was suitable for his daughter.

"Begging your pardon, sir," Lavery said, breaking his reverie. "We've passed Needles Point and are ready to make our final tack before entering Carlisle Bay."

"Very well," Gabe answered. "I will inform the admiral."

* * *

Lord Ragland's barge bumped alongside of *Peregrine*. It was sent out to help off load Sir Victor and the others of high standing. Buck had sent several of *HMS SeaHorse's* boats over as well as including Lord Anthony's barge. After being informed of their proximity to Bridgetown, Anthony had Bart ask Dagan to meet him below. There Anthony recommended to Dagan that he allow Lady Deborah and himself to act as guardians to Ariel until such time as definite plans could be worked out with regard to her future. Dagan had agreed, knowing it was the best all around. Heading back topside, Lord Anthony was thinking of how Deborah would respond to Ariel when suddenly he found himself lying flat, his bottom on the hot tarry deck.

"Damnation," Gunnells growled. "Mr. White, you've knocked the admiral on his arse."

Lieutenant Lavery, Lieutenant Davy, and Bart all rushed to help Anthony to his feet.

"I'm...I'm sorry, sir," White stammered. "I...I was rushing to inform his Lordship the guests (as the previous prisoners had been referred to) were departing."

Bart could see the youth was in a state of fear. "Don't worry about it, snotty. Yew's just done something the enemy 'as been trying to do for years."

Lord Anthony glared at Bart but was unable to be angry seeing the broad grin on his cox'n's face.

"My apology, sir."

"Apology accepted, young sir."

Witnessing what had happened, one of the tars spoke to a petty officer, "Lucky. Lucky 'e is. A lot of officers would 'ave 'ad him kiss the gunner's daughter."

"Aye," the petty officer agreed. "Now be back to your duties."

* * *

The signal for captains to repair on board was given the following morning. After the captains were given a cup of coffee and pastries Anthony nodded to Buck, who called the group to attention. *It was comforting to see the smiling faces of his captains*, Anthony thought. After pleasantries were exchanged, Anthony went over the events that had taken place since their departure, although it would have been unusual if word hadn't spread from ship to ship already.

"We have a convoy due within the month. It will be our job to escort it on to New York if we still have a foothold there...then on to Halifax." The pause brought about the chuckle, as he knew it would. "After we nestle the grocery captains in their respective ports, I intend we do some witch hunting...specifically the *Tidewater Witch*. I want our frigate back as well. I'm sure we can find someone to command her." Again there was laughter from the group. "If we can't take her, I want her...them, sunk."

Damn, Jepson thought, *not only is Bart right, but also his Lordship is out for blood.*

"We will meet again and discuss this in more detail the closer we get to the actual operation. Now, one of the jobs a commander-in-chief hates the most is convening of a court martial. However, as I previously stated, Lieutenant Mahan has lost *HMS Rapid*. Regardless of cause, when a captain loses his ship, regulations require he appear before the court. I am positive that once we hear of the circumstances surrounding the loss of *Rapid*, her captain will be acquitted."

Damme, Buck thought, *whether by intent or not, he's just let his captains know his wishes.* Hearing his name, Buck turned his attention back to the admiral.

"As I am the convening authority, Captain Buck will preside over the court. In addition, Captain Anthony, Captain Markham, Captain Taylor, and Captain Hazard will also serve. That will give us the required minimum."

Humph, Buck thought, *Hazard's confirmation has not returned yet. Oh well, he's the admiral.*

"Captain Buck."

Damme, there's my name again, Buck thought. "Yes, your Lordship."

"It would be my recommendation that Captain Jepson be appointed counsel for the defense."

"Yes sir," Buck acknowledged. *If this Mahan ain't acquitted with Jepson as his counsel, then he's a lost soul,* he thought, and then was relieved when he didn't hear his name again.

* * *

Bart and Dagan stood aft with Bart more or less leaning on the taffrail, enjoying a bowl of tobacco. Bart was examining his pipe between puffs.

"It's 'ard to believe but this pipe was once as white as a newborn baby's bottom."

The pipe, a hand carved meerschaum, was now a golden brown.

"Comes from burning the tobacco and your sweaty hand," Dagan advised. "Now tell me, Bart, how did Lady Deborah take to Ariel?"

"Oh, well enough. She greeted her kindly and had a servant girl show her a room. She told Ariel to freshen up while 'is Lordship did the same, and then they'd talk and get to know each other. Only it took 'is Lordship a sight more time to freshen than it did Ariel, even with Lady Deborah's help."

Bart had a grin on his face as he thought of the previous evening. "Seemed to me like 'er Ladyship was a bit more peaked after 'elping 'is Lordship."

By the time Bart had finished his story, Dagan was smiling. "When we got home, Faith hugged me and then took Gabe in hand. I didn't see him again until this morning. Lum and Nanny were there with that big old dog. Nanny finally said, 'You gots somthin to do, you better go on and do it cause them young folks got plenty catching up to do. I 'spect it'll take da rest o' the night.'"

Bart chuckled at Dagan's attempt to sound like Nanny. "Did she feed yew?"

"Aye Bart. That woman can cook. It's a wonder Lum's not as big as a whale. After supper, Lum broke out his lotz and played a few tunes."

"I miss the days of Gabe's singing and playing," Bart said, sounding melancholy.

"Aye, I remember on *Drakkar* when he, Stephen Earl, and Markham would get to singing verses. The whole ship would bust a gut laughing. He can't do that anymore. It wouldn't be seemly for a captain."

Shaking his head Bart agreed. "Yew knows, Dagan, we's getting old."

"That we are, Bart, but the alternative ain't worth a damn."

"No, yew's right there, mate."

Chapter Eighteen

The court martial was held in the great cabin aboard *SeaHorse*. It had taken a few days to get the officers and crew together. Lieutenant Lavery loaned Lieutenant Mahan a uniform and sword for the occasion. While most of the crew had been gathered as witnesses, Captain Buck talked with the member of the court. It was decided to keep the crew on hand, but they would only call the bosun, Mr. Murray; the master, Mr. Love; the first lieutenant, Mr. Wesley; and the ship's captain, Lieutenant Mahan.

It was 8 a.m. The bells had just signalled the forenoon watch. The hands went about their duties but in a quiet, somber manner. Everyone was aware of the court martial that was about to take place. The signal flags snapping in the wind overhead were enough to remind a forgetful soul. The shrill of pipes alerted everyone the admiral was now on board. The officers who made up the court were already aboard as well.

Inside the great cabin, a large mahogany table was set up so the court would have the light from the stern windows to their back. A group of five armed chairs sat behind the table for the court's officers. Off to the right was another armed chair for Lord

Anthony, who though not a part of the court would
be present.

Two small tables were set up facing the large
table. These were for the judge advocate and defense
officers. Off to the side, two rows of chairs were set
aside for the witnesses and the few spectators who
would be present. Lieutenant Lavery acted as provost and had escorted Lieutenant Mahan on board
the flagship. They were standing by the lee bulwark
when the marine sentry approached the two officers.

"They've ordered the prisoner to be brought in,
sir."

"Very well, Sergeant," Lavery said. He then
turned to Mahan and held out his hand. "Good luck,
Captain, though I'm sure you'll not need it. I know
each member of the court and they're all seaman.
They've all been tested in battle and they all know
what you went through."

Trying to put on a cheerful face, Mahan shook
the offered hand. "In that case, Nathan, I hope to
return your sword before the day's end."

Entering the great cabin Lieutenant Lavery
remembered his coaching. He walked to the great
table, stood at attention, and then placed Mahan's
sword on the table in front of Captain Buck.

"The prisoner is delivered to the court as
ordered, sir."

Buck acknowledged Lavery then asked
Lieutenant Mahan to take a seat, pointing to a chair
just to the left of the defense table. Lieutenant
Hazard had been appointed judge advocate. Buck
looked to him and said, "Carry on, Mr. Hazard."

Nervously Hazard shuffled through several papers. It was obvious he had been studying them prior to the prisoner being called. Once he got the papers in order, he picked them up with his one arm. He read the letter convening the court. Mahan had been given a copy of the letter and was told by Jepson it was routine. Finishing the page, Hazard put the paper down, picked up the next, and read his appointment letter to act as judge advocate.

Once this was done Hazard reviewed another document. He cleared his throat then said, "It's time to administer the oath to the captains sitting at the table."

Starting with Buck, as he was the acting president, each member stood, put his hand on the Bible, and took the oath. Hazard was hoarse and almost tongue-tied by the time the oaths had been administered to all the captains. *Damme*, he thought, *I'm glad there weren't thirteen captains as some court martial called for*. Then it was Buck's turn to administer the oath to Hazard. Once this was finished, Hazard went back to his desk and took a long drink of water from a waiting glass. He then shuffled around and picked up another paper. He cleared his throat, set the paper down and picked up the glass and downed the remaining water.

"Ahem." Holding the paper in such a way so as to pick up the most light he read, "To Lieutenant Patrick Mahan, Commanding Officer of the sloop, *HMS Rapid*, of sixteen guns. You are hereby required and directed to appear before a court martial for the loss of *HMS Rapid*...etcetera, etcetera. Lord Gilbert Anthony, Vice Admiral,

Commander in Chief, Windward Islands, West Indies."

Lieutenant Mahan was then called and asked to explain the circumstances surrounding the loss of his ship. The lieutenant appeared far less nervous than Hazard had. He requested permission to refer to his notes, since they could not be called official documents. Starting with the date, time, weather conditions, and ship's location, Mahan cited the first sighting of the French fleet and the approximate time they were fired upon. He continued his narrative to the point the ship was fired upon and then abandoned. He subsequently told of his and the crew's capture by the Americans and ended his testimony with his being part of the prisoner exchange. His report was so complete that he was not interrupted once.

When he sat down Buck looked to his fellow captains. "Does anyone have any further questions?"

Markham leaned forward, "Just one, Mr. President. Captain Mahan, to your knowledge, was the Colonials able to salvage or gain use of *Rapid*?"

"Nothing other than firewood, sir." This brought a chuckle to all in the great cabin.

"Thank you, Captain Mahan," Buck said. "You gave a fine report."

Wesley, the first lieutenant, was called and asked if he had anything to add to Mahan's story. "No sir, only that he was very calm during the whole ordeal."

Next, the master was called and, other than discussing his reviewing the charts with the captain and deciding on a favourable location to beach the ship, he had nothing to add. Gabe asked the master to explain "favourable location."

"The captain had decided to burn the ship to prevent the enemy from using her. He'd already dumped her guns as you recall."

After the members of the court agreed that they recalled that part of the report the master continued.

"The captain is a good man who cares about his people. He wanted to save as many as he could when he fired the ship. He didn't want anyone kilt needlessly. That's why we picked where to beach the ship, the most favourable location."

"Thank you," Buck said then had the bosun called. "Mr. Murray, you have heard the testimony given by your captain, first lieutenant, and master. Do you disagree with any part of their testimony?"

"No sir."

"Do you have anything to add?" Buck asked.

"No sir. They said it all."

"Thank you. You are dismissed. The court will recess for fifteen minutes."

Jepson had to stifle a yawn and rub his leg, which had fallen asleep. He'd not had anything to do since the proceedings had begun. Of course, he'd already talked to his Lordship and told him the boy captain had done a good job avoiding capture of his ship and saving lives.

It was less than fifteen minutes when the court martial was called to order. Entering the great cabin, the first thing Mahan looked for was his sword. The hilt was turned toward him. He'd been acquitted.

"Thank you, Lord," he prayed silently.

"Captain Mahan," Buck spoke. "The assembled captains that make up this court have found that you did act consistently with your duty by setting afire then running His Majesty's Ship *Rapid* on shore, in preference to falling into the hands of the French fleet or rebels...and you are hereby acquitted accordingly."

* * *

Refreshments were served after the great cabin had been put back to sorts. Anthony called Buck into a private conversation during this time.

"Tell me, Rupert, do you think Mahan would make a good flag lieutenant?"

Buck paused a moment while considering the question. "Aye, my Lord. I think he might. His report was clear, concise, and well put together. You can't fault his judgment with anything we've seen so far."

"Good," Anthony replied. Buck's evaluation was much as his was. "Now," he continued, "Pull him aside and put forth the idea."

"Me!" Buck exclaimed.

"Yes, you. He'd not deny me if I asked, but if you put it to him, and give him time to think on it and maybe even talk with Jep or one of the others. Then, if he responds positively, I'll have me a good flag lieutenant."

Nodding, Buck understood Anthony's reasoning. "I'll put it to him, my Lord, in a genteel sort of way."

Laughter could be heard in the adjacent area.

"That was one of Markham's and Gabe's little ditties I believe."

"I think you're right, Captain. Brings back memories does it not? Now let's go join the group before they drink up my best."

"No worries there, sir," Buck replied with a chuckle. "Bart and Silas are bound to have an adequate reserve stock."

Slapping Buck on the back, Anthony couldn't help but smile. "Aye, Captain. If they didn't, I'd think something was amiss."

Chapter Nineteen

The convoy sailed into Carlisle, the salute booming off the lead ship. Lord Anthony took his glass and watched the lead ship, a lithe new frigate. As he watched, he saw men standing by, prepared to trim the yards and braces. The shrouds were full of men as they raced aloft, ready to furl the sails.

"She's the *Phoenix*, thirty-six guns, sir." Anthony's new flag lieutenant, Lieutenant Mahan, spoke.

"A beautiful ship is she not, Patrick?"

"Aye sir," Mahan replied, still not used to being addressed by an admiral in such a friendly manner. Jep had been right about Lord Anthony and he was glad he had accepted the position.

"Signal for captain to repair on board."

"Aye, my Lord."

Turning to go about his duties, Mahan thought, *The signal midshipman probably already has the signal waiting.*

Captain Roger Frostbrier was a striking figure. A hearty, loud voice fit his giant muscled body.

"Had to give me a frigate," he told Buck. "Otherwise I'd have been bent double by the time I was thirty. Got so many knots on my head from forgetting to duck, it's a wonder I can still think."

Anthony liked the man immediately. After a glass of hock, they sat down and discussed the passage.

"They're better than most grocery captains," Frostbrier said. "War has been going long enough that most have had their fill of privateers."

"Did you encounter any?" Anthony asked.

"No sir, but we did sight a ship off Barbuda. My lookout swore it was a British frigate but when I tried to make contact she hauled her wind."

This set Anthony to thinking. He then told of the loss of the British frigate off Chesapeake.

"Might have been the same one but with two frigates and a brig escorting the convoy. A single ship would not have had a chance," Frostbrier opined.

More like she was a scout, Anthony thought, *sent to see when the convoy arrived, and then she'd beat her way back to get reinforcement.* There was little doubt in his mind the convoy would be attacked.

"Thank you, Captain, for your report. The governor, Lord Ragland, enjoys dining with new captains when they arrive. It is a way to keep himself abreast of what's happening in England, so expect an invitation from him. However, if you will do the honour of dining with me tonight, I will offer you some of the island's delicacies. I have my family here so we will dine ashore."

"Thank you, my Lord. It will be my honour."

"Very well, I'll have my carriage waiting at the dock at say 8 p.m."

"That is gracious of you, my Lord, and I'll be there at eight."

Back on *Phoenix*, Frostbrier's first lieutenant asked, "What's our new Lord and master like?"

"You wouldn't believe it, Mr. Raleigh. You wouldn't believe it."

* * *

Anthony had invited Sir Victor, Buck, Gabe, and Markham to dine that evening as well as Frostbrier and Raleigh, his first lieutenant. In addition to Gabe bringing Faith, Sir Victor had invited a recently widowed lady named Olivia Cunningham. Hers had been a May and December marriage.

Mr. Andrew Cunningham had been sixty and Olivia, known by close friends as Liva, had only been twenty-four. Mr. Cunningham had lived ten years after their wedding but had been a bedridden invalid the last two.

Buck's nod and "evening Liva" raised little doubt to those gathered that he was one of the lady's close friends, or had been at one point.

Lady Deborah had met the widow on several occasions and liked her bluntness and lack of pretense, even though it was said she was in the top five of the island's wealthiest. *It would take a strong man to handle her*, Deborah thought. After years of running the plantation, she would not be one to be content playing the dutiful little wife. Buck had the strength but the sea had Buck. But, as much could be said about Gil, yet while she didn't have him one hundred percent, neither did the sea.

Ariel looked around at the gathered guests and quickly asked Gabe, "Is Lieutenant Davy not coming?"

Damn, thought Gabe, *I should have invited him.* "I'm sorry," he finally managed. "Lieutenant Davy is attending his duties tonight. I'm sure he will make himself available for future engagements."

Ariel looked disappointed and as she walked away, Faith whispered, "Liar."

Gabe winced. He quickly excused himself and spoke to one of his brother's servants and asked him to round up Bart if he was still in the house. When Bart showed up, he and Gabe spoke quickly and quietly. Then Bart was gone.

The group made polite conversation, with Frostbrier providing the latest news and gossip.

"Tell me, sir," Lord Anthony requested. "What is the general attitude at home now that the news of the French has joined the Colonials?"

Frostbrier paused as if considering the depth of the question before answering. "The military seems to be concerned, sir. It will undoubtedly further strain our resources. It seems a given we will have to fight the Frogs on two fronts. However, once you get past the Navy and Army, the discussion is met with ambivalence. There appears to be a general lethargy from the public and even some in Parliament don't appear to be alarmed."

"They damn well will be when the Frogs cross the channel or worse, when Spain sides with them against us." Realizing he'd spoken with profanity and vehemence, Sir Victor bowed his head in embarrassment. "Please forgive my outburst and profanity, ladies. Lord Anthony, I beg your forgiveness for my breach of behaviour."

Lady Deborah was quick to speak, "Nonsense, Sir Victor. I wish more were as concerned and loyal as you are. I applaud you, sir."

"Thank you, my Lady. You are most gracious."

Both wine and claret was offered with small cuts of cheese and delicate cuts of meat and seafood.

Dinner had just been called when a doorman announced, "Lieutenant Davy to see Captain Anthony."

Ariel's eyes immediately lit up. Gabe excused himself then returned, making a show of folding a paper and putting it inside his jacket. Lady Deborah stepped forward and welcomed the new arrival.

"Shall we set another place?" she asked the young lieutenant.

"I'm not sure," he stammered. "I was told to deliver an urgent message to the captain, Madam."

This caused Anthony to look at Gabe, who gave a quick wink causing his brother to smile.

"I see no reason for Lieutenant Davy to rush back to the ship now that he's completed his errand," Gabe said.

"Good," this from Anthony. "Lieutenant Davy, would you honour us with your presence for dinner?"

"My pleasure, your Lordship."

During the meal, Frostbrier and Raleigh were kept busy, only it was more on what was the latest fashion and what plays were the talk of London.

While the dinnertime buzz was going on, Faith leaned over and whispered to Gabe, "You made that happen didn't you?"

"Aye, one of the benefits of being the ship's captain."

"There are other benefits as well," she whispered. "Some you're liable to reap later tonight."

* * *

After dinner, the men gathered as Lord Anthony broke out cigars and a decanter of brandy. Lieutenant Davy appeared unsure of what to do. He didn't feel comfortable with his superiors but didn't wish to stand around with the ladies.

This time it was Faith who came to the rescue. "Lieutenant Davy, do you know the game of whist?"

"Yes, Madam."

"Good. There's a cool breeze on the side porch. Would you mind taking Ariel there and teaching her the game? That way we will have a ready fourth when we decide to play."

"It will be my pleasure," he responded as he and Ariel fled the room, worried Faith might change her mind.

The conversation continued between Anthony, Sir Victor, Frostbrier, and Raleigh; this time it was a definite political conversation. Feeling a bit devilish, Gabe sidled up to Buck. "Liva, is it?"

"Aye."

"She's a very attractive widow."

"Aye."

"She's absolutely a prize catch."

"Aye."

"Damme, Captain Buck, is 'aye' the only word you know?" This from Francis Markham who had walked up unnoticed.

"Nay. I know more, but what she wants is more than I can give. Besides...she's rich."

"And you're not, with all the years of prize money you put up."

"Well there's that," Buck admitted. "I told her to give it till after the war. She said she was a woman with a woman's needs and she didn't know if she could wait. Therefore, I said don't, and I haven't been back."

This was a shock to Markham and Gabe. Finally Gabe spoke. "I apologize, sir. It was rude of us to press the matter, even in jest."

As the evening grew, Frostbrier stood and said, "Thank you for such a wonderful evening, sir. I wish I had orders to serve under your flag."

"I do as well, Captain. You have no idea how I wish for another ship to replace our sixty-four that was lost."

Making their way home Gabe thought of Buck and mentioned him to Faith. "Captain Buck sure looked lonesome tonight."

"He won't be for long."

"He won't?" Gabe asked, not sure he'd heard correctly.

"That's what I said," Faith flippantly replied.

"How do you know?"

"Cause I saw the note Liva gave to Deborah to give to Buck. He's to give Sir Victor time to drop her off ... drop her off, not come in. Then when the lights are out, he's to come to the door."

"Well, maybe she is willing to wait."

Not understanding what Gabe meant Faith replied, "Not for long I don't imagine."

Chapter Twenty

Francis Markham, Captain of *HMS Dasher*, plopped down in a chair and called for his servant.

"A glass, and sooner than later."

He'd just left a meeting on the flagship where he was told he was being placed in command of the convoy leaving in the next week or so. *Damme,* he thought, *and damn Gabe too.* He'd hung around after the meeting and harassed his friend.

"Couldn't happen to a better man...no worries or boredom. No worries about having a good sleep because you won't have time."

Had Buck not called Gabe, he'd probably have bounced a belaying pin on his smirk head, so he would. Now all he could think of was all the miles of herding a bunch of mules to Nova Scotia. Blast those merchants who sent ships to sea with hulls so ripe it would be a wonder half didn't flounder. Under-manned and overloaded, let the Navy protect us and for free. It was a poor card he'd been dealt but not one that others, including Gabe, hadn't already been dealt, he realized.

Ships from England carried goods to keep the war going. Then they'd head back to the West Indies to pick up cargoes of sugar, tobacco, and nutmeg, in addition to spars and masts that had been picked up in North America.

Sitting down at his desk after downing a glass of hock and ordering another, Markham went over the sheets given him by Buck titled "Signals and Instructions for Ships under Convoy".

"You'll be escorting thirty-three," Buck had said. "That's ten less than arrived. The other ten will go to Antigua then return and wait for the England bound convoy."

Well, he'd review and add anything he desired. "Remember," Buck had admonished, "keep it simple. Thirty-three grocery captains and all thinking they know better than you."

He'd warn them to keep up. Stragglers were fair game for privateers. Any ship that didn't keep up at night would likely find himself a prize at dawn. The Americans, and now the French, both knew their business all too well. He, Markham decided, would not be answering to Lloyds for negligence on behalf of some merchant.

* * *

The first hint of daylight showed on the eastern horizon, a typical West Indies dawn. Markham's first lieutenant could be heard bellowing out orders and men rushed to do their task, not wanting to feel some bosun's mate's starter.

The master reported, "The anchors hove short, sir."

"Any of our children appear ready to make sail?" Markham asked, speaking of the merchantmen.

"No sir," the master sadly answered.

It might wake the admiral but Markham felt he had to establish authority at the onset.

"Mr. Hawks," Markham called to his gunner. "I want a gun loaded with a bag of powder and fired toward the merchants. Unshotted mind you."

"Aye," the grinning gunner replied and called to his mates to prepare one of the bow chasers."

"Umgh!"

"Yes," Markham acknowledged his master.

"Might wake the governor same as the admiral, sir."

"That it might, sir."

Lord Anthony would not be awakened. He was already awake and watching through the stern window. He did jump when *Dasher's* gun was fired but continued to watch as the convoy ships quickly made ready to get underway.

"Got 'is point across 'e did," Bart said watching the convoy as well. "'E didn't make no friends firing that gun I'd wager."

"No, I don't imagine he did but he let them know he'd brook no lack of diligence to his signals."

Watching until the convoy was under full sail, Anthony could smell coffee, so he sat down at his table. "Bart, ask Buck to join us if it's convenient and then have them signal for Gabe and Jepson to repair on board. Silas!"

"Aye sir."

"I'll have coffee now but I expect three for breakfast."

"Aye, I'll put on more bacon. Would 'is Lordship care for a bit o' cheese and a pastry while we wait?"

The yes was on his lips but his hands were on his belly. It had, as Bart was fond of saying, "grown 'siderable" over the last year. He needed to exercise more and eat less. Did it...would it seem inconsistent with his rank to put in an hour each morning walking around the ship? He'd think on it.

Seeing Silas still waiting for an answer, he said, "I think a small pastry might be in order. And Silas, you know how Buck and Jepson like your coffee."

"Aye sir," the servant replied, and then added under his breath. " Same as you do."

* * *

The convoy got underway on the early morning tide. It was several hours later when two more of Lord Anthony's ships weighed anchor and set sail. The sails disappeared over the horizon just as the sun set. More than one glass was trained on the departing ships until they vanished from view. Lord Anthony closed his glass with a snap and handed it to Bart.

Sensing Anthony's mood, Bart started to say something encouraging. However, he remained silent. Gabe and Jep were sailing their ships deliberately into harm's way. They were to seek out the enemy and engage them in battle. When ships fought, men died. This was on his Lordship's mind. If something were to happen to Gabe, Lord Anthony would never forgive himself. At times it was best to be near...but silent. Bart was silent.

A small observation deck was built over the porch of a small house sitting on a slight rise. Lum and Nanny both stood by as Missy Faith watched her man...her brave frigate captain, sail away. She knew from the start of her relationship with Gabe that she'd always be in competition with his mistress...the sea. She had spent many hours talking to Deborah about the rivalry they each shared but could never win.

"I don't understand the hold the sea has on our men," Deborah had said. "But I'd rather share them with the sea than lose them to it."

"Damn!" Faith shouted when she could no longer see the sails on her man's ship. She rose suddenly and felt a wave of nausea sweep over her. Lum was quick to grab her as she staggered slightly.

"You feeling bad?" Nanny asked.

Fanning herself, Faith took a couple of breaths and replied, "Just some vapors. I feel fine now."

Lum could feel the cold clamminess in Faith's hand so he continued to support her.

"Get outta da way you old beast," Nanny shouted at Samson. "Lawd, he done got so big he blocks da doh."

Samson looked up, yawned, and then moved to let them pass.

"Don't talk so rough to my baby, Nanny."

"Yo baby. Child, dat dog near big as a horse. Baby...humph! You has spoiled him all right, worse than any child I ever seen."

Sensing he was being talked about, Samson looked up with his big old sad eyes, and then licked Faith's hand a few times. She stopped and knelt to pet the brute and was rewarded by several licks across the face.

"Kisses better than Gabe," Faith laughed, feeling much better now.

"Lawd, child! Yo mama's gonna look down and wonder where yo raising went. I promised to look after you when the Lawd took her home."

"You do, Nanny, you and Lum."

"Yeah well, Lum go put on some water to heat. After all that slobber she's gotta be scrubbed."

"Oh Nanny, Samson is clean." Then to emphasize her words she leaned down and kissed the dog again.

"It's a good thing Captain Gabe is gone, child. He see you do dat he ain't never gonna kiss you again. Hurry up wid dat water, Lum."

* * *

Gabe sat under the skylight enjoying a glass of sweet lime juice. Nesbit had promised supper within the next quarter hour. Dagan sat across from Gabe with a list of possible replacements for Paco, Gabe's cox'n who'd stayed behind in Saint Augustine.

"I've talked with the possible replacement," Dagan was saying, "and I believe Jacob Hex is the best prospect. He's bright, he can read and write, and was Mahan's cox'n."

"Why didn't he stay on board the flagship with Mahan?" Gabe asked. "As the new flag lieutenant, Mahan could have gotten him on board."

"I asked him that very question," Dagan replied. "Said he didn't want to get barnacles on his bottom."

This caused Gabe to laugh. Hearing the laugh, Nesbit thought to himself as he set dishes on a serving tray, *Never hurts to start out on the right foot*.

The smell of roast mutton smothered in onions, buttered carrots, potatoes, and hot bread filled the

air, as one by one, Nesbit uncovered the dishes as he
set them on the table. Gabe had been kicked back in
his chair munching on nuts and cheese. He now
rocked forward, sitting all four chair legs firmly on
the deck, his mouth watering over the prepared
dinner.

"Would you like a glass of wine, sir, or do you
wish another glass of lime juice?"

"Wine...wine would be fine."

Dagan nodded his agreement. Nesbit had long
stopped inquiring if Dagan would be present for a
meal. If he was there, he ate. If not...well, leftovers
never lasted long with the captain.

* * *

The convoy was in sight the following day at dawn's
first light. Gazing to larboard Gabe could make out
Pegasus. She was on station, as Gabe knew she
would be. He'd not want to be the officer on watch
who had let a helmsman drift off course...not with
Jepson as captain.

"Looks like a bunch of pregnant whales,
Captain."

"Is that so, Mr. Gunnells?"

"Aye sir, wallowing along as they are under a
soldier's wind. It's not surprising we caught 'em
quick as we did. Not a scrap more canvas than they
can get by with."

"I'll bet Captain Markham is about to bust a
gut." This was from Lavery.

"Aye," Gabe replied. He could picture his friend
trying to hurry along a convoy that was used to a
leisurely pace.

Once the sailing in convoy practice had begun, the merchants had no need to try to outsail the competition to the next port. Prices would all be the same. In the old days the first ship to arrive got the best prices for their goods. The convoy system had in effect levelled the playing field and neutralized competition for the most part. What they lost in prices they gained in keeping the ship. While the system was not perfect, it did cut losses to privateers significantly. It was not the duty any Royal Navy captain would choose, however.

As the sun rose, the ships sailed through a sparkling sea. At times the sun's rays seemed to dance across the small waves. A shout was given as some crew member spotted a school of porpoises. The school swam alongside for a while then, as if tired of the ship's slow progress, they effortlessly outpaced the frigate and were soon lost from sight. An hour or so later, a flying fish came inboard hitting a seaman in the chest. A shout of alarm from the unsuspecting seaman brought a chorus of laughter from his mates. Gabe went below to enjoy the last of the morning's coffee. It was just lukewarm but he didn't mind. He'd drunk cold coffee on numerous occasions and had come to like it that way.

A knock on the cabin's door was followed by the sentry's announcement, "Seaman Hex, zur."

"Come in," Gabe motioned with his hand.

The seaman came forward and stood at attention.

"Relax, Hex." Gabe wanted the man at ease as they talked. "Do you know why you were sent for, Hex?"

"Aye, I think so, sir. Belike the cox'n's duties."

Gabe nodded, "Nesbit, a cool glass for Hex."

When the glass of lime juice arrived Gabe motioned for it to be set on the table. "Sit down, Hex. Do you like lime juice?"

A grin creased the stocky sailor's face, "It'll do to wet your whistle, but it's not a proper drink, sir."

Gabe immediately liked the open candidness of the man. "And what would you call a proper drink?"

Hex seemed to be in thought, and then replied, "There are several answers that could all be right, sir. If I was out with me mates, rum is the only drink there is; if I was out with a lady, not some floozy, a glass of wine or maybe ale. But if I was around gentlemen, the only thing I'd consider would be bourbon whiskey."

Now this is intriguing, Gabe thought. General Manning had served this during the prisoner exchange at Norfolk and had, in fact, given Gil several bottles.

"Bourbon over gin?" Gabe asked.

"Aye sir, unless you just want to get drunk, then I guess gin would be the cheapest way to go. I've even tried the stuff the Rooskies drink...vodka I think it is. It was about the same as gin but made out of potatoes."

"I see you're a man who knows his spirits," Gabe said. "How'd you come by all this knowledge?"

"The bourbon is what we got while we were in prison. That is, if you had any money. I had a bit tucked away and won a bit here and there so I bought the bourbon."

"I see," Gabe said. "Do you play cards?"

"I have, sir."

"Well, let me tell you now, don't get into a game with Bart. Do you know who I am talking about?"

"Yes sir, Bart is well known to those forward."

This time it was Gabe who smiled. "And to most of those aft as well. Tell me about yourself, Hex. What's your given name?"

"Jacob, sir, took it from the bible. My father said with a last name like Hex the front one had better come from the scriptures. While my name is Jacob, my mates call me Jake."

"What did you do before the Navy?"

Hex looked sheepish, his eyes barely slits. "I was a smuggler, sir, or rather my father was and I often helped."

"Did he have many boats?" Gabe asked, thinking back to his days as a young midshipman when he'd been assigned to a cutter trying to run down a smuggling ring.

"Boats sir, no, not nary a one. My father sold the goods to different shops. He was the go-between man so to speak. He wanted me to know the business from top to bottom as it were, so I spent plenty of time between the coasts."

By that Gabe knew he'd made trips back and forth to France. "Were you from Deal?" Gabe asked.

"Aye, grew up in the shadows of Walmer Castle."

The smugglers of Deal were the stuff legends were made of. If Hex's father was in the trade, he'd probably been very wealthy and his son given a good education. Therefore, it puzzled Gabe why the man was serving before the mast.

"Hex, do you mind my asking why you're a tar?"

"We were set up, sir. An old employee of my father was a spy for the revenue service. A trap was set up and my father was killed. I was given a choice. Jail or sign up for the king's shilling. I took the shilling. But not before the spy had been given a grin from ear to ear."

Hex said this while making a motion like he'd sliced his throat. *He just as much as mentioned he'd committed murder,* Gabe thought. *Well, he'd be a good man to have on your side.*

Seeing the lime juice was finished Gabe asked, "Another glass?"

"If it's all the same with you, sir, I'll pass."

"Very well," Gabe replied with a smile. "Go find Dagan and tell him you're my new cox'n."

Now it was Hex who smiled. "Aye aye, Cap'n. You'll not be disappointed, sir. I promise you."

Gabe nodded. "I've no worry there...Jake."

*   *   *

A knock was heard, and then the sentry announced, "First Lieutenant, zur."

"A glass of lime juice?" Gabe asked as he drained the last from his glass.

"Er...no sir, I'll pass."

Thinking of Hex's reply, Gabe smiled. Seeing the look on Lavery's face Gabe quickly explained, "A thought just came to mind, Nathan. I was not being rude."

"Aye sir."

"What brings the first lieutenant down at this time of day?" Gabe asked, trying to lighten Lavery's apparent unease.

"It's about Mr. Hawks, sir."

"Mr. Hawks," Gabe replied.

"Aye sir. We didn't get a replacement for Lieutenant Wiley, sir, and I thought we could promote Mr. Hawks to acting third lieutenant. He's ready sir."

Damme, Gabe thought, *I'd meant to do that already, but so much had happened.*

"I'm remiss, Nathan. Young Hawks should have already been promoted as you say. Would you like to inform him?"

"Aye sir. It would be a pleasure."

"Then I'll expect to see him in the wardroom when I next receive an invitation."

"Aye sir...on Saturday."

Peregrine's wardroom had made a tradition of inviting the captain to dine on Saturday evenings when at sea.

Chapter Twenty-one

The seas were choppy at first light with a variable breeze. The mainmast lookout reported the convoy to larboard with *Pegasus* to starboard and slightly astern. Clouds were building to the northeast.

"Squalls by the first dogwatch I'd say," Gunnells volunteered.

Gabe nodded his acknowledgement.

"The type of weather Witzenfeld favours for his sudden attacks and sweeping up stragglers, I'd say." This was from Dagan, who had been silent until now, his gaze on the distant horizon.

"Aye," Gabe answered. "You feel we'll meet today?"

"Today or at dusk depending on the weather. Not later I'd say."

Those standing within hearing took this prediction as gospel; most looked at Dagan's predictions about events as they did the master's weather predictions. His name had risen in the crew's mess more than once, with some of the older seaman swearing his uncanny predictions came from another world. While some felt this was a heavenly gift others swore it was a curse from the bowels of

Hades. He was a gypsy they'd whisper, a fortune teller. At least one swore, "He's a soothsayer." The one fact on which all the crew agreed was that Dagan was a mystery.

"Sent to keep 'is eye on the cap'n," Tate, a former captain of the foretops would say. "I been with the cap'n off and on as man and boy. That was afore the rheumatism set in. The one thing I can tell you is we're safe while Dagan is around...most of us uns anyway. A few might get kilt but not as many as would be otherwise."

Taking a last gaze at the horizon, Gabe turned to his first lieutenant. "You may secure from quarters, Mr. Lavery."

To the northwest, clouds continued to build and the sky turned gray. The waves rolled, with some overlapping the previous one, causing a foam like appearance. More than one of the crew was doused by the salty spray. By noon the barometer had dropped but the wind was still moderate. It was the sea that seemed confused. The ship would roll from larboard to starboard one minute then pitch as the bow crashed through a rogue wave.

Gunnells made his way over to his captain as Gabe returned on deck after his dinner. Shouting to be heard over the groaning rigging, Gunnells stated, "I feel we are meeting with a blow of consequence."

"I don't understand," Gabe admitted.

"I believe we're dealing with two converging storms, one out of the north and another from the east. I think we are to the south of the convergence but it could still be bad enough."

"What do you recommend?" Gabe asked.

Gunnells appeared to think on his reply. Finally he answered, "Sir, I recommend we reduce sail to storm jibs and trysails."

"Very well, Mr. Gunnells, make it happen. Mr. Lavery."

"Aye, Captain."

"Have all loose gear secured. Double the ropes on the guns and have blocks placed under the trucks. Have the cooper check the water casks and make them fast. Also have the carpenter and his mates do a thorough check of the hull and the well."

"Aye aye, sir."

"Mr. Graf."

"Sir."

"Rouse out the sea anchor and bend the anchor cable to it. Be sure it's sheltered from the wind. Mr. Lavery."

The first lieutenant quickly returned to hearing distance. "Yes, Captain."

"I know you heard Dagan's concern that we'll meet up with the privateer before the day is out."

"Yes sir."

"Well, we need to be ready for storms on both fronts. I want chain slings rigged. We may not have time later. We'll feed the men after the ship has been made as ready as possible then douse the galley fires."

"Aye sir." Lavery continued to stand. He could see his captain doing a mental check list.

Finally, Gabe looked at Lavery, almost not believing he was still standing there. However, a smile crossed his face as he realized his first lieutenant knew him too well. He'd given his captain time to think of anything else before rushing off to do as ordered. "Ahem! I think it would be best to keep our lookouts fresh. Have them changed every two hours. Sooner if the weather worsens."

There were six posted lookouts. *This would take some doing,* Lavery thought.

"Lieutenant Davy."

"Aye," Davy answered the first lieutenant, knowing some task was about to be passed down. Would he act or reassign it? Seeing the stern look on Lavery's face as he approached he thought, *I'd better handle this myself.*

"Deck thar," the forward lookout called. "The convoy is reducing sail, sir."

Markham must have decided to continue any further under full sail was pointless. Did he also consider this the prime opportunity for the convoy to be attacked? Gabe wondered. Doubtless he did. Problem was he was helpless to prevent it. The goal was to prevent as few losses as possible. It was over a mile from Markham's lead ship to the rear of the convoy. Any enterprising rogue could cut out a ship and be over the horizon before an escort ship could come about and respond. *That's where we come in,* Gabe thought.

Rain began to spatter on deck. Suddenly Hex was there with Gabe's tarpaulin and a cup of coffee. "To keep you dry and warm your innards," he volunteered.

"Thank you, Hex," Gabe replied, glad he'd decided on the man to be his cox'n.

The foul weather persisted into the afternoon...the sound of thunder, one clap after another, followed by jagged streaks of lightning and sudden squalls with howling bursts of wind. Water sluiced down waterways and out scuppers as the bow continued to rise and fall plunging through one wave after another. The barometer fell to twenty-nine before it leveled off and a slight rise was noted.

The rain had slowed to a drizzle when the mainmast lookout called down from his wooden platform. "Deck thar, strange sails to starboard."

A chill went through Gabe at the sighting. Turning to Dagan he said, "It appears you were right, Uncle."

"Aye," Dagan responded. He'd felt it would be this day since sunrise. This would put an end to Witzenfeld...hopefully.

"Signal *Dasher* the sighting," Gabe ordered.

"Aye," Davy replied. He had been hoping for an uneventful watch.

Gabe looked at Hex. "A wet with Dagan and I before it gets too hot."

"Aye sir. I'll drink to your success and when this is over maybe we'll confiscate a proper drink off yonder rogues."

"A proper drink," Gabe quizzed.

"Aye, Captain, one of the buggers is bound to have a proper store of bourbon."

Shaking his head at the man's answer, Gabe turned to Dagan. "Did you check and see if Hex was related to Bart?"

"Only in spirit...only in spirit," Dagan replied.

"Well damme, I guess that's close enough."

Chapter Twenty-two

After a quick wet, and buckling on his sword, Gabe took the two pistols offered to him by Dagan. Hex had stood silently but observed Dagan, paying attention to every detail as Dagan made the captain ready for battle. Next time it would be his job...if there was a next time. Returning on deck Hex heard a whisper come from Dagan. He didn't make out the exact words but it sounded like Dagan was telling the captain...his nephew, to have a care. The captain's reply was only a smile and a pat on the shoulder. Hex felt he'd just seen the love of one man being passed to another much like a father to a son. A pang of jealousy came over Hex as he thought of his father. They would have had much the same relationship had his father lived.

Once on deck, Gabe was greeted by Lavery. "Three, no four ships, sir, on a course to intercept the convoy."

"Has *Pegasus* sighted the ships?"

"Aye sir."

Nodding, Gabe ordered, "Have *Pegasus* close with convoy."

"I...ah think he's already doing so, sir."

"Very well." Gabe knew Jepson would not wait to be ordered to take the obvious steps. "You've signalled *Dasher*?"

"Aye and repeated it as well to the convoy."

"That ought to tighten them up a bit then, Nathan."

Lavery knew when the captain used his given name, something was in the air. Be it festive or battle. It was his way of setting people at ease.

"The men have been fed?" Gabe asked, already knowing the answer.

"Aye sir. The old naval axiom...men fight better with a full stomach."

"Then we'd best be at our business. You may beat to quarters, Mr. Lavery."

"Aye sir."

It was almost magical how the ship came to life. Calloused feet rushed across the deck as the shouts of petty officers encouraged the men to their battle stations amid the sounds of a bosun's pipe and marine drummer. Powder monkeys hurriedly brought cartridges of gunpowder up for the guns. Pumps were rigged and the decks were sluiced with water then sand was liberally spread to give better grip. Gun captains were lighting lengths of slow match to smoulder in a tub until ready for use. Forward, the gunner with his mates was removing the tampion from the smashers.

Would they be close enough to use the big brutes? Did Witzenfeld have carronades? Gabe doubted it.

"Jake," Gabe called to his new cox'n.

"Yes Cap'n."

"My regards to the gunner and have him load grape on top of round shot."

"Aye aye."

Gabe could have shouted or ordered one of the midshipmen to carry the message but Hex needed to become known. "Mr. Lavery."

"Aye, Captain."

"I want a man with good peepers in the cross tree."

"Yes sir."

Having spread on more canvas *Peregrine* was trying to close with the convoy so as to intercept the privateers. If that was who they were. If not, they'd fooled the devil out of Gabe and may get a ball up the arse for their foolishness. The light was falling fast and so was the wind. Taking up his glass Gabe could see Markham had moved *Dasher* to windward. The situation was almost ideal for Witzenfeld. Unless a miracle happened the convoy escorts would be unable to prevent the dancing privateers from snapping up several prizes.

"Should we fire up a flare?" Lavery asked, a hint of nervousness in his voice.

"No, Captain Markham knows his business."

"Deck thar, two o' the buggers are making it for the convoy."

"What about the third ship?" Gabe shouted.

"'E jus seems to be picking 'is time, sir."

"Waiting to see what we do," Dagan volunteered.

"My thoughts too," Gabe replied.

"Deck thar, *Dasher* 'as come about on a new tack."

"He's going to challenge the privateer," Lavery said, his statement almost a question.

"What else can he do?" Gabe retorted, slapping his hand down on the fife rail. He thought to himself, *Hold on Markham, I'm coming.*

Flashes were seen in the distance and the lookout called down. "It's 'arder to see, sir, but I believes the pirates 'as fired on some convoy ships. They's taken a prize, sir. Two now."

Gabe climbed a few feet up into the shrouds. In the fading light he could see *Dasher* with flags a flying, bearing down on the enemy.

"They've taken another one, sir," the lookout called down.

"Like a shark."

Gabe turned to see who had spoken. It was Hex.

Seeing his captain's look Hex said, "Sorry sir, I didn't mean to think aloud."

"No apology necessary, Jake. I was thinking the same thought. A shark on a shoal."

The roar of a distant cannon was heard.

"*Dasher*'as fired, sir."

Frustration or challenge? Gabe wondered. *Dasher's* guns certainly could not be brought to bear at this point. It seemed like forever but in reality it could not have been more than ten minutes since the lookout had reported the first prize taken. At the rate they were going the privateers would soon be out of prize crews.

The distant sun seemed to linger on the horizon making visible the convoy. Then suddenly it was gone, taking with it the sight of action ahead.

"Take the glass," Gabe ordered a petty officer, then jumped the few feet to the deck.

The distinct sound of cannons not a mile away could be heard as muzzle flashes broke through the darkness.

"We should have been closer," Gabe said feeling defeated. "We were nothing more than spectators."

"He's like Colonel Meacham's man," Dagan said. "He's won a round but not the match. This time he's won a second round."

"Aye but the third one is ours. You can bet on it."

No one spoke during the interchange between the captain and Dagan. Cooper White, the new midshipman, took in every word. *We have to win the next round*, he thought. He'd seen too many die at Witzenfeld's cruel hand.

"Mr. Lavery." Gabe's voice broke the silence.

"Aye sir."

"Send up a flare. Keep the sky lit. I don't want some grocery captain to get a touch of nerves and fire a ball at us."

"Aye sir."

From the dark an unknown seaman spoke, "Don't worry Cap'n, 'e couldn't 'it the ocean wid a mouth full of baccy if 'e had to spit."

This was followed by chuckles. Then petty officers ordered the men to silence. The flares lit up the sky and *Peregrine's* company gazed at the merchant ships as they glided by.

"Scared bunch they are," Gunnells commented. "Otherwise you couldn't beat them into such a tight formation."

Peregrine was soon up to hailing distance with *Dasher*. "How are you?" Gabe called to his friend.

"We're fine," Markham called back. "A few scratches but nothing a little paint won't fix."

"Was you able to get a course...a direction they were headed?"

"Aye, north and west but who knows which course they took once they were out of sight. Gabe."

"Yes Francis."

"Go get the whoresons."

"I will."

"I wish I was going with you."

"So do I," Gabe replied. Then letting the speaking trumpet fall to his side Gabe thought, *So do I.*

Turning to his quarterdeck Gabe said, "Mr. Gunnells, did you hear Captain Markham's observation as to the direction the enemy has sailed?"

"Aye sir."

"Good. Then lay a course to follow. After that, if you will, you and Mr. Lavery come down to my cabin with your charts."

"Aye aye, Captain."

"Mr. Lavery."

"Yes sir."

"I feel a double tot can be given to the crew for their troubles."

"Aye sir."

As Dagan turned to follow Gabe below, he made eye contact with Hex and motioned for him to follow.

Chapter Twenty-three

Gabe sat at his dining table, going over the chart before him, while Lavery and Gunnells looked over his shoulder and pointed out possible destinations of the enemy.

"It would take a sizable inlet to shelter the three privateers and their prizes. Was anyone certain as to how many ships were taken?" Gabe asked.

"Four that I heard the lookout call down," Lavery said. "But they could have taken more before they broke it off. Four to six I'd say," he concluded.

"With our approximate positioning being just off the Georgia coast I'd say they have three possible choices," Gunnells volunteered. Using the stem of his pipe he pointed at the charts. "Cumberland Island is a barrier island just off the coast here. Used to be called San Pedro Island. General James Oglethorpe renamed it in honour of William Augustus, the thirteen year old Duke of Cumberland. Far as I know, the island has been mostly uninhabited since the Spanish attacks on the English settlements were put down. Still, some old forts and such left standing, I imagine. It'd be a good place to hide out and maybe store their plunder. It's not that far to the mainland so it could even be ferried over."

"Where else would you consider?" Gabe asked.

"Savannah is always a possibility. The river is deep and they could sail up it a ways."

"They could never be sure a British frigate wasn't there as well," Gabe stated discounting Savannah.

Clearing his throat the master took a deep breath and continued. "The only other place large enough to handle that many ships would be Beaufort or Port Royal. That's on the Georgia - South Carolina border."

"I know where that is," Gabe admitted. "No...I don't think it's there. I think Witzenfeld would have a place close by to keep down the likelihood of meeting up with a British squadron. What about these barrier islands, Mr. Gunnells? How many are there in the same proximity?"

"A slew of 'em, Captain. But not more than six that might fit the rascal's needs." Pipe bowl grasped firmly in his hand, Gunnells again used the stem to point. "From Cumberland, the next would be Jekyll, Saint Simons, Wolf, Sapelo, and maybe Blackbeard's."

"Blackbeard's?" Gabe laughed. "Do you think the rogue would dare tempt the old pirate's soul by stomping across his ground?" This brought a chuckle from the group. "No, Mr. Gunnells, looking at these depths on the chart for the various islands I think you are right. Cumberland seems like the obvious choice."

Turning slightly, Gabe asked, "What say you, Dagan?"

"Cumberland or Jekyll would be my guess."

"Then it's decided. Mr. Gunnells, lay us a course for Cumberland. Mr. Lavery, make sure our stern lights are lit. I don't want to lose *Pegasus* in the dark."

"Aye Captain."

"Nesbitt!"

"Sir."

"A glass for our guests, if you please." Turning to Hex, Gabe asked, "Tell me man, have you a voice? Can you play an instrument?"

"Aye, Captain, I can pluck out a tune or two with stringed instruments."

"And can you sing?"

"Well, Captain, some says I can and some says I can't."

Gabe cocked his head and stared at his new cox'n. "Well, tell me, who is it that says you can?"

Hex's face turned into a broad grin and his squinty eyes seemed to come to life and sparkle as he answered. "Them that says I can, are mostly those that are drunk."

Dagan burst out in laughter at the answer while Lavery and Gunnells tried to stifle their chuckles.

"Well damme," Gabe snorted, slapping his knees. "And them that say you can't are mostly sober. Is that it?"

"Aye, Captain, that's about it." This created another bout of laughter.

Once the laughter subsided, Gabe asked, "What's your favourite stringed instrument?"

Hex thought a moment then replied, "At sea, I'd say the mandolin is my favourite with the violin a close second. Ashore, the cello is my favourite. It's just too big and cumbersome to bring aboard ship. A slave on Antigua taught me to play a banjo and it's good for an up-tempo piece but not for a ballad or a love song."

"I've never seen a banjo," Gabe volunteered.

"Nor I," Lavery added.

So Hex explained what a banjo looked like. "It's the parchment paper over the metal hoop that gives it its unique tone."

The discussion then turned to mandolins and how they evolved from the early Spanish lute-like instrument to the popular eighteenth century version.

"I saw one in Barbados but it was more than I could afford," Hex stated with a sigh.

The master and first lieutenant took the lull in conversation to make their departures. Seeing his captain yawn, Hex felt it was time to go and asked permission to go topside for a smoke.

When all had departed Dagan called for another glass of wine for the two of them. Once served, Nesbitt was dismissed. Dagan then talked to Gabe and admitted his love and longing for Becky.

"Do you think you'll settle in the southern colonies after the war?" Dagan asked Gabe.

"Depends on how we are received. If the feeling is too strong against us, we may sell Faith's holdings and move to the West Indies. I don't think we'll live in England."

"Maria will never move," Dagan volunteered, speaking of his sister and Gabe's mother.

"Aye, I've thought about that."

"We'll discuss it more later," Dagan said, "when it's closer to a time for a decision."

Gabe nodded but didn't answer, the thought of his mother in the forefront of his thoughts. She had hit if off well with Faith and now the miles and a damn war had separated them.

"I love you mother," Gabe whispered as he stared out the stern windows.

Dagan heard the whisper but didn't say anything. Times had changed since Gabe had last been called a bastard. He'd matured in numerous ways. One of the most important was he'd come to understand the love his mother and father had felt for one another, a love that had thumbed its nose at the social standards of the time. A love that had cost Lord James Anthony professionally and politically and had caused his mother to be looked upon as a mistress or worse. But a love that had seen the two through the toughest of times.

Now, how would society look at Gabe and Dagan? Would they be accepted into Colonial America after the war or would they have to make their homes elsewhere? Dagan gave a sigh as he tried to push these and other thoughts from his head. He must concentrate on the enemy, on Witzenfeld. This had to be first on his mind...for the time being.

Chapter Twenty-four

Land was sighted at first light two days later. Jepson was rowed to *Peregrine* and, over lunch, Gabe and he decided that once Cumberland Island had been reached they would cruise offshore until dark and a scouting party landed to reconnoiter the area. Gabe had insisted, over Jepson's arguments, that he be the one to go ashore with the scouting party. Jepson gave in, realizing Gabe was much like his brother when it came to stubbornness. No wonder two of the family had made admiral and, in all likelihood, Gabe would be the third.

* * *

Peregrine and *Pegasus* cruised along under easy sail, reefed topsails with courses and topgallants furled to the yards. Anyone on the island who saw them pass would expect them to be the usual British patrol making its way up from Saint Augustine toward Savannah or maybe up to Charlestown. However, once the sun was down the two ships came about, unfurled the courses and topgallants, sheeting them home. They shook the reefs from the topsails and the ships became much like living creatures. They sliced through the water, white foam trailing to starboard as each new wave was attacked, the bow dipping and rising, spray coming over the fo'c'sle. The wind was on the larboard quarter driving the ships to their destination.

Gabe stood at the lee rail observing all. He gritted his teeth and tried to force himself to relax. It would be a couple of hours yet, he knew. All the plans had been made. The shore party had been instructed as to what duties they were to perform. Blades had been sharpened. The only firearms taken would be those by the marines. *I'll take a brace of pistols*, he thought. There was nothing left to do but wait.

The only sounds were the creak of the yards and an occasional whistling as wind rushed through the riggings. By tomorrow he might be dead, but tonight he couldn't help but feel the edge of excitement slicing through to his very soul. Would he ever be content to live a normal life...the life of a planter? How did a man face the roar of cannons one day and be content to watch sugar cane grow the next? Would he find contentment with Faith and a family or would he need the sea like some craved opium? Hearing the slightest of steps on the deck, Gabe turned to see Dagan.

"A night for thinking," Dagan said. "A peaceful night...for now."

"Aye," Gabe acknowledged. "For now."

* * *

Two longboats grounded gently as sailors jumped over the side and pulled them up further onto the beach. A wave was receding so that Gabe stepped into only ankle deep water. However, his lower legs were soaked as the next swell came in, pushing the now empty boats further up on the dry sand.

Looking at the captain's soaked boots, Hex whispered, "Nesbit ain't gonna like the shape them boots are in. He'll have to take saddle soap to 'em sure."

This brought a chuckle from a couple of sailors.

"Hush, damn you," Gabe hissed. He wanted to chuckle himself but stifled it. Who else but Hex would have not only thought of the damage the sea and sand was doing to his boots but would voice it? His way of putting the men at ease, Gabe suddenly realized.

Gabe turned to look at his new cox'n. His face was void of expression. *My reprimand appears to have had little effect,* Gabe thought. That was good. He didn't want a pouting cox'n.

Dark as the night was, a man had to be close to make out his features. The waves left a line of phosphorescence as they rushed in, died out, and retreated back to the darkness. Looking into the darkness Gabe could see no signs of the ships. He had ordered all lights be doused as they approached the island.

Turning inland, he whispered, "Where's Dagan?"

"Here."

"Dagan, you have the best eyesight. You pick a couple of men and lead off. Sergeant?" Gabe called.

"Sir." The reply was crisp even at a whisper.

"Leave two men with the boats then place another on that little rise. They are to keep a sharp lookout and keep their fingers off the trigger until they know who they're shooting at."

"Is there a password, sir?"

Gabe thought for a moment. *How many would remember if some elaborate signal was used?* "*Peregrine*, Sergeant, and the reply is *Pegasus*."

"Yes sir," the marine replied as he saluted, did an about face and assigned his men their tasks.

Moving at little more than a slow walk to prevent stumbling or falling, the party made its way across the island. It was covered with large dunes and between the dunes great stands of huge oak trees with moss hanging like a curtain from their limbs. Twice they had to make their way around ponds. Hex stooped by one, dipping his hand into the water and tasting it.

"Fresh water," he stated.

The party followed a game trail, which made the going easier. Rounding a small bend the men were met with a sudden blowing sound followed by a snort and a rush of feet as something bounded into the underbrush.

"Damme," Gabe hissed. "What was that?"

"It be a deer, sir," one of the sailors replied. "We come on 'em where they was bedding down."

Gabe could feel his heart pounding and realized he had been so startled he'd drawn his pistol without thinking. Calming down it took a few seconds to get his breathing under control. *It's a good thing the men hadn't been issued firearms*, he thought.

A man from Dagan's lead group was waiting when Gabe and the rest of the men approached the top of another small hill.

"They're there, sir, just over the rise. Dagan is waiting just a little further on. 'E said it might be best if the men waited here for now while you two talked."

Gabe nodded but didn't speak. As he started off he noticed Hex right behind him moving very quietly.

"Regular little city they got there," Dagan said by way of greeting.

Gabe couldn't believe his eyes. *Damme but Dagan is right.* Lanterns were hanging from poles at set intervals and a fire was ablaze here and there. Several tents had been set up and the laughter of men and women could be heard. Several ships could be seen in the distance lined up bow to stern. Off to one side, a large hulk seemed to have been turned into a trading place. Men were going up and down a make-do gang plank.

"Brothel," Hex volunteered. "An old guineaman turned into a pleasure palace of sorts. I bet you can buy whatever your heart desires from yonder hulk: women, gambling, you name it."

"I wonder how much his financier sees," Dagan said. "There's enough loot down there to set a man up for life."

"That's why it's here," Hex answered. "He probably sends one out of three prizes to Norfolk with a trusted accomplice. The rest he brings here. Pays the men for the prizes, then fills them with wine, provides them with women, then sells the plunder back to them."

Gabe and Dagan stared at Hex as he finished. "You seem to know a lot," Gabe stated.

"Aye Captain, you forget I was a smuggler's son. I can tell you, while the man could live forever off that treasure trove down there, it gets in your blood. It's not just about the money, not that it don't help, but it's as much about the chase and maybe a little vengeance thrown in."

Hex was a man with insight, Gabe decided. "Let's scout out the approaches then back to the ship," he said. "Dagan, you take the left and Hex will come with me to the right. We'll meet back atop the rise in an hour. If we get caught...well, don't talk."

* * *

An offshore wind made the row back to the ship easier that the row ashore. Jepson, along with his first lieutenant and master, met in Gabe's cabin on board *Peregrine*. Gunnells, Lieutenant Lavery, and Lieutenant Davy were already enjoying a glass when Jepson and his officers arrived. Gabe took Gunnells' charts and pointed out the locations of the ships on the chart.

"*HMS Drake* is anchored there and the *Tidewater Witch* here," Gabe said, pointing them out on the chart. "I didn't make out the third privateer. My cox'n thinks she may have sailed with a couple of prizes to Norfolk."

"What about shore batteries?" Jepson asked.

"None on this side of the channel. It's anybody's guess as to the mainland," Dagan stated. "There may be a few cannons on the guineaman, but I think the only guns we'll face will be those aboard the ships."

"Now, my plan is this," Gabe said.

"Did you see anyone living on the island?" Gunnells interrupted.

"Only on the beach. We passed an old settlement but it was deserted and going to ruin."

"That would be Berrimacke," Gunnells volunteered. "Dungeness built a fort and settlement back around 1742 when we were fighting the Dagos. It was said a lot of the Spaniards were eaten by sharks. It was told the sharks would swim right up into the shallows, grab a man alive or dead and head back to the deep."

"Jesus," Jepson whispered. "I hope most of them were dead."

"Aye," Gabe replied. Turning back to the chart, he stated, "Where the rogues have set up camp appears to be the widest section of the Cumberland Sound. It narrows here at Plum Orchard where there's a big bend. It widens and the Cumberland River empties into the ocean. Now my plan is this. *Pegasus* because of her shallow draft will enter at the northern entrance and make her way down to a point where you can block any ship trying to escape through that channel."

Gabe was about to recommend that Jepson have a good leadsman taking soundings but realized, before he spoke, that Jepson wouldn't need anybody pointing out the obvious. "The shore party will be made up mostly from *Pegasus's* crew but I'll have Marine Lieutenant York detail a squad of marines with Sergeant Sharp. He knows the lay of the land having made the reconnaissance earlier."

"What officer will you put in charge of the shore party?" Lavery asked.

"Since most of the men will come from *Pegasus* I was thinking of her first lieutenant. However, if Captain Jepson would rather keep him aboard, I'll send Lieutenant Davy."

"Parks can lead the shore party," Jepson stated. *He needs the experience*, Jepson mused.

"Good," Gabe muttered then added, "Dagan, have one of the men from your group assigned to Lieutenant Parks as a guide."

Nodding his acknowledgment, Dagan said, "I'll send Bond. He was a poacher in his day. He'll not likely let a herd of deer spook him."

Gabe couldn't help but wince at the words, true though they be. "Damn scoundrel," he hissed, and then looked down at the chart once more. "We'll land the shore party closer in this time; it will save the men some rowing. Hopefully our attack will be a complete surprise."

"When do you plan to start the attack?" Lieutenant Davy asked.

Gabe thought for a moment then looked at Jepson. "As soon as you are in position, send up a flare. I will be lying to, outside the southern entrance. When you set off the flare, we will enter with guns roaring."

"Hell of a wake up call I'd say," Davy volunteered.

"Aye, but a wake up call they'll not likely forget," Jepson added.

Chapter Twenty-five

Cooper White stood close to Lieutenant Davy. Since the day he'd been cast over the side of the *Tidewater Witch* at Norfolk, he'd come to like the young lieutenant. He had been friendly and was willing to offer guidance and instruction without being overbearing or condescending. He had proven to be an officer the men respected and gave that extra effort for. However, now just before the break of dawn, the lieutenant seemed preoccupied. He refrained from all attempts of small talk, something that usually made the watch go faster. Was he concerned about the upcoming battle? White didn't think so. The men in Lieutenant Davy's division had said he was a fierce warrior. Little did the midshipman know that Lieutenant Davy's mind was on Witzenfeld, his previous lieutenant.

Davy had contemplated suicide back in his early days as a young midshipman. Suicide...after committing murder. Had Dagan not intervened in his mystical way, Davy would have killed the evil Lieutenant Witzenfeld without remorse. Was this, the brother, as cruel and evil a man? Did he find satisfaction in hurting others? He'd overheard the captain and admiral speak about his treacherous ways, his being a turncoat and, worse yet, a man without honour. Would he be the last Witzenfeld he'd have to face? He hoped so. Lieutenant Witzenfeld and his brother were about as much as any family deserved. It was said the family had suffered due to the dishonour this latest Witzenfeld had brought on the family by his gambling and being a traitor.

I pray God you let me...us, put an end to it this day. He was starting to think about a family himself and didn't want to constantly look over his shoulders for old enemies or adversaries. That would be no way to start off a new life; a new life in which he could picture Ariel playing an important role. He had money. He'd saved more than most since he'd been basically dumped on the deck of *Drakkar* by a man who didn't want some snot-nose lad interfering with his relationship with the mother. He'd been hurt...hurt and resentful then, but not anymore. He'd found a home in the Navy. Men like the captain, who'd been a senior midshipman at the time, trusted him. He'd grown and matured since those early days and now hopefully he'd put to rest the name that meant torment and fear to a young lad. Today would end it. It'd have to.

A seaman clearing his throat brought Davy out of his reverie. The captain and Dagan were coming on deck. They had gone down for a cup of coffee an hour ago, as did Lieutenant Lavery and Gunnells. The ship had been at quarters for an hour now or near to it. *Peregrine* had been lying to, rising and falling with each lazy swell. The occasional slap against the hull by a small wave was the only sound in the pre-dawn hour.

"The lookouts have reported no signs from either *Pegasus* or the shore party," Davy reported without being asked.

Gabe looked at the sky. "It won't be long, David. Send young White for a cup of coffee or go down yourself for a quick cup."

"I'll send White, sir. Give 'im a chance to snitch a swallow for himself."

Gabe grinned. "You never did such a thing as a snotty, did you sir?"

Now it was Davy who smiled. "Not until I was trained on the sly by the senior midshipman. His last name was Anthony, I recall."

"Damme sir," Gabe replied, feigning dismay. "Surely you're not insinuating that I would have subscribed to such practices."

"Well sir, one does change as he ascends the lofty ladder to command."

"Humph! Send your snotty for a cup before duty calls."

As Davy turned away, Dagan whispered, "That one has changed. Our wee little David Davy is now a fine naval officer."

"Aye," Gabe answered. "I can easily see him walking his own quarterdeck."

Gunnells and Lavery now made their way toward Gabe. "Wind has freshened a mite, should help our cause."

Nodding, Gabe turned to the first lieutenant, "I want grape on top of ball for the first round. Load the swivels with canister."

"Aye, Captain, that will cut down a few if they are stirring."

Glancing again toward the sky, Gabe said, "We'll have them stirring soon I'm thinking."

"I hope Witzenfeld is here and not on the privateer that wasn't accounted for."

All heads turned and glared. "Damnation Nathan," Gabe cursed, "why'd you think such a thing, let alone voice it."

"Sorry sir," the lieutenant replied sheepishly.

"No worries, he's there."

Gabe thought Dagan had spoken but it had been Hex.

"Are you a sorcerer, sir?" Gabe snorted.

"No sir, but I don't know any smuggler, pirate, or rogue alive what's gonna sail off leaving all that loot there, in someone else's trust." Hex emphasized his statement by pointing his hanger toward the mouth of the inlet.

"Experience speaking again?" Gabe asked.

Now it was Hex's turn to look sheepish. "Aye Captain, you know my background."

"That I do, Hex, and it has provided valuable insight."

"Flare!" Dagan called before the lookout could even call down.

"Let's get underway, Mr. Lavery. Mr. Gunnells, set a course to bring us inside the channel."

Two Aye Captains rang out in unison.

Gabe then turned to Dagan. "Uncle, have a care."

"And you as well, Gabe. This will be a good day. I have a feeling...but it never hurts to keep your head down."

Hex listened to the interchange but didn't speak. More than once he'd heard Lieutenant Davy or Lieutenant Lavery speak of Dagan having a gift. A couple of the older hands even whispered such stories. None of which had he believed...until now. It was like cold steel running down his neck and back; a phantom that went deep and touched his very soul, something indescribable. There was definitely something special about Dagan. Was he mystical as some said? He didn't know. He'd heard of certain ones among the American Indians who had the gift. The power to see what no one else could. He wasn't sure about any redskin Indian. But Dagan had it. He'd bet his life on that.

Looking out toward the horizon, the first rays of sun were starting to show themselves, streaks of light penetrating the gray sky. The entrance into the channel lay just ahead. Amelia Island was to larboard and Pelican Banks to starboard. The gunner was forward with his mates. He'd be firing the carronades. Lieutenant Davy was stationing himself as the gunnery officer and gun crews were tying rags around their heads. It all seemed to be a dream, a dream in slow motion.

Shaking his head to clear his thoughts, Hex had one more thought come to mind. *By noon I'll be rich from my share of prize money or dead in a noble cause.*

Chapter Twenty-six

The leadsman called out his soundings from his platform in the chains. The findings were repeated and passed along by seaman to the quarterdeck. Thus far the charts had been accurate as to depth and width. *Peregrine* seemed to be flying through the channel. The wind blowing Gabe's hat off caused his hair to stand out not unlike the pennant flying overhead.

"Here's your hat, sir," Hex said. "You may wish to tie it on or I could take it below."

"I'll not be hampered with a string," Gabe replied harshly.

Without another word, Hex took the hat below.

"Permission to take in the mainsail, sir." This from Gunnells.

Realizing the speed was too great to accurately access the anchorage and attack, Gabe gave permission.

"Deck thar," the forward lookout called down. "Anchorage and ships sighted, sir. No sails being set."

"We have them!" Gabe roared, pounding his fist into the palm of his other hand. Excited, he grabbed a glass from its bracket and bounded up the shrouds. The ships at anchor appeared to be unmanned with no activity aboard, as the lookout had reported. Sweeping the anchorage with his glass, he could make out activity ashore. Something or somebody had alarmed them. *It was too late now*, he said to himself. Climbing down the shrouds, a thought came to him suddenly. Jumping to the deck he called for Lieutenant Lavery, Davy, and the gunner.

When the three had assembled, Gabe spelled out his sudden change in plan. "The first ship we pass is the *Drake*. We will fire all our swivels at the ship. Then you, Lieutenant Lavery, will take a boarding party, take the ship, and use her larboard guns to assist in taking the other ships. I'll lay *Peregrine* close by for your party to board. See the bosun for the boarding party and take a squad of marines."

Before Lavery could reply Gabe added, "Hurry now, time is short. Lieutenant Davy, you are to take over the first lieutenant's duties. Mr. Hawks, you will take charge of the guns. Mr. Druett, after the first round I want the smashers loaded with canister. I don't think the rascals will have time for much action with round shot, so we'll cut down the rogues and not destroy the ships if we can help it."

"Aye Captain," the smiling gunner replied, already estimating his share of prize money.

"We're ready, Captain." This coming from Lieutenant Lavery.

That didn't take long, Gabe thought but replied, "I'm glad to hear it, sir. I thought you'd decided on a nap before reporting."

This brought a chuckle from the men and a smile to Lavery, understanding the captain's ploy to set the men at ease.

"Mr. Gunnells."

"Aye Captain."

"Reduce more sail and pass as close astern to *Drake* as possible without buggering her."

This brought more smiles and chuckles. They were close now...almost ready and nothing but a few musket shots had been fired and those were from ashore.

"Activity on yonder ship," the lookout called down.

Well, somebody is finally awake, Gabe thought. Watching as the distance between the two ships closed, Gabe took his speaking trumpet and held it close to his lips.

"Just a bit closer...just a bit more."

A musket ball hit the deck with a thud, causing a splinter to impale itself in Gabe's hand. Feeling the sting, he ignored the wound, his eye and mind on the closing ship.

"Now!" he yelled. "Fire, fire as you bear."

The roar of the smashers was but a split second before the cannons fired. The sounds were deafening as the deck gave a shudder as pure hell was belched forth, the might of *Peregrine's* guns destroying all in its path.

No sooner had the guns fired when Lavery's voice could be heard, "Boarders away."

"No resistance, Captain," Hex offered.

Indeed, Gabe thought. Who could have lived through that to offer resistance? The pop of musket and pistol shot could be heard ashore but it was sporadic.

"Mr. Druett, yonder lies your next target," Gabe shouted pointing at the *Tidewater Witch*. "Fire when ready."

Boom!...Boom! Again tiny balls filled the air with a buzz, followed by cries of pain as men fell wounded and dying. Before another round could be fired into the *Witch,* a white flag was quickly raised in surrender.

"Deck thar, one of the brigs be getting underway."

"Which direction?" Gabe asked, his speaking trumpet at his lips.

"The utter one sir."

"Gawd," Gunnells growled. He ought to flog the London lubber.

Another crash and Gabe could feel the vibration in the planks beneath his feet. This last brought quick action and now white flags were raised over the remaining ships except for the beached guineaman.

Looking back toward *Drake*, Gabe could see Lavery standing on the poop deck as a British flag was being raised.

"Mr. White."

"Aye sir."

"Signal *Drake* welcome back to fleet. Mr. Davy."

"Aye Captain."

"Take a party of marines to yonder ship under a flag of truce. Explain that as they appear to be defenseless we will not fire on them if they lay down their weapons and march down to the beach, hands high in the air."

"Aye sir."

"Mr. Davy."

"Sir."

"Do not enter the ship. We don't know what lurks within its confines."

"Aye sir."

"Mr. Gunnells, if you will bring us around, I intend to board the *Tidewater Witch*."

"Aye Captain."

"Dagan."

"Aye."

"Gather a boarding party."

"Hex, break out my gig."

"Aye Captain."

"Mr. Gunnells, anchor so we can keep an eye on those three merchant brigs. Mr. Hawks, please assist the master as needed. Mr. Druett, if there's any belligerent activity aboard any of the vessels I will be obliged if you would quieten it with a load of canister from one of your smashers."

"Aye Captain. We's loaded and ready."

Nodding Gabe turned and almost ran into a surgeon's mate.

"What's the bill?" Gabe asked.

"A few splinters like the one in your hand, Captain; otherwise nothing to report."

Good, Gabe thought. "I suppose Dagan told you about the splinter," he said.

"No sir. It was your cox'n, Hex."

"Humm. Well, let's get it taken care of quickly. I've a ship to board."

Chapter Twenty-seven

A mulatto stood at the end of Witzenfeld's cot. She either was or had been a slave at some point; shackle scars still pointed out the obvious. She was slim and very beautiful. Her hair had a reddish brown hue and her flashing eyes were a soft brown. She was completely naked. Her breasts were proud but not overly large. She gave Gabe, Dagan, and Hex a look they would never forget. Though she must have been frightened by the sounds of battle she stood defiant, and contemptuous. She was the only thing of beauty in the cabin. The air was stale and reeked of alcohol and something Gabe couldn't make out.

Picking a pipe up off of the cluttered desk Hex volunteered, "Opium. No wonder the lout is in a stupor."

Witzenfeld lay crossways under a sheet on his cot. An empty bottle lay on the deck near a hand that was hanging off. He didn't stir. Gabe was aware of Dagan's eyes searching the cabin. Was it for some hidden rogue, a weapon, or more likely loot? Hex picked up a soft white linen gown and gave it to the girl. It didn't completely hide all the girl's nakedness but it made Gabe feel better. A knock on the outer door got Gabe's attention.

It was a bosun's mate. "Sir, we've done a quick look see and other than the dead men on deck the ship is deserted."

"Did you find anything of value?" Gabe asked.

"Nothing to speak of, sir. Course we ain't searched the hold." The bosun's mate's reply was such Gabe was sure the party had come upon something and it had already been hidden or divided.

"I see," Gabe said. "The nothing to speak of...has it been shared?"

"Aye," the sailor replied sheepishly.

"Very well, but mind you, I'll flog any man that tries to bring alcohol on board."

"Oh no sir, we'll not let that happen. We'll keep our peepers open for such contraband, Cap'n, and that's no error."

"I believe you will," Gabe replied, dismissing the man.

With so much to be taken, it would be a dumb sailor indeed to risk it over a bottle of rum. Seeing a length of rope lying across a chair Gabe took it and tied a slip knot at one end. He threw it over Witzenfeld's head pulling the knot tight around the man's neck.

"Is there any water in that pitcher?" Gabe asked pointing to the desk the dress had been on.

"There's water in the bowl but the pitcher is dry," Hex replied.

"Hand me the bowl then." Taking the bowl, Gabe poured the water over Witzenfeld's head. This brought forth a moan but little else. "Fetch me a bucket of water," Gabe ordered.

"Sea water, Captain."

"I don't care if it's bilge water, Hex, just fetch me a bucketful."

"Aye, Captain." When Hex returned he had two buckets. Seeing Gabe's look, Hex offered, "Case one wasn't enough, sir."

Gabe couldn't help but smile at his cox'n. "Well, Jacob, since you brought them down, you may have the pleasure of dousing our comatose pirate."

"Aye," Hex replied. *That's the second time he has used my given name*, the cox'n thought, which took away the sting of the captain's harsh reply from a few minutes ago. Also, the captain referred to the man as a pirate. This did not bode well for the fellow's chance of survival.

Dashing the first bucket of water over Witzenfeld caused him to rise, spitting and sputtering.

"I'll keelhaul the whoreson who just tried to drown me!" he roared.

Eyeing his captain, Hex waited for further instructions. He followed Gabe's eyes to the other bucket. Picking it up, without speaking, Hex tilted his head toward Witzenfeld as if to say *again*? Gabe's reply was an affirmative nod. This time Hex slowly poured the entire contents over Witzenfeld's head.

The rogue tried to avoid the water but the rope around his neck held him firmly in place. By this time, Witzenfeld had sobered enough to realize he'd been taken.

Seeing the man had his wits back, Gabe spoke. "In the name of the king, I arrest you for piracy."

Pulling the man to his feet, Gabe saw he had on slops. Handing the rope to Hex, he ordered, "Take the pirate to the master-at-arms and have him put in chains. No one is to see him until I give further orders."

"Aye," Hex acknowledged.

Turning to Dagan, Gabe spoke again, "Take the girl ashore and put her with the rest of the women."

Once on deck, Gabe could see *Pegasus* anchoring with the brig that tried to escape under her guns, and a British flag flying. Looking ashore, Gabe thought, *Well thank the Lord but that was easier than it had any right to be; now comes the hard part.*

Trying to take stock of the situation, Gabe decided to hold an officer's call. Making his way into the crowded gig, Gabe couldn't help but notice the bulging pockets of the crew.

Turning his head quickly so as to not be caught staring, he said, "Set me ashore, Hex. Then tell Mr. Gunnells he is in charge of the ship and he's to send the midshipmen and another twenty...make that forty hands ashore. After that give my compliments to Lieutenant Lavery on board *Drake* and would he be kind enough to join me ashore."

* * *

Once ashore, Gabe was quick to realize his men were vastly outnumbered. It was only the surprise and timing that carried the day...thus far. Lieutenant York had assembled the prisoners in a group and circled them with guards. A swivel gun was being set up on two sides of the circle. This addition would lessen any thoughts of overpowering the guards and taking control.

Most of the men were still dazed from the previous night's activities but they would soon have their wits about them. When that happened, things could get out of hand even with Marine Lieutenant York's extra precaution with the swivel guns.

Lieutenant Davy was approaching by himself. "Seeing the number of prisoners here, sir, I didn't think adding another twenty or so would be good so I had them tied together and left them under guard."

"Good thinking," Gabe said.

Lieutenant Parks made his way over to Gabe. "The damn cutthroats have more plunder than all the king's coffers. Damme, sir, but I believe we are all going to be rich men after today."

Thinking of the stuffed pockets of his gig's crew, Gabe said, "We cannot prevent the men from helping themselves to much of what's laying about but let's not let it get out of hand. Lieutenant York, if you will put Sergeant Sharp in charge of the prisoners, I'd like you to set up a central area to stage our...bounty."

"But sir," Parks put in, "there's gold and silver aplenty, but that's just part of it. That damn pirate could set up a city on this island. There's heaps of every imaginable cargo under those tents and huts. Drink of every description including fancy wines. There's barrels of gunpowder and weapons a plenty of every make and size. There's fancy expensive cloth, uniforms, shoes, sails, spars, navigation instruments, surgical supplies, medicines, hogsheads of sugar, coffee, flour, tobacco, and bales of cotton."

The excited lieutenant paused to take a breath. "Captain, I'm not sure we have enough ships to take it all back in."

Hearing a few grumbles from where the prisoners were located, Gabe said, "Well, first things first."

By that time, Jepson had come ashore followed by Lavery and Hawks. Hex and Dagan soon made their appearance.

"Captain Jepson, we need to do something about those prisoners. I don't want to leave anything of value behind so it will take all our manpower to load the ships. Take a couple of men with you and talk to the prisoners. Offer them parole, a boat to cross over to the mainland along with food and water."

"What about the women?" Davy asked.

"Send them with the men if they will go. By the way, should any man desire to join the King's navy...and you get a good feel about him, we'll sign them on today. I'm sure a few have been made to sail with the rogues against their wishes."

"Sir, those other men will never keep their parole."

"Aye, Mr. Hawks, you are right, but neither will I have to worry about waking with cold steel at my gullet."

"Aye, Captain, I see your point."

"Mr. Lavery, if you'd go aboard each of the ships and see if they are ready to put to sea I'd be grateful. Offer the same choices to anyone aboard and see if we can locate any of the merchant's captains."

"If we do, they'll claim half of our plunder," Parks volunteered.

"Aye, they'll claim it, Lieutenant, but without a proper ship's manifest they'll not get it. Now Hex, be a good fellow and inspect those fine wines for any damaged cases and pay particular attention to any of the bourbons you have mentioned."

"Aye, Captain, my inspection will be complete."

"As it should be," Gabe replied, "as it should be."

Chapter Twenty-eight

The entrance into Carlisle Bay was likened to an approaching fleet by the island's onlookers. Lord Ragland had himself rowed out to the flagship to be present when the senior captain reported in. Including *Peregrine* and *Pegasus*, seven ships filed into the harbour and dropped anchor. The signal for captain to repair on board was bent on and Gabe was quickly on his way to the flagship.

"Damme, sir, but what an operation," Lord Ragland exclaimed after Gabe completed his narrative. "You'll be knighted for this," he swore. "I can see the Gazette now."

Gabe hadn't thought of being made a knight, but looking over the pages of inventory, he knew he was set for life. Lieutenant Parks' words came to mind...we'll all be rich men after today. He just didn't realize how true those words were. To make things better, not a ship's captain could be found so no claim would be made.

"And you got the pirate as well." Lord Ragland was speaking again. "I'll try the turncoat myself. We'll hang him before the week's end."

"Humm!"

"You have objections?" he asked Lord Anthony.

"In theory no; I'd as soon string the man up from the yardarm and trial be damned. However, we have to think of our sailors. This man carries a Letter of Marque. We must prove, probably through diplomatic channels, that he stepped outside the letter with his actions and should be tried as a pirate. Who knows? Once we include all the evidence we recovered, even his own backer may want to hang him."

"Yes, you are right of course. Has Sir Victor left?"

"Yes, he sailed with the mail packet on the morning tide," Anthony answered. "Lord Skalla is here now. He is Sir Victor's replacement from the Foreign Office. I'm sure he will be most interested in the case."

"Yes, well, I'll leave it in your hands for now," Lord Ragland replied, arms crossed and hand on his chin. "We'll have a reception tonight, Captain Anthony, for you and all your men."

"Thank you, Lord Ragland, but it will take some time to secure, ah...the cargoes."

"Yes, of course. We'll have them brought closer ashore and discuss tomorrow whether to sail the ships to England, cargoes intact, or unload them here." Winking at Anthony, Lord Ragland added, "I'm not so old that after being away for weeks, if given the choice of a night at home with a beautiful wife or dining with the governor, which one I'd choose. We'll send out invitations to celebrate your victory later in the week."

* * *

The final decision had been to unload the military stores, ship supplies, wines and strong drink, as well as some of the clothing. The coins, plates, and cotton, along with other non-perishable goods were left aboard the ships to be sailed back to England along with the ships.

Anthony had discussed all the captured ships with Lord Ragland and it was decided the admiralty needed to make the decision about buying back a Royal Navy frigate. The brigs were needed to transport the "cargoes" back to England but the *Tidewater Witch* could be purchased right off. Jem Jackson would be promoted into her, and as a tribute to his captain, Nathan Lavery was given command of *HMS Viper*.

Lord Ragland's reception was therefore to celebrate two occasions: Gabe's successful operation and Lavery's promotion to command. Lord Skalla sailed away with Captain Ambrose Taylor under a flag of truce on *HMS Lizard* to discuss the possible trial of Witzenfeld.

The dilemma Gabe now faced was the first lieutenant opening. Davy, while a good officer, was not ready for the first lieutenant job. Discussing the vacancy with Lord Anthony, the new flag lieutenant cleared his throat and asked if he might make a suggestion.

"Certainly," Anthony replied. Thus far, Mahan had been everything he'd expected and then some.

"Sir, I'd like to recommend Lieutenant Wesley for the job. He's on board *SeaHorse* as a super-numerary. I've known him for years and he will do a great job I've no doubt."

"That's interesting, Lieutenant," Gabe responded. "On the way to the flagship, my cox'n let on I could do a lot worse than Wesley."

"I second his recommendation," Mahan responded with a smile, and then added, "Captain Anthony, don't let Hex's simple ways and speech fool you. Times were when I was sure he had as much say so on *Rapid* as I did. I'm sure you know his history. Had things been different some years ago it wouldn't be hard to imagine him walking some quarterdeck." Seeing Lord Anthony was puzzled by the conversation, Mahan discussed Hex's past and how he came to be a jack tar.

When Mahan had finished, Gabe added, "Think of an educated Bart."

"God help us!" Anthony exclaimed. He then looked at Gabe, "Would you like for the flag lieutenant to send for Wesley? Give you a chance to talk to him in a less than official setting."

"Aye, sir, I think I'd like that."

Without another word, Mahan headed out of the cabin. Once he had left, Anthony spoke to Gabe, brother to brother. "Was everything all right with Faith? Lady Deborah had seemed a little concerned as to her well being after their last visit." What he didn't say was Deborah wondered if Faith was pregnant. He knew if Gabe had been told of such he'd have told him by now. They discussed the reception for a while, and then talked of how grown Macayla was starting to act.

"Not like the colonel's daughter, I hope," Gabe replied unable to resist the urge to tease his brother over the spoiled little girl who had sailed with them from Norfolk.

"Heavens no, Deborah would never allow such behaviour and neither would I. Times were, I wished I'd had a belaying pin handy and considered having Bart fetch one. He was ready to toss the little she devil over the side himself."

They then discussed the likelihood of the Americans allowing Witzenfeld to be tried as a pirate.

Lord Anthony then said something that surprised Gabe. "Had I found him as you did, Gabe, I'm not sure I wouldn't have excused everyone then slit the bugger's throat, and then swore the slave must have done it. Of course, since she'd somehow escaped through a stern window there was no way of knowing for sure."

"I had similar thoughts," Gabe admitted. "And had Dagan been left alone, I've little doubt Witzenfeld would not have died trying to escape."

"Ah, but hindsight is perfect, is it not?"

"Aye, I can't argue with you there, Gil." Gabe then spoke of young Hawks.

"We have an examination scheduled," Anthony advised, but before any further discussion went on, the sentry announced, "Lieutenant Wesley, sir."

Rising, Anthony said, "I'll let you two talk. Silas."

"Aye, my Lord."

"Captain Anthony's glass needs to be refilled and see what Lieutenant Wesley might like."

"Aye, sir."

Hearing the exchange Wesley thought, *Damme, I've never been treated in such a manner.* Of course, he'd never seen or heard of a vice admiral excusing himself so that a captain and a lieutenant might converse either.

* * *

The crash of a ship's salute sounded across the harbor, its smoke drifting through the open stern windows to fill Gabe's nostrils. He didn't rise as normal to look out

Faith. She had been sick for the second or was it the third day in a row. She'd be fine when he got home but by the time he left at first light, she was sick again.

"It's that terrible smell on you," she'd complained.

Gabe had sniffed the sleeve of his work coat. Several odors seemed to mingle together: tar, oakum, and paint. He could identify them all but none were overpowering and certainly nothing more than usual.

The cabin door opened and closed without an announcement by the sentry. It had to be Dawkins or Hex as Nesbit was in the pantry banging around.

Hex's voice rang out. "Dispatch vessel, Captain."

"*Firefly*, Captain Hampton. I wonder what news she brings," Gabe said absently.

"My bet is you'll know by noon," Hex replied, then continued on, "I made sure Hawks was away on time for his examination and warned him to not try to do any last minute cramming. It'd only confuse him."

"Good," was Gabe's only answer.

Looking out the stern windows, Hex said, "You all right, Captain?"

Gabe explained Faith's sickness.

"I ain't no doctor," Hex said, somewhat unsure as to his word...but finally got out. "She sounds pregnant to me, Captain."

The change that came over Gabe was remarkable. "Damn, Jake, but I bet you are right. I think I'll go talk to her now."

"I'd wait a while were I you, Captain."

"Wait, why?"

"Unless I'm mistaken, I believe your new first lieutenant just shoved off from the flagship."

"Oh...humph. Well, I guess it would be rude to not greet the man. Maybe Faith will be more able to talk tonight."

"I'm sure she will," Hex replied.

Gabe then noted Hex staring out of the windows again. "What are you looking at?" Gabe quizzed.

"I believe that's a captain, I mean a real captain, in *Firefly's* boat. Not just *Firefly's* commander."

Gabe made his way to the window but the boat was passed by that time, and only the back of the captain could be seen. Still, it looked somewhat familiar to him.

From on deck the challenge "Boat ahoy" and the reply "Aye, aye" could be heard through the open skylight.

"That's your lieutenant," Hex stated as he handed Gabe the hat he rarely wore aboard ship. Seeing Gabe's look as he pushed the hat down, Hex said, "Be nice to set a fine example for the bloke's first day."

Gabe swallowed hard, not believing what he heard, then, seeing the grin on Hex's face, was reminded of his brother and Bart. "Damme, Jake," he hissed. "You're talking about a king's officer."

"Aye," Hex replied, the grin still on his face.

PART III

Newgate Jig

The pirate eyed the crowd outside
They came to see him hang
He'd once struck fear in many a man
By the mention of his name
Many a captain lost his ship
Their life blood to his blade
Many a young girl he had kissed
Till that dreadful day
Better he'd been struck down
Now resigned to his fate
It was like a circus outside
In the yard at Newgate

...Michael Aye

Chapter Twenty-nine

The following evening Lord Anthony and Lady Deborah were guests at Gabe and Faith's home. Uncharacteristically, Anthony had sent Bart over to inquire if Captain Buck may also be invited. Generally, when the admiral dined at his brother's house, it was strictly a family affair and Navy protocol was forgotten. Hex had not been surprised at this but was surprised at how included Bart and Dagan had been. Dagan was actually family, so after thinking on it, Dagan's presence made sense.

However, nothing could have prepared Hex one evening when little Macayla had entered the house, saw Bart sitting in a chair, and rushed over calling, "Uncle Bart, Uncle Bart, I got a puppy." So the old salt had a soft side, Hex realized.

Over a wet one evening, Bart had told him of his history with his Lordship. "Day will come yew and Gabe will likely have the same sort of relationship. Thing to remember is for all his rank and 'sponsibility, he's still a man. Being a man, times will come when he'll have his doubts and fears; same as me and yew. Only difference be he's the captain and can't let on none. That's when yews have to be a friend. Course it goes without saying yew has to keep yer trap shut as to what yew sees and hears. Won't be long and yew'll be family, jus like me."

Tonight, with the family and Captain Buck all together, Hex thought of Bart's words and felt humble to have been one of a very few to be at this gathering. After a bit of chitchatting, Gabe announced dinner was being served and it was time to be seated. Hex found himself at the end of the main table. Dagan had the very end, Bart was to the right, and he was to the left. Gabe sat at the head of the table and the guests had just grabbed a chair. After the main course had been finished and fresh glasses set out champagne was poured.

Gabe rose and quickly had everyone's attention. "I've invited you each here to enjoy the happiness that Faith and I share. Gil, Deborah, Rupert, it is my extreme joy to announce my lovely bride is with child."

A muffled sob was heard and the guests caught a glimpse of Nanny, a napkin to her eyes, as she fled. "Praise the Lawd, praise the Lawd," she cried until she was out of hearing.

"My congratulations!" Anthony exclaimed.

"Mine as well," Buck said.

Deborah had rushed around the table and was hugging Faith. Gabe caught Hex's eye and with a nod raised his glass in salute.

Later in the evening, after dessert, the men gathered in the den for brandy and cigars. Anthony cleared his throat. "Gabe, you saw the dispatch ship drop anchor I'm sure."

Gabe managed an "Aye, sir," while at the same time he tried to relight his cigar from a nub of a candle, all the time struggling to keep the melted wax from dripping on the table or floor. When he sat the candleholder down, the other men gave a collective sigh of relief. Realizing he'd gained an audience, Gabe stood erect and smiled.

"Damme boy, you had us worried there for a while," Anthony laughed with the others joining in.

"Such a feat with matches there on the mantle," Buck declared. This brought forth more laughter.

When the laughter had stopped Anthony spoke again. "As I was saying, I'm sure you all saw the dispatch vessel drop anchor. Well, in addition to the usual correspondence, she also gave passage to my new flag captain."

A look of dismay creased Gabe's face then he realized the significance of his brother's words. Addressing Buck, he grabbed his hand and shaking it exclaimed, "You've been made admiral!"

Dagan began clapping his hands and the rest followed. Faith and Deborah entered the room to see what the excitement was about. Hearing the news, they too congratulated Buck with a hug and a kiss.

Once the ladies departed Gabe, feeling devilish, asked, "Tell me, Admiral Buck, are we the only ones who know of your promotion?"

"There's a few who know," Buck replied. "Is there anyone specific you're speaking of?"

"Aye, that pretty widow lady, Mrs. Olivia Cunningham; but to you she's Liva, I believe."

* * *

A captain's call the next day at noon had Lord Anthony's dining room crowded. Rumor was rampant as to why the sudden gathering. Once refreshments had been served, Anthony announced Buck's promotion to the group. He then introduced the new flag captain, Sir Winston Swift KB. Once seeing the man, Gabe recognized him and realized why he'd looked familiar when he had had the fleeting glimpse as he was rowed from the dispatch vessel to the flagship.

Captain Swift had been one of the captains on the board for Gabe and Markham's lieutenant examination. He had seemed firm but fair. Still, he'd take some getting used to. Buck had been with Anthony so long he seemed like a permanent fixture. Well, Buck would let him know of the admiral's ways.

After the congratulations, Buck announced all those midshipmen who had passed the recent lieutenant exam. Most of the captains already knew. Of the two dozen who'd taken the examination, sixteen had been passed; of those, twelve had been made lieutenant immediately. The rest would have to wait for an opening.

Lord Anthony then called the discussion back to order and announced the captured brigs, their cargoes, and the captured frigate would be sailed back to England as soon as the ships could be made ready for sea. "This shouldn't take more than a couple weeks to get everything together. By that time, the dispatch vessel would or should be back and would sail with the group. Admiral Buck will hoist his flag on *Peregrine* for the return trip. Along with *Peregrine*, Captain Hazard on *HMS Fearless* will also be an escort vessel."

* * *

For the islands it was an unusually cold day. The wind blew a rain that seemed to be coming down sideways and in sheets. The palm trees were bent double and dead palm fans blew across the narrow streets and walkways. Gone were the usual idlers who normally filled the benches outside the taverns. The young men were huddled up at home instead of buying rounds at the bar, running up their father's tab.

Hex tugged down his hat and pulled his tarpaulin closer. The crew for the captain's gig were seating themselves and getting ready for the row ashore. Gabe had put off departure for an hour but with no letup in the weather he had to go, rain or not. A Navy captain did not keep the governor or the admiral waiting. He had been told to report at Government House at 3 p.m. It was now 2 p.m. If he had left at one, he could have had a quick lunch with Faith and maybe an hour of personal time together. Since the discovery of her pregnancy, Faith had been very affectionate and more than willing to share an intimate hour or so when the opportunity presented itself.

Captain Taylor had returned with *Lizard* the previous evening just at dark. Lord Skalla had been taken ashore immediately. Gabe had little doubt that it was his return that necessitated this meeting.

The gig was like a bucking horse. Gabe tossed his cloak over his shoulder as he made his way down to the gig, careful to not slip on the wet, slippery battens. He could feel the wind ruffle his hair and tug at his queue. *Lord, don't let me get tangled in my sword and fall arsehole over tea kettle into the gig, or worse, the ocean.*

Hex had the gig crew turned out well in spite of the inclement weather. The tossed oars were painted a bright white and stood in a perfect line. Each of the crew had their tarred hats pulled low and the checkered shirts were already soaked. Gabe felt a pang of guilt at having to rouse out the crew on such a day. Hex had stationed himself by the tiller after assuring his captain was safely in the boat. Seating himself in the stern, Gabe waved to Wesley, who had stood at the entry port until the gig shoved off.

The tide was on the ebb and they were rowing against the wind. He'd give the men money to buy a wet before they returned to the ship. That would take a bit of the sting out of the return trip. Passing the flagship, Gabe saw his brother's flag at the foremast. He was staring at it when the gig was suddenly lifted from the stern and launched forward. Water flooded over the bow. The oarsmen were tossed about and a cry was heard forward where one of the men's arm was shattered.

"Bail...bail men, use your hats or we'll be swamped," Hex shouted as water was up over his ankles.

A small bucket lay next to Hex. Gabe reached for it and joined in the bailing. The gig was sluggish but maintained headway and soon the boat had been almost emptied. Once ashore, Gabe looked at his soggy uniform and wet shoes. He still had forty minutes. He'd go by his house and put on dry shoes. He'd have Nanny take a towel to his coat but otherwise he'd have to make his apologies for the uniform.

* * *

Rain beat off the window panes in Lord Ragland's office. A small fire was in the fireplace. Seeing Gabe's appearance, Lord Ragland motioned him closer to the fireplace. "Here, Gabe, get closer to the fire; see if it won't help you dry out. I don't want you to catch a chill." Shivering, Ragland continued, "Not a fit day for man or beast."

Mulled wine was served and Gabe was introduced to Lord Skalla.

Looking at the timepiece on the mantle, Lord Anthony said, "I'm concerned the flag captain is not here yet but you've stated you have another appointment, so Lord Ragland don't delay the meeting any longer on my behalf."

"Thank you, sir. I do have another appointment so we will go ahead or rather I'll let Lord Skalla give his report." Turning the floor over to the foreign office agent, Lord Ragland whispered to a servant and brandy suddenly appeared. Apologizing for interrupting Lord Ragland declared, "The mulled wine is good but my achy bones cry for something of more substance." A sniffer was poured for each of the men and the meeting resumed.

"As I was saying," Lord Skalla began, "we anchored at the mouth of the river and sent a boat in with a lieutenant under a flag of truce. We were soon approached by a guard boat and escorted to Norfolk where we anchored for the evening. General Manning was requested and on the evening of the third day made his appearance. He had been in Wilmington, North Carolina. Had we known or been told we could have met him there. Regardless, after our conversation I produced documents signed by Captain Anthony and Captain Jepson. General Manning invited me to supper the next evening. He sent one of his men to accompany me to his home. There we supped with a gentleman who was said to be Witzenfeld's privateer backer. After several questions were asked which I answered to the best I could we were interrupted by a knock at the door. It seems Witzenfeld's main lieutenant had been rounded up. He was forced to answer some harsh and incriminating questions. When asked why he'd been party to such underhanded schemes the man simply replied, 'For my life. Had I divulged what was going on I'd have been a dead man. Me and several others wanted no part in the scheme but we did want to live. Our lives and that of our families wouldn't have been worth a farthing if we'd told.' The sincerity in the man's voice spoke volumes. In the end, General Manning gave me a letter charging Witzenfeld with treason and piracy. The man's Letter of Marque was revoked and his backer said for what he'd cost him he'd hang the whoreson himself. The bottom line, gentleman, is we've been given the go-ahead to try the man as we please."

A general discussion ensued and it was decided that Lord Ragland would have jurisdiction as the man's actions were treasonable and he was considered a pirate.

"We'll try him Friday and hang him Saturday at sunrise. Give the local folks a bit of entertainment."

Anthony had no qualms with regard to hanging the man, but he'd never been one for public spectacles. Before he could voice his objections, there was a knock on the door.

Answering the door, Lord Ragland turned to Anthony. "It's your flag lieutenant, Admiral. He says it's urgent." Mahan was ushered in and Anthony knew from the man's paleness something was terribly wrong.

Lord Ragland had poured a glass of brandy. Handing it to Mahan, he said, "Take a drink man and then tell us what the matter is."

Taking the glass and downing the amber liquid in one long swallow, Mahan looked at Anthony and said, "It's the flag captain, sir. I fear he's drowned."

An uncontrollable shiver shook Gabe as he recalled his near accident.

"Damn," Lord Anthony cursed. "Are you sure?"

"Fairly certain, sir. A couple of the gig's crew managed to swim to the nearest ship. The rest of the men and the gig are still missing."

For all the men in the Navy, it was precious few that knew how to swim. For two men to have survived it was strange indeed.

"Keep a close lookout and watch the beaches. Something might turn up yet." By that Anthony meant bodies frequently washed ashore. *Damn*, he thought again, *the man hadn't even unpacked his chest yet.*

Chapter Thirty

A memorial service was held for Captain Swift and the other drowned sailors the next day. It was strange holding the service for a man that was hardly known to you. It was only fitting the service be held aboard *SeaHorse*. The captain's ship, but a ship he'd never sailed...never even weighed anchor. As a sign of mourning, the yards were set cockbill.

As Lord Anthony, Lord Ragland, and finally, *SeaHorse's* chaplain spoke, the men were silent. Each thinking, but for the grace of God, he may have been one of the dead.

One sailor had whispered to his mate, "Ole King Neptune must have been looking for a new crew to take the captain and the tars." Dagan heard the comment and realized just how deep superstition ran in the common hand. "Why else would a squall hit the harbour when it did, if it wasn't for the king of the deep needing sailors," the hand whispered.

Gripping a shroud, Gabe looked to the sky. The gray, angry sky of yesterday was gone. The sun's rays streaked down and reflected off the calm harbour waters. Calm, clouds, storm, squall. No one knew what the morrow would bring. Off to larboard was a flock of squawking gulls. Gabe watched as they hovered, then dove for some tiny fish that made the mistake of being too close to the surface. The chaplain had raised his voice to be heard over the squawking. A futile attempt, as the gulls came closer to the ship, drowning out his voice. Finally they flew away. By that time the chaplain had given up and asked the assembly to bow their heads in prayer. Once the service was over, Lord Anthony's captains and Lord Ragland met in the admiral's dining area.

"Silas."

"Yes sir."

"Broach a bottle of that bourbon General Manning gave me."

"Aye sir," Silas replied, a bit reluctant to pop the cork.

A bottle would only go around once with all these people. That didn't leave even a good swallow and there were only six bottles left. Well, he'd see Bart didn't get a glass and that was no error.

"A nasty business," Anthony said, addressing his captains. "We'll have to make some changes until I can get a new flag captain. Any recommendations, Admiral Buck?"

Pleased that Anthony had used the term admiral, Buck cleared his throat before he answered. He'd taken a gulp of the bourbon and felt the burn all the way down the back of his throat. A slight hack and his voice returned. "I would be willing to stay on until a new man could be sent."

"Nonsense. You'll do just as your orders state. Captain Markham."

"Aye, my Lord."

"Your first lieutenant, is he ready to command?"

"Aye."

"Good. You will be my temporary flag captain and your first will have temporary command of *Dasher*. Tell the man the first permanent command that comes along will be his."

"Thank you, my Lord. You honour me."

Amused at Markham's discomfort Anthony thought, *Your words are correct but your tone tells the truth*. Of course, Anthony couldn't blame the man. To be a dashing frigate captain one day and tied to the admiral the next with little expectation of more than a tedious day to day existence was a change most would wish to avoid. A time would come when the flagship would up anchor and attend some mission, possibly even do battle with the enemy, but those possibilities were the exception.

Well, the good thing is, it would look good on his record, and it was only temporary.

After the discussion of who would fill in for the departing Buck, the upcoming trial for Witzenfeld was discussed.

"How do we inform the man's family of his disgrace and execution?" Lord Ragland was asking.

Lord Ragland was having a difficult time, knowing the family; he wondered just how much one family could take. Anthony knew the difficulty of writing letters. They had gone through Captain Swift's belongings and found a recent letter from his sister. That was the only correspondence found in his chest so Anthony surmised she was the man's next of kin. Gabe had promised to hand deliver the letter as the lady lived in Portsmouth. That was their home port and, at any rate, Gabe would visit his mother who lived in the city. Well, it will bring an end to an otherwise dreadful chapter in their lives.

Anthony's mind had drifted and it took him a moment to realize the governor was still talking about Witzenfeld's family.

"Aye," he responded. "An end."

* * *

Witzenfeld was defiant until the end. The trial lasted only a day and would have been less had not the defense brought forth a point of order. It dealt with a matter of jurisdiction. Since the man had "run" from his service with the Honourable East India Company, did they not have the right to be a part of the trial? It was decided the procedural question might delay the carrying out of the man's sentence but, from a legal point of view, would not change the verdict. The decision, based on the major from the provost marshal's office, was that to delay carrying out the sentence was cruel and would cause undo suffering.

Markham hearing the major's legal view whispered to Gabe and Jepson, "Since when is carrying out a hanging sooner than later cruel?"

"Aye," Jepson agreed. "But as long as there's breath there's hope."

What was surprising to Gabe was the man's last request. Hex and Lum were playing the fiddle and mandolin as Nanny cleaned off the table. Gabe had just lit his pipe and Faith was sitting in the chair next to him reading. The knock when it came was unexpected and the message more so.

"It's Witzenfeld," Gabe announced to Faith and the others. "He's asked to speak with me."

"Must you go?" Faith asked.

"It's hard to turn down a condemned man's last request," he said.

Hex had put down his instrument and gathered a cloak and Gabe's sword. In the dresser where Gabe had laid his hat was a pistol. Hex had recently cleaned the gun and knew of its existence. He looked at the gun, turned away then as an afterthought, turned back, took the pistol and tucked it into his waistband. There was very little crime on the island but the gaol was situated in the worst part of Bridgetown. *It would never hurt to be prepared*, he thought.

Following Gabe out the door, Hex leaned over and whispered to Lum, "Find Dagan. He's playing cards with Bart. Send him to the gaol."

Lum picked up his hat and departed out the rear door. The guard at the gaol, a sergeant, apologized for rousting out the captain.

"We generally try to make they last hours easy, zur. Sometimes they wants to talk, sometimes they don't. I 'ope the captain understands."

Gabe assured the sergeant he did and was led down a dimly lit passage with cells on both sides. At the end of the passage was a wooden door. Passing through the door was a small open area. Beyond that a set of bars ran the width of the room. The cell was dark, damp, and smelled moldy. High on the back wall was a small window which let in enough fresh air to make the room and cell bearable. Beside the door were a small table and a single chair for the guard. When a man was sentenced to death a twenty-four hour guard was placed outside his cell.

Inside Witzenfeld's cell a small candle burned from a holder mounted on the wall. In addition to a wooden cot, a single chair was all that made up the furnishing inside the cell. Seeing Gabe enter, Witzenfeld made his way to the bars and stretched out his hand as if to shake hands in greeting.

The guard was quick to say, "Beggin' the captain's pardon, it's against the rules to touch the prisoner."

Nodding his understanding Gabe spoke, "You sent for me?"

"Aye that I did; I didn't believe you'd come. I'll ask you to forgive my humble surroundings," Witzenfeld stated, his arms making a resigned gesture. "It insults a gentleman's nostrils to be sure but, alas." Again he made the resigned gesture. Seeing Gabe's impatience, Witzenfeld said, "I'd offer a glass but without money the scoundrel of a guard brings only water."

Gabe looked at Hex who was standing just to the side. With the slightest of nods Hex fished out a coin and gave it to the guard. "A bottle if one is available."

Eyeing the coin, the guard replied, "Thank you, Gov'ner, I'll be right back."

"Where to start?" Witzenfeld's voice was very humble and subdued. "My family has been a thorn in your side for some time have they not, Captain Anthony?" Not giving Gabe time to answer the man continued. "I never got along with my brother. He was a coward through and through. He only got commissioned because of the family name. Of course that was before my problems with the Honest John Company. Still, as much as I disliked the shit, he was my brother."

Witzenfeld took a deep breath then sighed. "The reason I requested you tonight, Captain, is to say I'm sorry for the trouble my family has caused you. That and to find out exactly how my brother died. They say he jumped over the side, that he committed suicide. I never believed that. He was too much of a coward. I also hear Dagan put a hex on him."

The use of "hex" made the cox'n take note. He'd made use of the guard chair while Gabe stood at the cell.

"Does Dagan really have the power to put a hex on someone?" Witzenfeld asked. "They say he's got special powers. I never believed in such but a man who was there swore Dagan whispered a hex on the boy and he jumped over the side."

The sound of the door opening made Witzenfeld look toward it. "Speaking of the devil," he said, "there's Dagan now."

Too late Gabe realized his mistake. Turning to see if it was Dagan who entered, Witzenfeld's hand shot out. He had a torn length of sash in his hand and he quickly looped it over Gabe's head and pulled back as hard as he could. With his feet on the bars for leverage, he pulled on the cloth with all his might, choking the air of life from Gabe.

Hearing Gabe gasping, Hex was at the bars in a flash. He pulled the pistol with one hand and using the heel of the other cocked the gun in one motion. Gabe's face was already turning blue as Hex thrust the pistol barrel between the bars pointing it at

Witzenfeld's chest and squeezing the trigger. The explosion was deafening in the confined space. The impact of the ball knocked Witzenfeld back onto the cell floor, crimson flooding over his shirt. Gabe fell forward into the guard, who dropped the bottle to catch the captain. Taking in gulps of air, the color had just returned to Gabe's face when Dagan rushed through the door with his sword drawn. He had just entered the building and was being led to the cell when the pistol shot rang out. Seeing the still smoking pistol in Hex's hand, Dagan laid his hand on the man's shoulder. "I thank you for doing my job. But for you, Gabe ..." Dagan sighed but didn't finish the sentence. He didn't have to; his expression said it all. Leaning forward, his hand still on Hex's shoulder, Dagan found his words and whispered, "I'll not forget this."

Neither will I, Hex thought, his palms sweaty and hands shaking. *Neither will I.*

The next morning Gabe was summoned to the governor's office. Lord Skalla and Buck sat in cushioned chairs while Lord Anthony stood next to the fireplace, his hand resting on the mantle.

After hearing Gabe's report of the previous evening's events, the men were silent, each deep in thought.

Finally, it was Lord Skalla who broke the silence. "It's a good thing your man had sense enough to go armed. Otherwise we'd had to try the bugger again. Damnable waste of time that would have been."

Gabe's head had been drooped, shamed at letting himself be duped so. Hearing Skalla's words, he looked up seeing a smile on the man's face. They were all smiling.

Chapter Thirty-one

On Saturday before the scheduled Monday sailing, one of the last convoys before hurricane season sailed into Barbados...what was left of the convoy, that is. The *Romney*, an old fifty gun ship, was towed into port. Water gushed over the side as pumps struggled to keep her afloat. A sail had been jury-rigged to what was left of the mainmast. The largest of the merchantmen was giving the tow. A small frigate and a brig were the only other Royal Navy ships. Out of a convoy of thirty vessels, six merchantmen and three naval vessels completed the voyage. The probability the *Romney* would make it to the dockyard was anyone's guess.

Aubrey Byrd had been the *Romney's* first lieutenant. Only he and one other officer survived. "It was the French!" Byrd exclaimed when he reported aboard the flagship.

"How many and what size ships were they?" Anthony demanded.

"I'm...I'm not sure, sir, six or eight warships, maybe a handful of privateers."

"What size, man...how many guns?"

"The largest a sixty four, a couple of heavy frigates...had to be forty-fours and the rest smaller frigates or corvettes." The man was drained. To get more may have overtaxed him and he'd been through enough.

"Bart."

"Aye."

"Call away my barge."

"Aye.

"Lieutenant Byrd, my servant will fix you a hot meal then you lie down and rest. We'll talk more later."

"But sir, I must get back to the ship. They need me."

"I believe I'm capable of seeing what's best for the ship and that the crew is taken care of," Anthony replied tersely. Then seeing the man's hurt, he relented and said, "You've done enough, sir. Let someone else share the burden."

"Thank you, sir."

"Lieutenant Mahan."

"Aye, my Lord."

"Send over one of the surgeons, the bosun, and carpenter. Let's see if the ship is salvageable."

The stench of burned ropes, wood, and wounded men filled Anthony's nostrils as he boarded the *Romney*. Guns lay on their sides. The regular clank of pumps that defied the sea filled the air. Inspecting the captain's quarters, the companion ladder was cocked and loose. The captain's quarters were a charred mess. The two stern guns lay at the end of their tackles, one of the gun's barrel split open where it must have taken a direct hit. The unmistakable stain of blood was spread over the deck. The men on the main deck were removing broken timbers, cordage, and tattered sail. The wheel was broken and the mast merely stumps.

An old sailor approached Anthony's group. As he neared, Anthony realized he was the master. "This old lady will live to swim and fight another day, sir." The pride in the old salt was touching. The men from *SeaHorse* were arriving now. If, like the old master said, she'll live to swim and fight another day then they'd better hurry.

Getting back into his barge, a carpenter's mate knuckled his forehead as Anthony was being rowed around the ship. "Checking for damage twixt wind-'n-water, sir," he said by way of explanation.

Once back aboard *SeaHorse*, Anthony took the leather courier's bag Byrd had brought over and took out the dispatches. Doing a quick overview, one letter caught his attention. French fleet sighted off the Azores. Possible destinations were felt to be Nova Scotia, America, or even the West Indies. *I wonder if Romney's captain had been aware of this*, Anthony thought.

"Bart."

"Here sir."

"Send for the flag lieutenant."

"Aye."

The two men must have collided in the passageway as the two were back in seconds, Mahan rubbing a red spot on his forehead.

"Are you injured, sir?" Anthony asked.

"No, my Lord."

Looking at Bart he saw no signs of injury, but rather than give the man something to fuss about later Anthony inquired, "And you, Bart, are you injured?"

"Not so's yew'd notice."

"Very well. Lieutenant, have a signal bent on for all captains to repair on board after the noon hour."

"Aye, my Lord. Is that all?"

"Yes...no," Anthony changed his mind. "Have *Romney's* lieutenant ..."

"Byrd, sir, Aubrey Byrd."

"Yes, well have him attend the meeting as well." Anthony had been contemplating an idea for an hour and finally decided.

* * *

As the first of the captains were piped aboard, Anthony walked to the windows and out on to the gallery. There was heaviness within him. Was it due to sending any of his captains out knowing they may have to do battle with a superior French fleet? Must they always have to face a superior force? Out-gunned and outmanned at every turn. Damn the politician that put Englishmen in harm's way without supplying their needs. Damn them all.

Since that morning, the wind had risen slightly. Clouds had gathered and drops of rain began to patter on the gallery rail and deck. Stepping back inside Anthony waited until the last captain had been seated and a glass had been served. It was interesting to see the solemn expression on his men's faces. They had all seen the convoy limp into Carlisle Bay. He was sure more than one had boarded the once proud ship and those that hadn't boarded the ship had heard of the utter destruction from those who had. Not the boisterous, bantering group that usually filled the great cabin. All were aware it could have been them...that they may be next.

"Gentlemen, it's a sad day for us as we mourn for those who have given their all. It appears the French are out again. I have read dispatches that allude to this and, in fact, yonder ship lays the proof. Starting tomorrow all ships that depart on patrols will do so in groups of two or three. A superior force is not...I repeat, not to be engaged if at all possible. I know, being the firebrands that you are, that's hard to swallow. However, you must know communication with the flag is most important. The protection of this station is our mission. Monday I had planned to send *Peregrine* and *Fearless* to England as escorts for the brigs and...recovered frigate. Those plans have changed somewhat. Captain Anthony and Captain Hazard will go as planned but I'm also sending Captain Jepson. George, your job is not to get caught up in battle but to carry the word should an engagement take place. I pray not. The other change I've..." Looking at Buck, Anthony paused and retracted his word. "We've decided to put Lieutenant Byrd in command of the *Drake* along with *Romney's* surviving crew. We will, of course, add as many men as we can to help man the ship. You understand, Lieutenant Byrd, command of the frigate is temporary. However, being in command will surely get the admiralty's attention and put you in position for another command even if it's not the *Drake*."

Lieutenant Byrd didn't get the usual hoopla and ribbing but a toast was drunk in his honour and a few gave a slap on the shoulder as they departed. He was not one of them.

Speaking to Bart later, Anthony said, "I'd have thought they would have been more congratulatory."

"Nay," Bart replied flatly. "He's got the stench o' death on 'im, that one does. They're afraid."

"Of what?" Anthony asked, disbelief in his voice.

"Of it rubbing off," Bart replied matter-of-factly. "Jack tar or officer, they's all alike when it comes down to it. They can smell the death, see it. He could bathe everyday for a week and it would be the same."

Chapter Thirty-two

Gabe felt a raindrop run down the nape of his neck. It had started the previous evening and rained until the early dawn hours. The riggings, sails, and deck were still damp. There was just enough wind to provide a chill from the wetness. However, the effect was just enough to wipe away the cobwebs in his head. He'd never been a good riser, probably never would be. Now 9 a.m. was his idea of a good time to rise.

Gabe walked up the sloping deck and spoke to the quartermaster at the wheel. They had secured from quarters an quarter hour ago. He watched as the ship's company prepared for another day. The lookouts had reported the convoy of ships to be on station but otherwise the sky was free of sails. The brigs were each manned by a skeleton crew; just enough to work the ship. *Just like a merchant would do,* Gabe thought, seeing it in a humorous light.

A master's mate had been put in charge of each of the brigs. Their instructions had been simple: keep station on *Peregrine* and if the group was attacked run for England. Let the warships deal with the enemy.

Hearing Hex call his name, Gabe knew Nesbitt was finished with breakfast: strong hot coffee, fresh pastries and cheese. A light but satisfying breakfast, much different from his last one ashore. Nanny had fried up some salty tasting ham and served fried eggs, grits, and biscuits. They had fig preserves to go on the hot buttered biscuits. A feast fit for a king. The typical southern breakfast. No wonder Lum had developed a belly. It was not unusual when friends stopped by that they politely asked if any of Nanny's biscuits were leftover. There had been no friends over that morning; however Gil and Deborah had come over for a short visit the night before their sailing. Hex and Lum had packed a few last minute supplies in a chest and headed to the ship.

Gabe was dressed and at the door when Faith came to him again. Her kiss had been long and passionate. Her breasts were crushed against his chest. He could feel her heartbeat and feel the hotness of her breath as she kissed his neck. The next thing he knew they were making love. Spent from their passion Gabe laid flat, Faith in his arms. Rising on an elbow Faith kissed him again. The sight and the touch of her breasts excited him all over again but he had no more time. He returned the kiss and hurriedly got dressed. The shift Faith put on did little to hide her beautiful body. Her stomach had just the slightest pooch...a sign that their baby was growing.

Reaching for his hat, Faith smiled. "I wondered if I had the same pull as the sea."

"Aye," Gabe responded taking his hat. "That and more."

"Take care," she whispered. "Your child will need his father's hand."

"His?" Gabe asked.

"Aye Captain," Faith replied in a mocking way.

"What makes you so sure?"

"Nanny says it's a boy. She says she can tell by the way I'm carrying it."

"Humph! I never heard of such a thing."

"Well, there are things about your old boat we don't know about but you do. So you see you don't know things Nanny does."

Ship, Gabe thought. Ship, not boat, but he didn't correct her. If Nanny said so then so be it. She had a fifty-fifty chance of being right. And if she was wrong, Gabe was certain some excuse would come up.

Seeing his second lieutenant, Gabe called to him, "Good morning Mr. Davy."

"Morning Captain.

"I hope you enjoyed your time ashore."

"Aye Captain, that I did. I wanted to tell you, Captain, when we get back Ariel and I plan to get married. She was reluctant at first." Davy then leaned forward and whispered, "Cause of her past you know. Said she was a soiled woman. But I told her I loved her and that's all that mattered."

"Well, congratulations David," Gabe said, using the lieutenant's first name. Then as an afterthought spoke again, "Have you spoken with Dagan?"

"Aye Captain, we've had several long talks."

"Well, again, I congratulate you, sir. She's a beautiful woman."

"Thank you Captain, but there's one other thing. Well sir, we'll be married when we get back and I'd like to ask you to be my best man. I hope I'm not out of order, sir." Davy must have seen the stunned look on Gabe's face.

Placing his hand on Davy's shoulder, he said, "No, you're not out of line. You honour me and I'm humbled by it."

Later, finishing his second cup of coffee, Gabe's mind still was going over his times with the midshipman from his fiery stance against Witzenfeld to their last battle.

"Deep in thought, Captain?"

Gabe looked up to see Buck. Not just Buck anymore, now it was Admiral Buck. He told Buck about Davy and how he'd matured in such a short time. Speaking of a short time, Gabe quipped, "It didn't take long for you to get your flag."

"It's the war," Buck replied. "I'll bet half the active captains retired rather than fight this cause."

Gabe was quick to note the use of cause, not war. "Aye," he replied. "I was told by Sir Victor we had a lot of yellow admirals," speaking of the captains promoted then taken off the active list the next day.

"There has to be, else I'd not been promoted."

"There's likely to be more promotions with the French in the war and Spain likely to join."

Hearing Buck's words, Gabe thought for a minute then said, "The Honest Johns say the sun never sets on the British Empire but I tell you truly sir, I feel we are an island unto ourselves."

"Aye," Buck agreed, and the two sat in silence, each deep in his own thoughts.

* * *

"Sail ho!" The lookout called down. "Sail off the weather bow."

Hearing the lookouts cry, Gabe, Buck, and Dagan raced up the companionway.

"Deck thar, more sails, sir, one's a ship-of-the-line. More sails, sir, six sets of sail. They wear French colors, sir."

Gabe called to the signals midshipman. "Make to the squadron 'enemy in sight'. Mr. Wesley, beat to quarters if you please and clear for action."

"Aye Captain."

Thinking of his last action Gabe thought, *Hopefully the outcome will be different today.* Turning to Buck, he forced a smile. "We fight under your flag today, sir."

Buck looked up at his blue rear admiral's flag flying at the mizzen. Would this be his first and only occasion to fly it into battle?

Seeing Buck's expression, Gabe held out his hand. "We'll not let you down, sir."

"You never have, old friend," Buck replied, taking the hand.

"Deck thar, I make it a sixty-four, two forty-fours, two corvettes and a brig."

"The brig will go after the prizes," Dagan volunteered.

"Mr. Gunnells, bring her closer to the wind. Alter two points to larboard if you will."

"Aye Captain."

"It will be a while yet, Gabe. I'll go change," Buck said, then headed below.

All about Gabe, men made ready for battle. Nets were being strung up; gun captains were harassing their crews. Powder monkeys ran with charges in their hands, tubs with slow match were situated. The deck was strewn with sand. Wesley was telling him the ship was cleared for action. It all seemed to be happening at once.

Though he couldn't see it, Gabe knew that down below the surgeon loaned to *Peregrine* by the flagship was setting up his line of instruments. Tubs would be set up for wings and limbs as amputations were carried out. Pray God he didn't suffer such an injury.

Before Gabe knew it, Buck was back on deck in his gleaming new uniform, the sun reflecting off the rear admiral's star.

Before he could speak, Buck ordered, "Go below and change."

Gabe knew the order was for his sake. Clean fresh silk was thought to cause less infection if one was wounded. Once his uniform was changed, Hex clipped on his sword and handed Gabe his hat. Hex had seen Gabe clutch the leather pouch around his neck and whisper, "Faith."

On deck Wesley was nervous; it was obvious in his speech. "He intends to engage," he said.

"What would you expect?" Dagan answered.

"Th...that's a sixty-four and two forty-fours."

"Would you run?" Dagan asked. The question seemed to calm the man as if he resigned himself to whatever fate may bring.

Gabe had just made it back on deck when the French sixty-four bearing their commodore's flag fired. Orange flames erupted from the double line of black muzzles.

"My God, the Frenchy is headed toward the brigs."

Seeing this Gabe called out, "Mr. Gunnells, alter course to yonder brig."

"Aye Captain. Two can play this game."

Generally a small ship was left out of battle but with the French commodore headed after the cargo ships Gabe felt his only course of action was to go after the French brig. The commodore would have to allow his brig to be sunk or come to its rescue. Gabe felt he'd do the latter.

Chapter Thirty-three

Gabe watched the ships as they closed.

"Look at the fresh paint," Dagan volunteered. "They're not long out of port."

"We'll have to fire on the up roll," Buck stated, neither man hearing the other.

The French sixty-four seemed to tower above *Peregrine*. She had done as Gabe expected. As Gabe headed for the smaller French vessel, the French commodore turned away for the British brigs.

"He thinks he can scoop 'em up at his leisure he does," Gunnells said.

He might be right, Gabe thought. Watching the approaching French squadron he could see the frigates were less than two miles and the sixty-four less than a mile. Calling to the signal midshipman, Gabe ordered signal 'independent action.' Hazard must have been expecting the signal as he immediately changed tack.

"He intends to go between the frigates," Gunnells stated.

"Aye," Dagan responded. "He knows it puts them at a disadvantage. The French will fear hitting their own ship if the guns aren't aimed precisely."

"We are almost up with the brig," Hex volunteered.

"Take in the courses," Gabe ordered. It was time to shorten sail. "Prepare to engage to starboard, Mr. Davy."

"Aye sir."

"Mr. Druett, I want those smashers speaking loud and often today. They may make the difference."

"Aye Captain, we'll sing 'em a tune they'll not likely forget."

"Mr. Davy."

"Sir.

"I want that brig's mast cut down."

"Aye sir."

"Mr. Gunnells, bring her up to pistol shot range then bring her across the stern."

"The Frenchy looks like she'll overreach us," Hex volunteered.

"It'll be close," Dagan replied, "but Gabe will put the brig between us so she will only be able to use the guns on the upper deck."

"I knew he was a smart one," Hex said.

"Aye," Dagan replied with a smile. "I taught him well." This brought a general chuckle from the crew within hearing.

Watching as the distance and gap closed, Gabe thought Davy had waited too long but gun by gun the starboard battery fired. Smoke and flames belched forth and a loud crash was heard. As the smoke cleared somebody could be heard cheering wildly.

Both of the brig's masts had been hit. Only the stays kept the forward mast from toppling over the side. The mainmast was shattered with only a splinter of itself holding on. It was already leaning and once the stays parted the whole thing would be down. The ship was listing to starboard. A mass of tangled rigging lines and broken spars dangled precariously. Any type of wind and it would all be in the ocean.

Gabe didn't have time to survey more of the damage. "Now, Mr. Gunnells."

The deck tilted sharply and *Peregrine* crossed the brig's stern. The sixty-four tried to follow suit but someone yelled, "She's in irons, by God."

Buck stood next to Gabe and excitedly yelled, "The Frenchy cut it too close. Without sails or headway they're going to collide."

Gabe was afraid to hope. Could their luck be this good? Then it happened; the two French ships ground together amid the downed riggings. The bowsprit impaled the brig and was tangled in the mass. Buck swore.

"Bring us around, Mr. Gunnells. Cross the big Frenchy's stern. Mr. Davy, fire as you bear. Mr. Druett."

"Aye Captain, we're ready."

Shots crashed overhead as the French sixty-four was able to get some of her guns to bear. A few balls hit the hull making *Peregrine* shudder.

"We'll receive more before we are in position!" Buck bellowed.

Gabe nodded but didn't speak. The voice of the bosun could be heard as he had men swarming aloft to repair damage.

"Look," Hex yelled, calling Gabe's attention to the bow of the sixty-four. Men with axes were trying to cut away the mess that locked the ships together.

Gabe wiped smoke from his eyes. More shots erupted from the Frenchy tearing away part of the poop and cutting down two men. The air was filled with curses as the gun captains urged their crews to reload and run out.

Severed standing and running rigging hung down and waved in the wind. Forward, Gabe heard the unmistakable sound of the smasher firing. As they passed the last gun to bear, Gabe bellowed for Gunnells to put down the helm. *Peregrine* answered and the stern of the sixty-four was exposed.

Decking exploded around the wheel and Gabe saw Gunnells go down. As the sixty-four's stern guns fired the helmsman was still at the wheel and it was intact. Davy had trained his gunners well. Each gun was laid perfectly and shot after shot poured into the unprotected stern. The smasher had silenced the French stern guns and the cannons fired round after round into the ship.

"That did it for her rudder!" Druett shouted.

"Come about and another broadside," Gabe ordered.

The quartermaster acknowledged Gabe's order and, without being hit by another French ball, another broadside poured into the sixty-four's stern.

"Bugger the bastard good!" Hawks shouted.

Once the smoke cleared, the whole stern of the once beautiful sixty-four was shot away and the rudder was gone.

"You don't want to take yonder ship?" Wesley asked.

"No," Gabe replied. "Lady Luck was good to us and she's out of action. To press it may mean losing this ship and our cohorts. No, we'll make for the frigates and lend a hand. We still have not won this battle."

"Aye Captain," Wesley replied thinking, *I should have known that.*

* * *

The battle between *Drake*, *Fearless*, and the remainder of the French ships was definitely favoring the French.

Thinking back on the *Romney*, how her mast and decks had been riddled with canister, Gabe called, "Mr. Davy, Mr. Druett, I want canister on top of ball for every round."

The men acknowledged Gabe's order.

"Lieutenant York."

"Sir," the marine answered.

"Have your men man the swivels. I want to pour as much grape as possible over the Frenchmen's deck."

"Aye Captain."

Hazard was working both starboard and larboard batteries as well as he could. One of the corvettes was now falling down wind. The mast and rigging was shot away and stays parting letting it fall over the side.

However, *Fearless* was taking a beating. Gripping his sword, Gabe prayed as he watched the ship keel over from the onslaught of the large French frigate.

"We must get closer," Buck stated, knowing Gabe's need to come to their friend's rescue.

"Look there!" Hex shouted.

Against orders, Jepson poured a broadside of his tiny pop guns into the French frigate.

"He's distracted them!" Buck yelled.

"Aye, now get away," Gabe said. "Get away, Jep, now!" He realized he was shouting but could not be heard above the noise.

The entire broadside including the smashers fired, the deadly mixture of ball and canister sweeping the Frenchy's deck. Men were falling everywhere on the French frigate. The wheel was shot away, parts of the bulwark were flying in the air, all mixed with the thud of iron tearing into the wooden ship. A bright flash was seen as a gun exploded.

"Must not have swabbed the barrel," Dagan volunteered.

Not surprising, Gabe thought. *Peregrine* now shuddered as balls from the other forty-four pounded into her deck. One of the midshipmen collapsed in front of Buck. Most of one arm had been shot away. Buck quickly tied a piece of rope above the boy's stump.

"Get him below," he ordered a couple of seamen. As he rose, his hands were wet and sticky from the boy's blood.

Another broadside slammed into the ship and the wheel was shattered. One of the helmsmen tried to rise but fell dead, his life's blood pouring over the deck. Hex and another hand grabbed the broken wheel.

Gabe bellowed, trying to make himself heard above the din of battle. "Mr. Druett, can you work both smashers?" It was no use; the noise was too great.

Another hand had been grabbed to help with the wheel, so Gabe sent Hex to speak to Druett. They needed both forward guns working. If he needed hands there were enough guns out of action their crews could be sent to help.

"Damme, but it's a hot one!" Buck exclaimed as he picked up his hat. Some sharpshooter had nearly found his mark but only succeeded in putting a ball through the admiral's hat.

Where's Drake? Gabe wondered; *had Byrd lost his nerve? Fearless* was in a bad way. The momentary reprieve given by *Peregrine's* onslaught had been forfeited with the arrival of the other forty-four. Another broadside slammed into *Peregrine*. The entire larboard bulwark was hit sending exploding timbers and splinters flying into the air. Beside him, Dagan flinched as a quill size splinter impaled itself into his arm. Hex was down but seemed to be rising; no visible injury could be seen. *We can't take much more of this*, Gabe thought.

The bang of swivels along with the uneven roar of *Peregrine's* guns showed they still had some fight left... but to what end? The sound of a full broadside was heard but it took a moment for it to register in

Gabe's mind that they didn't take any hits. However, he didn't have time to consider the implications at the moment.

Feeling a gust of wind Gabe yelled to the helmsman, "Hard over!" If somehow he could escape from between the two forty-fours there might be a chance. A quick glimpse of *Fearless* as they inched ahead of the French frigate was heartbreaking. The ship was doomed. The main topgallant staggered and plunged to the deck as Gabe watched. The forward mast was gone. Only a couple of figures could be seen moving on deck but amid the smoke and carnage her remaining guns still fired. *They had no chance*, Gabe thought. *They never did*.

"Dagan," Gabe called. He'd have to stand in for the master. "Man the braces! Put up your helm."

Peregrine gathered speed despite her torn sails flapping in the wind. Gabe was oblivious to the shrieking balls from the French sharpshooters that thudded into the planks beneath his feet. The blast of the swivel from the fighting top stopped the rain of balls. The scarlet coat of one of the marines flashed before his eyes as the man fell from aloft. Men were firing down from the taller forty-four. *Peregrine's* deck tilted as the men held the wheel and suddenly they were on a collision course with the forty-four.

"Ease your helm," Gabe ordered. Dagan nodded and spoke to the helmsman.

Realization suddenly came over Buck. "You're going to ram her." It was a faultless decision but one that would likely cost Gabe his ship.

It would give the brigs time to escape. Too late the French realized Gabe's intention. They'd been so caught up in their battle with *Fearless* that only one gun fired before they were rammed. However, its effect was devastating. Several men from the starboard carronade were cut down, canister shot raking the entire crew and cutting them to bloody ribbons as it toppled the smashers. The screams and cries of pain were drowned out by the crashing timbers as *Peregrine* rammed into the side of the forty-four. Water gushed into the opening created by *Peregrine's* bow. The sound of firing aft caused Gabe to turn and see *Drake* delivering a broadside up the other frigate's stern. The French captain in his haste to punish *Peregrine* forgot about *Drake*. Too late, they paid the price. A terrific explosion rocked the ship and a ball of flames rose into the sky.

Gabe could feel the furnace-like heat reach his ship. "Douse the sails," he ordered.

"Sir...sir," Wesley was calling. "The French is sinking. We have to cut away or they'll pull us down with them."

Men stepped over the strewn bodies to chop away at the bowsprit and timbers that locked the two ships together as if in a death grip. A shout from the French ship made Gabe look up. The French captain, his coat stained in blood, raised his sword in salute. As Gabe watched the man fell to his knees then toppled forward onto the deck, his sword clanging down, landing a foot or so from Hex. Picking up the sword he made to give it to Gabe.

"No," Gabe said refusing the offered sword. "Give it to our admiral. It should be his."

Chapter Thirty-four

The remainder of the voyage was slow. For the first week burials interrupted the daily routine. *Fearless* had been lost along with many of her crew. Miraculously, Hazard had come through unscathed. While in the process of freeing *Peregrine* from the sinking French frigate, *Drake* had come alongside to offer assistance. Gabe was shocked to find Jepson had boarded the ship and took command.

"I could see she had no guidance so I boarded to offer help. I found Byrd leaning against the mast clutching his chest. Seeing me, he uttered, 'Thank God' and slid to the deck. He was dead."

Gabe couldn't help recalling Gil telling him about Bart's words: *He's got the smell of death on him that one does.* Bart was right. Gabe thought of Byrd's last words: *Thank God.* That had been truer than anyone could have imagined. Had it not been for Jepson's quick action the outcome would have been far different.

"You never fail to come to the Anthony's rescue, do you," Gabe had said in all sincerity to Jepson.

"I'll see you a captain yet," Buck promised Jepson.

Had the French commodore not signaled for the remaining corvette to close with the flag and protect it, things might have gone much differently. They had been lucky and they all knew it. If the brig and the sixty-four hadn't collided there was little doubt in Gabe's mind that his wife would be a widow now...his child fatherless.

* * *

Gabe, Jepson, and Hazard were sharing a glass at the George Inn when the messenger arrived. "Sir, I've been looking for you everywhere. The admiral requires your presence." By that, he meant the port admiral.

As Gabe rose, the lieutenant looked down at the glasses on the table and at the paper the men had been reading and discussing. Motioning for the serving girl, Gabe ordered a glass for the lieutenant.

"Oh, no sir, I couldn't. I've been searching for you for awhile. It was your mother who said you could be found here."

"It's getting cold out," Gabe said. "You sure you don't want a glass."

"Yes...well, a quick glass wouldn't hurt." Seeing the paper the lieutenant spoke again, "The Gazette did you proud, sir. A wonderful article, I read the report. It was kind of Admiral Buck to give you all the credit. You and your fellow captains that is," the lieutenant added, not wanting to offend any of the other men at the table.

The headline had read, "Captain Gabriel Anthony, son of Admiral Lord James Anthony and brother to Vice Admiral Lord Gilbert Anthony met and defeated a much superior French squadron."

The end of the article had projected Gabe would be knighted for his acts. What the paper didn't say was how many good men were lost. Some killed, others maimed. Gunnells had lost an arm. It would be some time before he would walk another quarterdeck, if ever.

The drink came and the messenger downed it in one swallow. Arriving at the port admiral's office, Gabe was greeted by the admiral then told he had been summoned to Whitehall by Lord Sandwich himself. "They must have something in store for you, Captain, as the First Lord personally signed the order and sent a special courier to deliver it."

* * *

A brisk wind shook the coach as it rocked along the cobbled streets to Whitehall. As soon as the coach stopped, a doorman opened the door and assisted him down. "This way, please."

Did the doorman know who he was? Gabe wondered. Had some signal been passed to him by the driver? Gabe wasn't sure but followed the man as he opened the door. Walking down the hall he couldn't help but remember his first trip here in company with his brother. A lot had changed since then. He had been lucky, maybe more so than he deserved.

When handing the secretary his papers, the man spoke in a loud voice. "Captain Anthony, sir. It's good to see you. The First Lord has been awaiting your arrival." The man's voice carried and Gabe could feel the stares of the other captains, lieutenants, and workers in the great hall. He overheard one man swear, "Damme, he's only a boy." Before Gabe could sit down, the secretary was back.

"Lord Sandwich will see you now, Captain."

An angry appearing captain gave Gabe a cold look as they passed outside the First Lord's door. "You interrupted his visit," the secretary said in a whisper.

"Gabe," the First Lord greeted him. "My God, sir, but you've set England aflame with your heroics. This damnable war has gotten everyone down so. Your acts have raised spirits. Damme boy how did you beat an entire squadron?"

"I wasn't alone," Gabe answered, not comfortable with all the accolades.

"Just like your father and brother," Lord Sandwich quipped. Walking to his desk, he picked up a few sheets of paper. "A letter from my friend, Lord Ragland; he states he sent a similar one to the Prince Regent. He has stated...nay, *demanded* you be knighted. I've no doubt you will be." Pouring two glasses of claret, Lord Sandwich handed one to Gabe. "I hear your ship is in a bad way."

"Aye," Gabe replied slowly. It will take months to put his *Peregrine* back in shape.

"Well, we'll discuss another command for you. We have decided *Drake* was a lawful prize and will purchase her. Based on both Admiral Buck's and your recommendations we will put Hazard in command. Too bad you didn't capture one of the corvettes. It would have been a good ship to give Jepson his step up. He will get it soon however.

Good man, Jepson. Your brother was quite right to promote him and give him a command."

Hearing a knock Gabe knew his time was up.

"Do you have a place to stay here in London?" Lord Sandwich asked.

"Yes, my Lord. My sister and her husband have a house here."

Smiling, Lord Sandwich spoke. "Ah yes, your brother-in-law, Hugh. Not satisfied being a country squire, he now dabbles in politics. Course he's on the right side, at least for now."

As Gabe was ushered from the First Lord's office the clerk asked, "Would you give us the address where you'll be staying, sir, so that we may be able to reach you on short notice?"

* * *

The servant girl who answered the door looked Gabe up and down. "Yes?"

"I'm Captain Anthony," Gabe announced.

Before he could get any further a squeal pierced the air. "It's Uncle Gabe, Mother, Uncle Gabe is home."

The servant girl barely had time to step aside as Gretchen raced to Gabe and hugged him. Gretchen had grown over the years and had changed from a little snit to a very attractive young lady. The squeal hadn't changed however. Hugh and Becky came from the study. Becky hugged Gabe and Hugh shook his hand vigorously. The group then went into the library where a small fire was burning in the fireplace to ward off the evening chill. Refreshments were ordered and served. Gretchen sat down beside Gabe and hugged his arm to her.

Hugh said, "Damme, Gabe, but you are the toast of the town. Nay, all of England."

Becky rose from the chair she was sitting in and crossed over to the couch. Sitting on the arm she leaned over, her arm around her brother and kissed his cheek.

"Father would have been so proud of you," she said. "Every time I look at you I see him as he was when I was a little girl." Gabe could feel a tear drop from her eye and run down his face. "Oh damn it, Gabe, I love you so much. It tears my heart apart every time I think of you and Gil in ..." Becky had to pause as she sniffed and wiped her eyes. Sniffing again she continued, "In those sea battles. One day you'll be hurt...or worse."

The two were still hugging when the servant came to announce dinner. *So this was England's hero,* she thought. *He's a handsome devil to be the fire-eater the paper made him out to be.*

Epilogue

Gabe sat on the edge of his bed. It was nine o' clock. *The proper time to rise*, he thought. He could hear voices below. Dagan and Gabe's mother no doubt. The brother and sister had spent a lot of time together since returning to Portsmouth. When they had got back from London, Hex had asked for and been given a few days to visit relatives in Deal.

"Don't murder anybody," Gabe had half-joked, not sure the man had completed his vendetta against those who taken his family down. Pouring water over his toothbrush Gabe attempted to brush away the aftertaste of cigar and drink. The celebration last evening at the George Inn had been a continuation of one that had started in London.

Gabe had been knighted. He was now Sir Gabriel, Knight of the Bath. His mother had stood next to Becky and Gretchen during the ceremony. Tears of joy streaming down Becky's face, damned if his sister...yes, his sister, didn't cry at every turn. Gretchen had held his mother's hand. Hugh, along with Hazard and Jepson, had stood behind the women, Dagan and Hex to one side. Admiral Buck along with Lord Sandwich stood with several men from Parliament across from Gabe's family and friends. *Had Gil and Faith been there it would have been perfect*, Gabe thought. The family had celebrated that night and the next day Hugh had taken Gabe in tow to see his banker.

"You are far too rich to put all your money in one bank or with one investor," Hugh declared. "You need to diversify."

So with Hugh's guidance, Gabe invested in the Honourable East India Company, a shipbuilding company that needed cash to update its yards to fulfill its contracts with the Navy. He also bought lands including a hundred or so acres next to Deborah's on Antigua, through an agent Hugh knew well and trusted.

"How did you know about the shipyard?" Gabe had asked.

"I'm not interested in politics just for politics," Hugh admitted with a smile.

* * *

Gabe had finished dressing and was making his way down to the kitchen for a cup of coffee when a knock was heard. His mother's servant answered the knock and ushered the visitor into the kitchen where Gabe sat. Recognizing his visitor, Gabe rose and pumped the man's hand.

"Stephen Earl! Damme, sir, but it's good to see you. Sit down. I'll get you a cup of coffee."

After the men talked for awhile catching up on old times Earl leaned back and asked, "Have you heard Buck has lost his flagship?"

Gabe, who was leaning back in his chair as he usually did, rocked forward, concern on his face. "How?" he asked.

"Gaol fever," Earl answered.

"Typhus!" Gabe exclaimed as a chill ran through his body.

"Aye, I'm sure they cleaned all the gallows-bait out of Newgate to man the flagship. Those whoresons were probably riddled in louse and it didn't take any time to run through the crew. I hear seventy men are dead already and the captain is down with chills and fever. Likely he'll die too. The whole ship is quarantined and they say they'll try the new method to get rid of the fever."

"What's the new method?" Gabe asked. "I haven't heard of it."

"They burn sulphur in cans letting the smoke drift throughout the ship until every nook and cranny has been fumigated. This was recommended by some Doctor Lind."

"Well, that's too bad about Buck."

"I don't know," Earl replied, his eyes bright and his smile mischievous. "Our new admiral has been given another flagship, *HMS Trident*, and you have been given command of her. She's a sixty-four but sails like a frigate. She's one hundred and fifty-eight feet long and forty-five feet in the beam. Her main gun deck carries twenty-six twenty-four pounders; the upper gun deck carries twenty-six eighteen pounders. There are ten four pounders on the quarterdeck and they are replacing the nine pounders on the forecastle with smashers."

"How is it you know so much about this ship?" Gabe asked curiously.

"Because she was, is mine," Earl answered. "That is until we have a change of command."

"But...but what about you?" Gabe muttered.

"Oh, I have orders for a seventy-four. I'm to be Lord Anthony's new flag captain."

* * *

Later, after assuming command of *Trident*, Gabe sat with Buck in the admiral's dining room. Nesbit was serving refreshments and the men had finished discussing the need to complete Buck's staff before sailing. Dawkins had decided to retire so Gabe also had an opening to fill. The sound of an approaching boat was heard and, in a matter of minutes, the first lieutenant was announced.

Handing a leather bag to the admiral he stated, "Just arrived sir."

Taking the bag, Buck thanked the lieutenant. He opened it, took out his orders, broke the wax seal and began to read. "Um huh, yes, as I expected." Folding the papers he looked at Gabe. "Orders sure enough."

"May I ask where?" Gabe said.

"Yes. When the squadron is complete, we are to make up a group patrolling the southern colonies. Savannah, Georgia will be our homeport."

"Savannah," Gabe repeated.

"Aye," Buck answered. "We've taken the city and our job is to make sure we keep it."

Gabe only half heard. His mind was on Faith. How would she take the news? Would her people welcome her back being married to a British sea captain? *Too many questions,* Gabe thought. But at least he was going back. Back to Faith and their child...a boy child if Nanny was to be believed. A boy child.

Appendix

HISTORICAL NOTES

The French signed a treaty with the Colonies and in April 1778 Comte d'Estaing sailed from Toulon with a squadron of one ninety gun ship, one eighty gun ship, six seventy-fours, three sixty-fours, and one fifty gun ship and several frigates. The cruise took eighty-five days. Lord Howe received word just in time to move his ships from the Delaware River where they would have been bottled up if the French had taken even an average amount of time in passage. Lord Howe's squadron escaped but the twenty-eight gun *Mermaid* was trapped. The British sailed to New York where Howe anchored his small squadron just inside Sandy Hook. The French fleet arrived on July 11th, and everyone expected a great battle. However, the depth of water over the bar at the entrance of the channel was only twenty-three feet. The majority of the French ships required twenty-five feet. On the twenty-second of July a spring tide raised the water over the bar to thirty feet. Howe ordered his squadron to prepare for immediate battle; however to everyone's surprise the French sailed away. Had the French succeeded in crossing the bar and a broadside to broadside battle taken place there would have been little doubt as to the outcome.

Having been in the United States Navy, I spent a lot of time in the Tidewater/Norfolk area. Because of that I wanted to include some of the area's history in this book. The comments about the dockyard are basically out of the history books.

The Rathskeller was a bar I visited when I was a young enlisted man. The bar was just as I described it in the book, only the location was different.

The burning of Norfolk was much as I describe. On January 1, 1776, by order of John Murray, also known as the Earl of Dunmore, British ships in Norfolk Harbour began shelling the town with heated shot and hollow shells containing live coals. The shelling began at 4 a.m. Landing parties helped the fire along. The town's Tory (Loyalist) population fled but the Whig (Patriot) forces worked to drive off the British. However, they did nothing to put out the fires. In fact, the Whigs set more fires to prevent British use of the town. Damage to the town by the Whigs exceeded that done by the British, destroying 863 buildings. The British bombardment destroyed only 19 properties.

With my background in medicine I felt it only natural to include a couple of medical emergencies. Abdominal problems during that era were usually a kiss of death. Bart survived his appendicitis due to luck and a skilled surgeon. The use of alcohol or any other antiseptic was uncommon. In fact, some took their blood stained aprons and hands as a status symbol. It wasn't until Louis Pasteur's germ theory in 1865 that hand washing and disinfectants were routinely brought into use.

The use of hemp to help sedate Bart for his operation was mostly of my own making. The smoking of opium was used to induce a deep drug induced sleep but it was rare to find this type of opium readily available in the colonies during this period of time. Laudanum or opium and saffron were available as an oral or liquid medication. However, it was thought to cause nausea and would not have been used in a large enough dose to operate on the abdomen. Hemp was a large cash crop during the eighteenth century and George Washington felt his hemp was superior to tobacco. Ben Franklin started the very first hemp paper mill. Prior to that it was used to make ropes and lines for ships.

The Declaration of Independence was drafted on hemp paper and Betsy Ross sewed the first American flag out of hemp. Therefore, I felt hemp, which was a common plant, could be a probable alternative to opium.

Typhus, also known as gaol fever or ship's fever, was a devastating disease. Articles can be found where a large portion of a ship's company would be made up of prisoners from some gaol. On more than one occasion the disease was carried aboard a ship by louse infected felons. The entire ship's crew was soon infected and many died.

The yellow admiral was a post captain who had usually outlived his usefulness. However, since the rank of rear admiral was based on seniority alone, upward mobility was almost non-existent. To get around this captains were promoted to rear admiral one day and retired the next. This allowed deserving captains the ability to be promoted. However, this practice didn't take place until after the Napoleonic War, many years after I promoted Buck. Hey, it's fiction. The fact remains that a lot of Royal Navy officers retired rather than fight their American cousins. Because of this some were promoted far quicker than they would have been otherwise.

Alarac Bond mentioned the yards being set "akimbo" in one of his books. Another term, the one I chose was cockbill. When a ship's captain died the yard were set "akimbo" or "cockbill" when the ship returned to port. It was a sign of mourning the loss of the captain. It was Alarac Bond and Jim Nelson's insight that was the stimulus for my poem "Final Victory."

Age of Sail Glossary

aft: toward the stern (rear) of the ship.

ahead: in a forward direction.

aloft: above the deck of the ship.

barque (bark): a three-masted vessel with the foremast and mainmast square-rigged and the mizzenmast fore-and-aft rigged.

belay: to make a rope fast to a belaying pin, cleat, or other such device. Also used as a general command to stop or cancel, e.g., "Belay that last order!"

belaying pin: a wooden pin, later made of metal, generally about twenty inches in length to which lines were made fast, or "belayed." They were arranged in pin rails along the inside of the bulwark and in fife rails around the masts.

binnacle: a large wooden box, just forward of the helm, housing the compass, half-hour glass for timing the watches, and candles to light the compass at night.

boatswain's chair: a wooden seat with a rope sling attached. Used for hoisting men aloft or over the side for work.

bosun: also boatswain, a crew member responsible for keeping the hull, rigging and sails in repair.

bow chaser: a cannon situated near the bow to fire as directly forward as possible.

bower anchor: the name of the two largest anchors carried at the bow of the ship. The best-bower to starboard and the small-bower to larboard.

bowsprit: a large piece of timber which stands out from the bow of a ship.

breeching: rope used to secure a cannon to the side of a ship and prevent it from recoiling too far.

brig: a two masted vessel, square rigged on both masts.

bulwarks: the sides of a ship above the upper deck.

bumboat: privately owned boat used to carry out to anchored vessels vegetables, liquor, and other items for sale.

burgoo: mixture of coarse oatmeal and water, porridge.

cable: (a) a thick rope, (b) a measure of distance-1/10th of a sea mile, 100 fathoms (200yards approximately).

canister: musket ball size iron shot encased in a cylindrical metal cast. When fired from a cannon, the case breaks apart releasing the enclosed shot. (not unlike firing buckshot from a shotgun shell.)

Cat-O'-Nine Tails: a whip made from knotted ropes, used to punish crewmen. What was meant by being "flogged."

chase: a ship being pursued.

coxswain: (cox'n) The person in charge of the captain's personal boat.

cutter: a sailboat with one mast and a mainsail and two headsails.

dogwatch: the watches from four to six, and from six to eight, in the evening.

fathom: unit of measurement equal to six feet.

fife rail: the uppermost railing around the quarterdeck and poop.

flotsam: Debris floating on the water surface.

forecastle: pronounced fo'c'sle. The forward part of the upper deck, forward of the foremast, in some vessels raised above the upper deck. Also, the space enclosed by this deck.

founder: used to describe a ship that is having difficulty remaining afloat.

frigate: a fast three masted fully rigged ship carrying anywhere from twenty to forty-eight guns.

full and by: a nautical term meaning proceed under full sail.

furl: to lower a sail.

futtock shrouds: short, heavy pieces of standing rigging connected on one end to the topmast shrouds at the outer edge of the top and on the other to the lower shrouds, designed to bear the pressure on the topmast shrouds. Often used by sailors to go aloft.

gaff: a spar or pole extending diagonally upward from the after side of a mast and supporting a fore-and-aft sail.

galley: the kitchen area of a ship.

gig: a light clinker-built ship's boat adapted for rowing or sailing and usually used for the captain.

glass: shipboard name for either the barometer, a sand-glass used for measuring time or a telescope.

grapeshot: a cluster of round, iron shot, generally nine in all, and wrapped in canvas. Upon firing the grapeshot would spread out for a shotgun effect. Used against men and light hulls.

grating: hatch cover composed of perpen-dicular, interlocking wood pieces, much like a heavy wood screen. It allowed light and air below while still providing cover for the hatch. Gratings were covered with tarpaulins in rough or wet weather.

grog: British naval seaman received a portion of liquor every day. In 1740, Admiral Edward Vernon ordered the rum to be diluted with water. Vernon's nickname was Old Grogram, and the beverage was given the name "grog" in their disdain for Vernon.

gunwale: pronounced gun-el. The upper edge of a ship's side.

halyard: a line used to hoist a sail or spar. The tightness of the halyard can affect sail shape.

handsomely: slowly, gradually.

hard tack: ship's biscuit.

haul: pulling on a line.

hawse: the bows of a ship where the hawse-holes are cut for the anchor cables to pass through. The space between the stem of a vessel at anchor and the anchors or a little beyond.

heave to: arranging the sails in such a manner as to stop the forward motion of the ship.

heel: the tilt of a ship/boat to one side; a ship normally heels in the wind.

helm: the wheel of a ship or the tiller of a boat.

holystone: a block of sandstone used to scour the wooden decks of a ship.

idler: the name of those members of a ship's crew that did not stand night watch because of their work, example cook, carpenters.

jetty: a manmade structure projecting from the shore.

jib: a triangular sail attached to the head stay.

John Company: nickname for the Honourable East India Company.

jolly boat: a small workboat.

jonathan: British nickname for an American.

keel: a flat surface (fin) built into the bottom of the ship to reduce the leeway caused by the wind pushing against the side of the ship.

ketch: a sailboat with two masts. The shorter mizzen mast is aft of the main, but forward of the rudder post.

knot: one knot equals one nautical mile per hour. This rate is equivalent to approximately 1.15 statute miles per hour.

larboard: the left side of a ship or boat.

lee: the direction toward which the wind is blowing. The direction sheltered from the wind.

leeward: pronounced loo-ard. Downwind.

Letter of Marque: a commission issued by the government authorizing seizure of enemy property.

luff: the order to the steersman to put the helm towards the lee side of the ship, in order to sail nearer to the wind.

main mast: the tallest (possibly only) mast on a ship.

mast: any vertical pole on the ship that sails are attached to.

mizzen mast: a smaller aft mast.

moor: to attach a ship to a mooring, dock, post, anchor.

nautical mile: one minute of latitude, approximately 6076 feet – about 1/8 longer than the statute mile of 5280 feet.

pitch: (1) a fore and aft rocking motion of a boat. (2) a material used to seal cracks in wooden planks.

privateer: a privateer is a captain with a Letter of Marque which allows a captain to plunder any ship of a given enemy nation. A privateer was **supposed** to be above being tried for piracy.

prize: an enemy vessel captured at sea by a warship or privateer. Technically these ships belonged to the crown, but after review by the Admiralty court and condemnation, they were sold and the prize money shared.

powder monkey: young boy (usually) who carried cartridges of gunpowder from the filling room up to the guns during battle.

quadrant: instrument used to take the altitude of the sun or other celestial bodies in order to determine the latitude of a place. Forerunner to the modern sextant.

quarterdeck: a term applied to the afterpart of the upper deck—the stern area of a ship. The area is generally reserved for officers.

quarter gallery: a small, enclosed balcony with windows located on either side of the great cabin aft and projecting out slightly from the side of the ship. Traditionally contained the head, or toilet, for use by those occupying the great cabin.

rake: a measurement of the top of the mast's tilt toward the bow or stern.

rate: Ships were rated from first to sixth rates based on their size and armament:

First rate line of battle: 100 or more guns on 3 gun decks

Second rate line of battle: 90 to 98 guns on 3 gun decks

Third rate line of battle: 80, 74 or 64 guns on 2 gun decks

Fourth rate below the line: 50 guns on 1 or 2 gun decks

Fifth rate frigates: 32 to 44 guns on 1 gun deck

Sixth rate frigates: 20 to 28 guns on 1 gun deck

ratline: pronounced ratlin. Small lines tied between the shrouds, horizontal to the deck, forming a sort of rope ladder on which the men can climb aloft.

reef: to reduce the area of sail. This helps prevent too much sail from being in use when the wind gets stronger (a storm or gale).

roll: a side-to-side motion of the ship, usually caused by waves.

schooner: a North American (colonial) vessel with two masts the same size.

scuppers: Drain holes on deck, in the toe rail, or in bulwarks that allows water to run into the sea.

scuttle: any small, generally covered hatchway through a ship's deck.

sextant: a navigational instrument used to determine the vertical position of an object such as the sun, moon or stars.

ship's bell: the progress of the watch was signalled by the ship's bells:

1 bell	½ hour	5 bells	2 ½ hours
2 bells	1 hour	6 bells	3 hours
3 bells	1 ½ hours	7 bells	3 ½ hours
4 bells	2 hours	8 bells	4 hours

ship's day: the ship's day at sea began at noon; the twenty-four day is divided into watches measured by a four-hour sandglass.

12:00 P.M. to 4:00 P.M. - Afternoon watch

4:00 P.M. to 8:00P.M. – Dog watch (this is broken into 2 separate sections called the first and last dog watch. This allows men on watch to eat their evening meal.

8:00 P.M. to 12:00 A.M. – First watch

12:00 A.M. to 4:00 A.M. – Middle watch

4:00 A.M. to 8:00 A.M. – Morning watch

8:00 A.M. to 12:00 P.M. – Forenoon watch

shoal: shallow, not deep.

shrouds: heavy ropes leading from a masthead aft and down to support the mast when the wind is from abeam or farther aft.

skiff: a small boat.

skylark: to frolic or play, especially up in the rigging.

skylight: a glazed window frame, usually in pairs set at an angle in the deck to give light and ventilation to the compartment below.

slew: to turn (something) around on its own axis; to swing around.

spar: any lumber/pole used in rigging sails on a ship.

starboard: the right side of a ship or boat.

stern: the aft part of a boat or ship.

stern chasers: cannons directed aft to fire on a pursuing vessel.

tack: to turn a ship about from one tack to another, by bringing her head to the wind.

taffrail: the upper part of the ship's stern, usually ornamented with carved work or bolding.

thwart: seat or bench in a boat on which the rowers sit.

topgallant: the mast above the topmast; also sometimes the yard and sail set on it.

transom: the stern cross-section/panel forming the after end of a ship's hull.

veer: a shifting of the wind direction.

waister: landsman or unskilled seaman who worked in the waist of the ship.

wear: to turn the vessel from one tack to another by turning the stern through the wind.

weigh: to raise, as in to weigh anchor.

windward: the side or direction from which the wind is blowing.

yard: a spar attached to the mast and used to hoist sails.

yard arm: the end of a yard.

yawl: a two-masted sailboat/fishing boat with the shorter mizzen mast placed aft of the rudder post. Similar to a ketch.

yellow admiral: a term used in Britain to denote a post-captain promoted to rear admiral and placed on the retired list on the following day. The yellow admiral was created after the Napoleonic War.

zephyr: a gentle breeze. The west wind.